YETI LEFT HOME

AARON ROSENBERG

NEOPARADOXA
Pennsville, NJ

PUBLISHED BY
NeoParadoxa
A division of eSpec Books
PO Box 242
Pennsville, NJ 08070
www.especbooks.com

ISBN: 978-1-949691-91-7
ISBN (eBook): 978-1-949691-90-0

Copyediting: Greg Schauer, John L. French
Interior Design: Danielle McPhail
Cover Art and Design: Mike McPhail, McP Digital Graphics

Stock Art Components:
Tent Campsite, Voyageurs National Park, Minnesota © Steven Schremp, www.shutterstock.com
Retro style travel poster or sticker. United States, Minnesota © Teddyand-Mia, www.shutterstock.com

Section Break and Accents:
Foot ornament, art vector design © martinussumbaji, www.fotolia.com

DEDICATION

For Jenifer, Adara, and Arthur—
nothing beats your love and support.

With special thanks to Raphy, Hildy, and Adara
for their fantastic work as beta readers!

CHAPTER ONE

THE BOY GLANCED UP AS THE DOOR OPENED AND GAWKED AS A MASSIVE figure filled the frame, blotting out any view of the sun beyond like a large boulder had just been rolled in front of the entrance. After a frozen instant, the figure lumbered forward, ducking to clear the crossbar, a gust of frigid air sliding into the space ahead of it like a herald clearing the path. The small bell affixed to the door's upper edge tinkled as it slid shut. Now the boy could make out features on the approaching shape: thick white whiskers and shaggy brows under a battered baseball cap, a worn plaid shirt that perhaps had once been red and was now closer to pink as it strained over a broad chest and around thick arms, equally faded jeans tucked into massive work boots, enormous hands each clenched around — a trio of fish.

It was that last detail that brought the boy up short. He blinked, stared again at the strange scene, and rubbed his eyes.

But yes, this giant of a man had entered the small restaurant hauling three fish in each hand.

And what fish they were! Large, thick, and golden, they almost seemed to glow in the foyer's dim light. They had to weigh ten, twenty pounds apiece, yet the stranger had them hoisted up like a cluster of paper lanterns, dangling several feet above the scuffed linoleum floor.

"Wylie!" That sound burst, not from the giant but from the man behind the cash register resting atop the battered counter halfway between the door and the far wall. "What're you doing? Those go round back!"

The massive figure shrugged, the motion like an earthquake rippling across a strangely checked landscape. "Kyra said the door was busted," he mumbled, his voice low and gruff but surprisingly gentle.

"Oh. Yeah." The Roadside Diner's owner, Roy, sighed. "Okay, sure, bring 'em on through. Thanks." Then he turned back to the boy's father, standing before him, the bill in one hand and his wallet already clasped in the other. "I hope everything was good?"

"Fine, fine," the boy's father agreed, never even noticing the towering stranger behind him. But the boy, Jason, barely heard the exchange. He had turned to watch as the big man—Wylie—stomped past. This close, there was a strange smell, musky like something he'd sniffed at a zoo. Or a circus. Nor was it the fish—this was more of an animal smell, he thought, dry and earthy.

"You're really tall," Jason said softly, glancing up and up and up, and the man stopped to peer down at him.

"And you're not," he agreed, and Jason saw teeth flash behind the thick beard. Long, sharp teeth.

"Your teeth are really big," Jason noted next. He glanced down, closer to his own height, where those large hands still held the fish. "And your nails..." Here he trailed off. "They're really long, too," he finished finally. Because they were. Long and sharp-looking. Less like his own nails, or his parents', and more like—claws.

The man stared at him a second. Then he winked. His eyes were oddly yellow, Jason thought. Not like his Aunt Margot that time she'd been sick or his Uncle Don when he'd had too much wine the night before. No, these were really yellow.

Like a wolf's.

Then the giant continued on his way, stepping around the counter and disappearing through a swinging door there. Jason heard noises beyond that, dishes clattering and water running, and people speaking, and he smelled food. The kitchen.

A sudden burst of color before his face interrupted his musings— a lollipop, the disc a vivid green, held out to him by Roy, who was leaning over the counter with the sugary offering. "Thank you," Jason remembered to say, accepting the sweet. He tugged the wrapper off and stuck the treat in his mouth as his parents shepherded him out the door and toward their car to continue on their way to his grandparents.

He glanced back toward the little restaurant once as he hopped into the back seat, looking for that strange man. But the hulking figure did not re-emerge, and Jason soon forgot about him as they drove away.

"Wow, I think you scared that kid half to death!" Roy said as he stepped into the kitchen and joined Wylie where the enormous man stood off to one side, still clutching those fish. "Good thing I had a lolly handy—a little sugar and all's right with the world again."

"Sorry." Wylie shrugged, glancing down at his big feet. "Kyra said—"

"Hey, no worries, man," Roy told him, slapping Wylie on the arm. He felt bad—he knew how sensitive the big man was. "Okay, show me what you got."

In response, Wylie hefted the fish even higher, their fanned and mottled tails level with his head. In the brighter lights of the kitchen, Roy could see not only the gold of the scales, shading to olive on top, but the five darker bands around each one, the white tipping the bottom of each tail—and the sharp teeth filling each mouth.

"Walleye, huh?" He stroked his chin and the tiny tuft of hair there—being around Wylie always made Roy a little self-conscious about his scruffy little beard and the way his hair was starting to thin up top. Though at least his was still dark! Another strike against the shy, beleaguered fisherman—he couldn't be any older than mid-thirties, yet all his hair was already white! "Nice ones, too." Which they were—each fish had to be at least two feet long and probably weighed in at a good ten pounds or more. Yet the fisherman held them up like they were nothing. "Okay, yeah, I'll give you top dollar for them, of course." Which he would. Both because they were handsome fish and walleye were always tasty, but also because Wylie was one of his best suppliers.

Whatever else could be said about the big man, he knew how to fish!

Twenty minutes later, Roy shook his head. "Sure you don't wanna stick around?" he asked again. "Kyra's got a real nice chowder going, fresh bread's just come outta the oven, even got a few slices of pie left."

His companion perked up at the sound of that last item but finally shook his head. "I shouldn't," he said softly, his eyes dropping to his boots again. "Don't wanna break anything again."

"Hey, it was one time, man! Coulda happened to anyone!" Which wasn't strictly true, of course—most people couldn't dent one of the heavy steel work tables they used in the kitchen even if they tried. Wylie had practically bent it in half just by leaning on it. That was years ago, but the guy had clearly never gotten over it.

Which was a shame. Because he sure seemed like he could do with a few more friends.

Seeing he wasn't going to talk the fisherman out of leaving, however, Roy sighed and glanced over to Kyra. She was already approaching them, carrying a heavy paper bag, clearly full, the top neatly folded and stapled. Good old Kyra.

"Chowder, bread, and two slices of pie," she said, offering Wylie the bag with a warm smile. "Enjoy it, okay?" She was always taking in strays, and would spend half her time cooing over the kids that came in if she wasn't back here running things, but that was okay. She had a good heart.

"Thanks." Wylie accepted the bag, and for a second, Roy thought he saw a hint of an answering smile beneath that heavy beard. So, the big man could feel joy after all! "I'll stop by again soon as I've got another good catch."

"Sure, sure," Roy told him, tapping the big man on the arm as they headed back toward the dining room and the exit beyond. "No worries, man. Just take care, okay?" Wylie waved as he headed outside, ducking through the door. Roy watched him go, the cold night swallowing even such a giant up without a trace after a few minutes.

He couldn't imagine being alone all the time like that. But apparently, it worked for Wylie, and that was what mattered.

Two long-time regulars, Ginger and Gary, hollered at him, and Roy put those thoughts aside as he wandered over, a smile sprouting on his face as he went to chat.

CHAPTER TWO

WYLIE KANG RELAXED AS HE BROUGHT HIS BATTERED GREEN PICKUP TO A halt by the sturdy log pillar. "Home again, home again," he muttered as he shut off the engine, shoved the door open, and stepped out of the truck. "Finally." Reaching back into the cab, he snagged the paper bag Kyra had packed for him and the larger, heavier one from the town's only decent grocery. Then, pushing the truck's door closed again, he turned and trudged toward his home.

Embarrass was not exactly a large town—perhaps six hundred people in all—but even that was too many for Wylie. That was why he lived way out here instead. Technically, he was still within city limits, if only barely. More importantly, he lived right on the edge of Heikkila Lake, his back door opening onto a short, sturdy pier that projected out a good twenty feet onto the surface of the lake. He never had to go more than a few dozen paces to sit and fish or take a quick swim.

Crossing the short distance from his truck—the pillar marked the end of the rough road, such as it was—to his cabin, Wylie glanced around, studying his surroundings out of old habit. But there was no one about and nothing stirring. Even the water lay still. Good.

"Honey, I'm home!" he sang out as he pushed open the always-unlocked front door and crossed the threshold. "Oh, wait—I'm not married."

The cabin wasn't very big and had only a single room, plus a bathroom and closet off to the side, so it didn't take more than a few steps to cross the space and plunk his two bags down atop the kitchen counter. It had once been smooth white porcelain, but that had worn and yellowed and cracked long ago, so Wylie had ripped that out and replaced it with a simple slab he carved from a downed white oak, trimming out a hole for the sink, and then nailing the slab in place and sanding it smooth. Though initially, he'd replaced the surface out of mere expediency, Wylie had grown to appreciate the wood's golden hue and the subtle streaks that ran through it. Over the years, he'd lavished a fair bit of care on the countertop, trimming its edges for a cleaner line, keeping it sanded smooth, and even treating it with wood oil to bring out its natural shine.

And if it looked out of place in such a ramshackle home, what did he care? It wasn't like anyone else ever had to see the place.

Transferring the groceries into his fridge, Wylie pulled a single long-neck beer from the four-pack, holding that back to have with his dinner. The remaining cash from Roy went into an old coffee can on the window ledge above the sink. Then, beer in one hand and dinner sack in the other, he turned back toward the front door, or at least that general vicinity, stopping short of the entrance to plop down in his recliner instead.

It hadn't been easy to find a chair that could accommodate him—Wylie was over seven feet tall, after all, and weighed nearly four hundred pounds. He'd searched long and hard, using the town's public library and, more specifically, its one computer. Then there'd been the issue of how to pay for it—he didn't have a credit card or even a bank account, so in the end, he'd had to save up, bring his money in cash to the one bank, and get them to cut him a money order. Then he'd had to wait while they'd shipped it to him. But when this beauty had finally arrived, and he'd carried it in and then sat down, letting its microfiber cushions envelop his back and rear and cradle his arms and legs and neck...

This, he'd thought, *must be what Heaven feels like.*

Which reminded him. Setting the beer and bag on the floor for a moment, he undid his shirt front, his big fingers clumsy on the tiny buttons as usual. Then, leaning forward, he shrugged it off and tossed it into the far corner, onto his bed. Ah, that was better! The boots came off next, and he flexed his toes, enjoying the cool air flowing across them and over his bare arms and chest. The cabin had no heat, not that he needed any, and the windows were open as usual, allowing the cold, crisp air to wind its way in off the lake. There was a northeasterly cant to the breeze today—he could always tell. Wylie breathed deep and smiled, settling back into his chair. Yeah, that was a whole lot better.

After all, where would a Yeti be without the cold?

Fetching the remote from where it hung in its holster off the chair arm, he turned on the set. Other than the recliner, the TV was the only expensive item in the entire place, but it was a beauty — sixty-five inches, 5k, OLED stereo speakers, with a built-in smart TV function. There wasn't any reception out here, of course, but he'd installed a satellite on the roof and could get all his shows without a problem. Could probably go online, too, if he really wanted. Which he rarely did. TV was enough for him.

Flipping around, he finally settled on an episode of *Magnum, PI*. The original, not the revamp — he liked that one okay too, but there was just something fun and soothing about the classic version. Plus, even though he couldn't imagine ever wanting it for himself, Wylie enjoyed watching Magnum and the others running around in Hawaii's warmth, heat, and greenery. Once the opening credits finished, he tore open the paper bag, extracting the canister of chowder and the foil-wrapped oblong that was the bread. Both were still warm, which was more than enough for him. He happily tore chunks off the bread, dipping it into the chowder and then stuffing the whole soggy mass into his mouth while he watched Magnum drive that fancy red sports car and leap in and out of trouble, taking the occasional sip of beer to wash it all down.

Yeah, this was the life.

Later, after finishing the food — and both slices of pie, despite a momentary thought of saving one for tomorrow — and then shoving the empty soup container and crumpled ball of foil and torn bag into a trash bag, Wylie finally shut off the television and got ready for bed. There wasn't a great deal to do, of course. He brushed his teeth — he'd bought a heavy-duty electric toothbrush for that, which proved far faster and easier than trying to scrub at each fang by hand! Splashed some water on his face. Used the toilet. Then shucked his jeans and collapsed on his bed, which groaned beneath the weight but did not collapse. He hadn't bothered to turn on any other lights, and the windows stayed open all night, every night.

For a few minutes, he just lay there, hands behind his head, staring up at the ceiling. His feet dangled over the side, of course, but he was used to that, and when ready to actually go to sleep, he'd just roll onto his side, curling up a bit to fit all of himself atop the mattress. For the moment, it was enough to lay here and think back over the day's events.

It had been a stressful one, as it always was when he had to go into town. Not that he didn't like Roy and Kyra per se, he just always had to be so careful around them!

Then there had been that boy. That had been interesting. It had happened once or twice before. Children seemed to perceive more, or maybe it was just that they didn't have that filter most adults developed, the one that told them, "No, that can't be real, you're imagining things," and convinced them there was some other explanation for what they were seeing. Which was why most people just saw him as a really big, really hairy guy with bad teeth and long nails.

It was only the rare one — or the small child — who saw him as the supernatural beast he truly was.

Beast. Wylie snorted. Yeah, some beast. Living in an old shack, selling fish for beer money, watching old TV all day. I'm a real terror, all right. A danger to every man, woman, and child.

He chuckled again, then scrubbed one hand over his face, stifling a yawn. Well, this beast needed his beauty sleep — not that it would help any.

Tomorrow was another day. And there'd be more TV to watch, maybe some dishes or clothes to wash. And, of course, there'd be fish out there in the lake, just waiting to be caught.

Too bad there wouldn't be any more pie. But he had no one but himself to blame for that.

That night, Wylie dreamed. Usually, when that happened, he had only vague recollections, disjointed images or sounds, random snatches of color or music, or a half-remembered face. Often, he dreamed about the shows he watched, imagining he was in them himself, driving that sports car or flying that helicopter or chasing down that bad guy.

Not this time, though.

This time, he was himself, and the world was the one he knew, cold and clear and clean, the snow smooth and untouched, the trees dusted with it, the moon hidden behind clouds but the way still clear. He was running through the forest, his wide, flat feet barely denting the soft snow as he leaped with great long strides, his fur blending into the snowy landscape, his passage making only the faintest whistle against the wind whose path he was following, letting the cold itself guide his motions. His nostrils flared, and he stopped suddenly, reaching out to catch himself against a tree, his claws stabbing deep into its bark. There!

Up ahead, he heard a sound, just a whisper of movement. A scent tickled his nose, sour and sharp.

Men. There were men up ahead.

Creeping closer, Wylie crouched down, peering between trees and over fallen trunks half-buried by snow and dirt and time. Now he could hear voices and the crackle of a fire. The trees ahead had a yellowish cast to their far side, reflecting the flames, and he snuck toward them. Yes, there was a campfire going. Three men sat around it, warming their hands and passing a bottle back and forth as they laughed. Rifles rested at their sides, and Wylie's lips curled back in a silent snarl at the sight.

Hunters. He hated hunters. Killing for meat was one thing. But for sport? That was wrong. And using guns? That was wrong, too. They should use knives, or clubs, or, better yet, bare hands. The weapons nature gave them. Not these... tools. It gave them an unfair advantage.

Although, he thought, flexing his claws and baring his fangs, *even with the guns, I'd hold the advantage.*

But that wasn't the sort of thing he did. Not anymore. Not for a long time now.

This wasn't reality, however. It was a dream. And in the dream, Wylie did not turn away. He did not return to his cabin, and his television, and his bed. Instead, he rose to his feet and, with a terrible roar, leaped forward, over the log, into the center of the campsite. His big feet came down on the fire, snuffing it out and plunging the spot into darkness—a darkness he could see through just fine.

And then there was nothing but swift motion, growls, wet tearing sounds, and screams. Screams that echoed against the trees before cutting short, leaving little behind but a few last gasps—and a terrible howl, the exultant cry of a beast victorious.

Wylie woke with a start. The sun was just starting to inch up over the horizon, the first rays slowly lightening that farthest edge of the sky. A few industrious birds were already out and chirping, the water of the lake lapped against the shore, and he thought he could almost hear the fish deep within it circling about, taunting him and daring him to come out after them.

With a grunt, he sat up, rubbing his hand through his hair—and then stopped, holding the offending limb before him for inspection.

Caught upon his claws and dusted across his furred fingers were scraps of something rough and almost scaley. A dry, brittle material that shredded easily, releasing a pungent odor. Tree bark, and fresh.

But how had that wound up all over his hands when it had not been there the night before?

CHAPTER THREE

TWO DAYS LATER, WYLIE FOUND HIMSELF BACK IN TOWN.

Normally he went at least a couple weeks between visits, staying away until he'd eaten the last of the fresh food he'd bought, drunk the last of the beer, and was down to his last few cans of beans and boxes of mac n cheese, the emergency staples he kept for when everything else had run out.

But this time, he found he had no choice. Because even worse than being low on food, he was nearly out of life's most vital necessity:

Toilet paper.

It was impossible to think that anyone who had not grown up out in the wild, as he had, could truly understand. But when you'd spent the first few decades literally rubbing your backside up against trees or swiping at yourself with handfuls of dried—you hoped!—leaves, that first time that you crept into an empty cabin off-season and, wandering through the place, happened upon the bathroom, and that roll of fluffy white paper hanging there beside the toilet?

Forget the recliner, even. If there was anything closer to Heaven than using actual, honest-to-God quilted toilet paper, he couldn't imagine it.

That cabin had been his first taste of what life could be like. A roof over your head, walls around you, running water in the sink, a flush toilet, a stove and a fridge—and toilet paper.

He'd gotten scolded when he'd gone back home, but it had been more than worth the trouble. And, a few days after, Wylie'd returned to that cabin. Spent a few hours exploring it, studying the clothes he found hanging in the closet, the blankets folded in the cedar chest by the foot of the bed, and turning the knobs on the sink and on the stove.

The third time, he'd gotten more daring. Stretched out on the bed—which had protested mightily but endured—and fallen asleep, luxuriating in its softness, like sleeping on a cloud.

The trouble for that one had been far, far worse. But it was much too late by then. Wylie was hooked.

A month later, he'd been right back at that cabin. That was when he'd figured out how to turn on the television. Watching that, flipping through channels for hours on end, had been like a crash course in "being human." And, when he'd emerged from the cabin almost a week later, he'd been stuffed into a pair of sweatpants and a rain slicker—the only clothes there big enough to even remotely fit him—with an old Lakers cap perched atop his head and a pair of sunglasses hiding his yellow eyes.

That was the day Wylie Kang had truly been born.

He'd moved around a bit since then, scrounging and saving money doing odd jobs in between hunting and fishing, eventually buying this place for cash, so he didn't have to keep breaking into cabin after cabin. Got his truck used off an old retiree, found customers like Ray and Kyra, and settled into a routine.

Never looked back.

Which was why, when he'd noticed the toilet paper roll was getting low and, reaching for a replacement, had grasped nothing but air, he'd felt a moment's panic. He couldn't go back to bark and leaves. He just couldn't!

So instead, he'd hopped in his pickup and driven back into town. There were actually a few stores in Embarrass, but Wylie always went to the same one: Trapline. Mostly a liquor store, the place also carried basic supplies, food, and even live bait. They had everything Wylie needed—including toilet paper—and that saved him from having to go to multiple places, which would have meant dealing with more people.

Stepping through the front door, Wylie waved at Linda, who was manning the counter today. She smiled and waved back, all without ever really looking up from her phone. Linda was in high school or community college or some such, Wylie forgot which, but she worked here most weekday afternoons.

He knew his way around the store, of course, and immediately headed straight toward the "paper goods" aisle. If he'd realized his TP supply had been nearly out, he'd have picked up more the other day, but that's how it always went. You never realized what you had until it was almost gone.

This time, to be safe, he snatched up two large packages. That should keep him for a while! But just as he turned to head back out front and pay, he heard the front door jingle. Then an unfamiliar voice.

"Hoping you can help me." It was a woman, he could tell that much, her voice deep and strong and with that same no-nonsense tone he'd heard from people at the post office or the licensing board. Serious. Official.

"Sure, whaddya need?" Linda asked. "We got beer, wine, and liquor of all sorts, over this way. That way's the groceries, over there's office supplies, and that's the live bait area, over there. We—"

"I'm actually just after some information," the woman said, cutting her off, and Wylie edged a little closer, peering over the shelves. He could make out the back of a head—dark hair, pulled into a thick braid. Taller than Linda, who wasn't small herself, and solidly built. Jeans, leather jacket, boots.

And a long hunting knife hanging from her belt on one side, with a large holster on the other.

Definitely looked like someone who knew how to handle themselves.

"I'm looking for someone," she said as Wylie focused again. "Probably travels a bit but passes through regularly. Big. Quiet. Keeps to himself, mostly. Probably lives outside town?"

Wylie caught his breath and ducked back down just as Linda glanced in his direction. "Huh," she replied, popping her gum, which he knew she only did when she got annoyed at someone. "Yeah, no, don't think I know anybody like that. Sorry. Did you want to buy anything?"

"Thanks. Maybe some other time." There were footsteps, quick but not hurried, solid but not heavy, and then the door rang once more.

Wylie waited another minute or two before stepping into view.

"Sounds like you're gonna have company, maybe," Linda said, ringing up the toilet paper even before he'd set them down on the counter. "Everything okay?" He was surprised by the look in her eyes— was that concern? She had lied for him, after all. He'd always been polite to her, but he wouldn't have thought they were friends.

"Hope so," he answered, digging out some cash and handing it over. "Thanks." Then, scooping up the toilet paper, he headed out to his truck.

It was the only vehicle in sight besides the baby-blue VW Bug Linda drove, and Wylie wasted no time hopping in and peeling out, heading back to his cabin as fast as he could legally go. But he turned off a block later, pulling over to the curb to think for a minute. Then, instead of heading straight home, after all, he got back on the road, took the first right, and headed to the Roadside Diner instead.

He needed to know who that woman was and what she wanted with him. And Ray and Kyra were the closest things to friends he had here. At least Ray usually chatted a bit when he came into town. And Kyra always fed him. That had to count for something, right?

No sooner had he pulled up outside the restaurant, though, than Ray was slipping out the front door and making a beeline for the truck, a heavy paper sack clutched under one arm. Like he'd been waiting for Wylie to show.

"You've got trouble headed your way, son," the restauranteur stated as he approached. "Some woman was just in here looking for you. I didn't tell her nothing, but Jimmy couldn't keep his mouth shut." Jimmy was the waiter and busboy. He didn't like Wylie much, ever since the time he'd been hitting on some girl, and Wylie had told him to knock it off.

"What's she want with me?" Wylie asked, leaving the truck idling but hanging his arm out the open window as they talked.

Ray shook his head. "Nothing good. Seems there's some folks got killed a night or two back, out in the woods past you. Torn to shreds, she said, like a bear or wolves or something. She said she just wanted to know if you'd seen anything, but—" He frowned. "I don't like the way she looked when she said it. Less like you were a possible witness and more like you were the wild dog yourself." He patted Wylie on the arm. "I was you, I'd clear out for a few days, maybe. She'll nose around, not find you, and move on to pestering somebody else." He proffered the sack. "Kyra packed you up some grub, should last you a day or two at least."

Wylie accepted the bag, settling it onto the seat beside him. "Tell her thank you for me," he said. "And thank you." Ray nodded, raising a hand as he backed off a few paces. He stayed there, half-waving, as Wylie pulled away.

This time Wylie didn't take any detours. He needed to hurry and hope she hadn't beaten him there. Because, based on what Ray had said, he had a feeling he knew who—or what—this stranger was:

A Hunter.

Not like a person who hunted deer or bear or anything, either. No, Hunters went for much rarer game and far more dangerous.

They hunted supernaturals.

Like him.

That's why the questions. Torn to shreds, ripped apart, asking about someone big and strong and solitary—yeah, she wasn't tracking any wild dogs or rogue bears. She was on the trail of a supernatural killer.

And if Jimmy'd blabbed about him, she might already have a pretty good guess as to what Wylie was. A Yeti—big, strong, fast, clawed and fanged, likes the cold.

Easily capable of tearing a man to bits.

She'd figure she'd found her killer. And, like most anyone who hunted something dangerous, she'd be trained to shoot first and question later. If at all. Which meant he wasn't going to be able to talk his way out of this.

His only choice was to run.

Unbidden, a memory came over him as he drove.

"Steer clear of Hunters," his father'd said. "They're nasty, and they love to kill our kind, take trophies, brag about it after. That's what did for your ma. Got careless, got caught, got dead."

"They're just people with guns, right?" his little brother'd asked. "We can handle those, no problem."

But their father had shaken his head. "Trust me on this," he'd warned, as serious as Wylie'd ever seen him. "You ever see a Hunter, don't even think about trying to fight. Just run. Fast as you can, far as you can. Stay safe, stay hidden, and stay alive."

Which was exactly what Wylie planned to do now.

Pulling up at his cabin, he was relieved to not see any other vehicles in sight. Nor did he catch scent of anyone human having been there. Leaving the food bag on the front seat, he rushed inside. The advantage of having only one room was, there wasn't any place to hide, so a quick glance was enough to confirm that he was still alone.

That wouldn't last, though. He had to move fast.

Reaching under his bed, he hauled out an oversized gym bag in classic camouflage. He'd got it from a clothing company a while back as a free gift when he'd ordered a whole bunch of shirts all at once. Now he shoved all those shirts into it, along with his jeans, gloves, and hats. Next, he ducked into the bathroom and grabbed his toiletries, including the shampoo and conditioner from the shower—he bought the big family size and went through it fast. All that went into a plastic bag, which was added to the gym bag, along with the coffee can from the kitchen windowsill. Then he got his tackle box and both fishing rods. Those went out to the pickup, the box on the floor with the food bag, the gym bag on the seat, the rods slung across the gun rack in back—it had come with the truck.

That only left two things. Heading back into the cabin, Wylie snatched the blanket off his bed and wrapped it around his TV, which he unplugged. Then he hauled that out under one arm, his recliner with the other. The recliner went in the truck bed—he had a tarp back there, which he tossed over it and secured to the tie-downs around the lip, locking the big chair in place. The TV he lay down between the recliner and the cab, screen down. That should keep it safe as well.

Then, his two most precious possessions safely onboard, Wylie climbed back into the cab and started the pickup. He frowned as he pulled away, studying the cabin—somehow, even though it didn't look any different on the outside, it felt empty now, hollowed out.

He wondered as he drove away if he'd ever see the place again.

CHAPTER FOUR

SEVERAL HOURS LATER, WYLIE SLOWED TO A STOP AND GULPED.

"Wow," he whispered.

There, ahead of him, soared a tableau he never had, could never have even imagined. Buildings towered into the sky, their gleaming tops brushing the clouds. They all appeared to be either shining metal or some sort of white stone that almost glowed in the sunlight, though there were all different styles and shapes—some had clean, squared sides and flat tops, others were more layered and their tops more chiseled, and some were rounded, like a cluster of pillars or columns all huddled together for warmth, or the sculpture of a bouquet whose heads had all been shorn away, leaving only the gathered stems. It was absolutely amazing, and he knew his eyes were wide as he took it all in.

Minneapolis-St. Paul. The Twin Cities.

He had never realized buildings could get so big, or that a city could have so many of them.

How many people must live here? he wondered as he stared. Though still a good ways away, he could make out the zooming shapes of cars driving along the roads there, and already there were more people than he'd ever seen in one place. Heck, it was probably more people than he'd seen his whole life put together!

But then, that had been the whole point.

He'd stuck out like a sore thumb back in Embarrass. "That one big, hairy, bearded guy who lives off by himself, doesn't talk much. Who knows what he gets up to out there?" Yeah, not all that hard to find.

So, he'd figured, why not go someplace he'd be almost impossible to find? Some place with so many people you'd never be able to pick even someone like him out of the crowd?

Only problem was, what did he know about crowds? Or cities? Sure, he'd made it here.

So, what the heck did he do now?

Well, first thing's first. He couldn't just sit here—he'd pulled the truck off onto the shoulder, but even so, people were honking as they drove past. He needed to get back on the road, make his way into the city proper.

And, seeing as how it was well into afternoon, and the sky was already starting to darken in the east and blush in the west, he should probably find a place to stay for the night. He could figure out his next steps come morning.

With that in mind, he started driving again. Only now, in between glancing up and gawking at the skyline, he was peering about, looking for something he'd never searched for before—a hotel.

He finally spotted a great big rambling place with three or four floors and a massive peaked roof. "Country Inn & Suites," he read. Well, that sounded fine.

Pulling into the big parking lot, Wylie saw that there were plenty of empty spaces. Good. He didn't want to have to deal with too many people just yet. Better to ease into things. Shutting off the engine, he reached into the gym bag, finding the coffee can and extracting some of its contents. Then he started to hop out but paused. He wasn't in Embarrass now. Better roll up the windows and lock the door. Just to be safe.

The place's front doors were wide and made entirely of glass save for their heavy metal frames. They slid open as he approached, and he had to remember to duck as he stepped inside. A second set of doors stood just beyond that, and then there was a big, wide room with a floor of orangish tiles. At the far end was what looked like some sort of dining room, chairs gathered around tables and a counter along one wall, but his attention went to the long desk to his immediate left and the young man standing behind it.

"Good afternoon, and welcome to Country Inn and Suites," the man called as Wylie stomped over. "How can I help you?" He didn't look much older than Linda, short and stocky, with pale blond hair brushed back from his face and round glasses. The nametag on his shirt read "Bill."

"I need a room," Wylie answered. At least he had some idea how this worked, thanks to all the TV he'd watched! "For tonight. Just me."

"Of course, sir." Bill turned to the computer in front of him—Wylie hadn't even noticed it at first because it was tucked down behind the upper part of the desk—and tapped a few keys. "I can put you in a room on the third floor if that's all right?" He glanced up and smiled. "It's eighty dollars for the night, plus a refundable forty dollars for damage and incidentals. I'll just need your driver's license and a credit card."

Wylie was still reeling a little at the price—a hundred and twenty dollars? Just for a room for one night?—so it took him a second for the rest of that sentence to sink in. When it did, he blinked and shuffled his feet. "I'm paying in cash," he explained, his hand going to the money he'd stuck in his jeans pocket. He was pretty sure he'd brought in enough to cover that.

"That's fine," Bill replied, "but I will still need a credit card for incidentals. Hotel policy, I'm afraid." He gestured toward a sign on the wall behind him, and Wylie squinted a little to make it out. Sure enough, it said exactly that.

"I don't have a credit card," he tried again. Which caused the young man to frown.

"Ah, I'm sorry," he answered. "I really am. But I can't rent you a room without one."

Wylie blinked at him again, but although he flushed and looked away, Bill apparently was not going to change his mind. With a sigh, Wylie turned and headed back out.

There were bound to be other hotels, after all.

He was right, of course. There were other hotels. A lot of them, in fact, and quite a few dotted along Highway 35, the route he'd come in on.

Unfortunately, all of them seemed to have the exact same rule.

"How do you expect people without credit cards to survive?" Wylie demanded after the fourth place had told him the exact same thing.

"I've never even met someone without a credit card," the guy behind the counter—this one's name was Tommy—replied. "Not until today, anyway." He shrugged. "Sorry."

Wylie growled but cut off when he saw Tommy flinch, the poor kid's face going white. "Yeah, whatever." He stomped out. It was dark now, and he was getting tired, plus his rear ached, and his legs and back and shoulders. He didn't normally spend this much time crammed into the truck. Should he just give up, he wondered as he climbed back in yet again, hauling the door shut behind him. Find some place to just park instead? Even drive back out of the city a little ways and pull off the road? He could sleep in his recliner, he'd certainly done that often enough, and it wasn't like he needed heat.

But he wasn't ready to resign himself to that just yet. There had to be someplace that would take him, even without a stupid credit card!

"The U-Turn Motel," he read on the sign. "Sure, why not?"

It wasn't much to look at compared to the big, fancy hotels he'd tried so far. *But maybe that's for the best,* Wylie thought, pulling up in front of the low, single-story building that stretched in a wide U around the parking lot. Doors lined the walkway beneath a sturdy roof. So, each room had its own entrance? He could work with that!

The first door had a sign reading "Office" over it, so that was where Wylie headed. Sure enough, inside was the same sort of long desk he'd seen at every other hotel, though this one looked a bit more rundown and a bit less polished. The man behind it was a good deal older, too, paunchy and balding. "Rooms're fifty a night," he said as soon as Wylie ducked into the office—no sliding glass doors here! "Plus a forty-dollar security deposit—you get that back when you leave."

"I don't have a credit card," Wylie told him, figuring he'd better get that out of the way first. "That a problem?" He didn't mean to come off quite so terse, but he was exhausted and frustrated.

"Naw," the man—no name tag on this one!—replied. "Cash's fine." He held out a hand. "Driver's license, security deposit, first night's rent."

Wylie handed over his driver's license and then peeled a fifty and two twenties from the wad in his hand.

"Sign here," came next, as a heavy register was pushed across the desk. Wylie did so—he'd never been very good at writing. His fingers were so big and his claws so long, but he'd worked hard on getting at least a passable signature, and the man barely glanced at it before handing back his license, along with a receipt and a key. "Room twenty-four."

"Thanks." Wylie felt some relief as he exited and started down the walkway, glancing at each room number in turn. At least that had worked out!

As luck would have it, number twenty-four was at the far end of the second U, which put it right by where he'd parked his truck. That was just fine. Opening the door, Wylie stepped in and glanced about him. The walls were rough pine, a bit like his cabin. The ceiling was lower than he'd like but tall enough that he could at least stand straight without bumping his head, and it was an unbroken sheet of white. The bed looked big enough for him to manage, and there was a chair, a TV, a dresser, a bathroom he could just squeeze into, and a closet. There were also two windows, one in front and one in back.

Well, it would do.

Going back to his pickup, he grabbed the gym bag and tackle box and food and brought them in. Then shoved the existing chair into the corner, put the TV in the closet, and dragged in his own, setting them up instead. Ah, that was better, he thought as he opened both windows as far as they would go — there was a cold front moving in from the east, which felt lovely — tossed his shirt on the bed, settled into the recliner, and kicked off his boots. In a way, it was almost like home.

Snatching the paper bag from the little bedside table he'd set it on, Wylie peered inside. Ah, Kyra was a queen! There was another carton of chowder, several more slices of pie, another roll, something like it but a bit longer and heavier, he suspected was a sandwich, and two round, flat-topped serving containers. He opened the first one to find pot roast, new potatoes, carrots, and gravy. The second proved to hold fried chicken, mashed potatoes, corn, and cole slaw. There were also two water bottles, so Wylie extracted one of those, along with the fried chicken plate and the pie.

He'd eat, then watch some TV, then get some sleep.

In the morning, he'd come up with a plan on what to do next.

And, he thought with a smile as he ripped into the drumstick, the salty crunch of the batter exploding in his mouth, *maybe I'll even do a little exploring.*

After all, it wasn't every day a Yeti came to the big city.

CHAPTER FIVE

WYLIE WOKE TO RAISED VOICES.

"Wha—?" He flailed a bit, dragging himself up and out of the re-cliner, his eyes still half shut. The voices were loud and fast. Two of them, a man and a woman. But, he realized as his brain slowly regis-tered the fact that he was still alone in the room. The sound was com-ing from the room next door.

It sounded like an argument, though he couldn't make out the words. The man sounded angry, the woman alternately angry and... frightened, maybe? Wylie wasn't sure. What he did know was that it was only—he squinted at the clock on the bedside table—six in the morning.

"Keep it down over there!" he bellowed at last.

Instant silence.

"Ah, better," he grumbled and flopped back down. But, after a few minutes of tossing and turning, he finally had to sit up and admit the truth:

There was no going back to bed for him.

"Well, that's just great," he groused as he dragged himself into the bathroom. He ached all over—the price he often paid for sleeping in the chair—and the shower was too small to hold his bulk, so he had to content himself with splashing water on his face. Then he stuffed him-self back into a pair of jeans and a shirt—a dark grey today, to match his mood—snagged one of the caps from his bag—a Minnesota Wild one he'd picked up somewhere—and headed for the door.

His hand already on the knob, he paused. Was it smart to leave his stuff out in the open like this? Probably not. So, he shut the windows and the curtains and, after taking out a few bills, tucked the coffee can deep into the bag, which he slung up on the shelf at the top of the closet. Then he grabbed the "Do Not Disturb" sign and, as he exited, slipped that onto the doorknob, making sure he had his key and that the door was shut securely behind him.

There. Much better.

Making his way to the office, Wylie wasn't all that surprised to see the same unnamed man behind the desk. This place didn't look like it had a whole lot of staff. "Checking out or extending your stay?" the man asked. Again no "hello" or "good morning" or "how was the room?"! But he hadn't come here for good manners, Wylie supposed. And a place that was willing to take him without one of those blasted cards could get away with a whole lot, in his book.

"Extending," Wylie replied, placing another fifty on the counter. "One more night."

The money disappeared, and the man made a notation on the log book beside Wylie's name from the night before. "You got it. Need maid service?"

"Naw, it's all good." There didn't seem to be anything more to say, so Wylie turned and headed back out. He had tonight's lodgings taken care of, so that was good. That just left the day—and figuring out what he was going to do with himself in general.

Could he just head back home in a few days? Maybe. It depended upon how persistent that Hunter was and how much she thought he was the killer she was after.

From what he knew about Hunters, Wylie had to assume the answer to the first question was "very" and to the second "a whole lot."

Which meant he should stay away a little longer, just to be safe.

He couldn't just sit around his motel room all day, though. Both because it'd drive him nuts—not the solitude, he was used to that, it was having other people shouting and stomping around nearby!—and because he'd run out of money if he didn't find a way to earn some while he was here.

But it wasn't like he could just go fishing. He wouldn't know where to start, where the best fish were, and even if he caught something, he'd have no idea where to sell it.

He'd have to think of something else. But to do that, he'd need a better idea of the city itself.

So, it was time to do some wandering.

It turned out that he was quite a bit farther out than he'd realized. Wylie'd hoped to just walk toward downtown, but when he asked a random woman in the parking lot how long that would take, she just laughed at him. "How many days've you got?" she asked in reply.

So, he hopped back in his truck instead.

Steering back onto the highway, Wylie was surprised to find that the cityscape he'd admired last night had completely disappeared. Now all he could see was the road ahead of him, hills and grass to either side and here and there, a big building off in the distance. Not one of the skyscrapers from before, however—these looked more like warehouses or stores, big and boxy.

Apparently, he had just been at exactly the right angle and elevation when he'd looked before. Strange. Of course, that also meant those towers were probably even bigger than he'd first realized, which was impressive.

Now the only question was how to get to them.

He drove for a while longer, passing sign after sign for various streets and roads whose names he didn't know. Then, all of a sudden, the countryside fell away. The road continued on, but now it was alone in spanning a vast river, the asphalt transformed to stone.

He was crossing the Mississippi. And there, ahead of him, rose the cityscape again at last, now even bigger and bolder than before.

He'd made it!

A few minutes later, the bridge transitioning back into a normal street with buildings beginning to spring up on either side, Wylie passed a sign that said, "public parking, next left."

Okay, Wylie thought. *I can use that.*

He turned left and, sure enough, found a large parking lot on his right. It was already more than two-thirds full, but he maneuvered his pickup into an empty space without difficulty. The parking wasn't free, it seemed, judging by the meters at the front of each space. He dug into his pockets for change, finally coming up with a handful of quarters. "Max time reached," the meter informed him after he'd fed those into the slot one at a time. He took the little slip of paper it offered and, following the instructions on it, returned to his truck to place that on the dash.

He had, apparently, the rest of the day — the spot was paid for until seven, and then parking was free until morning again. Interesting system.

"Right, time to see the sights," Wylie told himself. "And maybe," he added as his stomach grumbled, "find some grub."

Walking the streets proved to be an interesting experience. Embarrass had paved roads, of course, but there weren't really any sidewalks — the town was too spread out to need them. Here, Wylie was hard-pressed to find dirt in between all the concrete and asphalt covering the ground. The sidewalks felt stiff and unyielding beneath his feet, and he was glad for his boots — he hated to think what'd it be like to walk on such a surface barefoot!

The buildings were a lot more numerous than he was used to, of course, and closer together. Every block had at least one, if not more, and many were four, five, six stories tall.

And the people. There were so many of them! He was used to only seeing perhaps a dozen at a time on the rare occasions when he ventured into town. Here, he'd counted more than that before even making it out of the parking lot. Most of them were varying shades of white, but he did spot a few with darker skin, ranging in size from tiny to nearly his size. He even spotted a man with purple hair and a woman whose long locks were as white as his own.

That last one made him blink a bit. She was tall and slender, and her hair was long and loose, flowing about her as if caught up in a breeze, though the air felt still. There was something ethereal about her, the way she moved like she floated over the ground instead of walking, the dreamy look in her eyes, that made Wylie stop and stare. She noticed, but instead of recoiling or running, she ducked her head as if she were the one embarrassed. That made him glance away quickly, feeling bad for discomforting someone else, though he supposed it was better than screaming.

Yes, this place was definitely not what he was used to.

He'd only gone a few blocks when he spotted another strange new thing. A truck was pulled up along the side of the road, but it wasn't empty like the rest. Nor was it a plain, boring vehicle. This one was painted a bright, cheery blue, and along the side, there was a wide opening with an awning overhead, as if someone had cut away the panel and hoisted it up. Several people waited in line, and as Wylie watched, the first one got to the opening and said something to the two girls working inside. A moment later, one of them handed him a lidded cup. Steam was escaping from it, and Wylie smiled. Even from here, he could tell what that was.

Lumbering into line, he was careful not to step too close to the woman in front of him, a wee thing heavily bundled in a thick coat, scarf, hat, mittens, and boots. He knew the size of his own feet only too well! They shuffled forward slowly, and he had time to study the menu written in bright chalk on the blackboard beside the window. There were various coffee flavors, and hot chocolate, and tea, plus a few things to eat like scones and biscuits and cookies. The prices made him blanch a bit—six dollars for a cup of coffee? Three for a cookie?—but the novelty drew him on, as did the rumblings of his stomach. Finally, the tiny woman in front of him had placed her order and stepped aside, and suddenly it was his turn.

"One large iced coffee with milk and sugar, please," he said, making sure to speak each word clearly. "And a cookie. Chocolate chip."

The girl at the register—also small, he thought, and with hair an interesting shade of dark red he wasn't sure could be natural—stared at him. "Iced?" she repeated.

"Yep."

She frowned, still studying him a second, then shrugged. "Nine." He handed her a ten, and she passed him back a single dollar. Then he stepped to the side to wait.

It only took a minute, then the other girl handed him a large cup and an enormous, thick cookie wrapped in plastic. "Straws're there," she said, gesturing at a dispenser to the side, next to a napkin holder. "Have a good day!"

"You too. Thanks." Her words warmed him more than any coffee would—they were about the first kind ones he'd had here so far! He stepped aside to let the next customer up, snagging a straw and some napkins as he moved off. Shredding the straw wrapper and sticking the drinking implement through the small hole in the cup's lid, he raised it to his mouth and drew in a long, deep sip.

Ah!

He'd never much cared for hot drinks—or hot food—but the first time he'd ever smelled coffee, cooked over a fire by some campers he'd spied on years ago, he'd been hooked by the aroma alone. And when he'd broken into that cabin, he'd found a can of ground coffee in the cupboard.

It was the same can he had stashed in his bag back in the motel room.

That first time had been a revelation, and over the years, he'd actually learned how to brew coffee properly. But this! This was amazing! It was deeper and richer than what he made and sweeter, too, without a hint of bitterness. Two sips and he could already feel it flowing through his veins, blasting away any last hints of fatigue, filling him with vim and vigor.

Of all the things he wished his father and brother and cousins had discovered and come to appreciate, coffee topped the list.

The cookie proved to be excellent as well—sturdy enough not to crumble away when he bit into it, but not hard at all, a little tender and a little chewy, sweet but with a hint of salt to counter that, the chips more like chunks, not gooey at all and rich like the coffee.

All in all, he had to admit it might even have been worth the nine bucks.

Thus fortified, Wylie studied his surroundings anew. The building behind him was two stories but took up the entire block and had interesting features like flat columns and strange ridges just below the roofline. A black metal railing ran along the side, with empty tables and chairs he suspected got more use in milder weather. Across the wide street stood a grouping of much taller buildings, tan and white and very geometric, but with trees lining their fronts to break up the monotony. Across the other way were a pair of tall buildings, one all grey and metal and very modern-looking, the other reddish stone and far more embellished. Wylie was surprised at how wide the streets and the sidewalks were, and how, even though there were so many buildings about and often quite tall, he could still see so much of the sky. He'd thought he'd feel a good deal more closed-in, more claustrophobic, in the big city. This wasn't so bad!

He was still considering that as he walked, picking a direction at random and winding up going past the trees as well as a row of people waiting at a small semi-enclosed glass hut and a boy in a red cap scrawling a fanciful landscape on the sidewalk with large chalks. There were other people about, and although Wylie did his best to give them space, he still took up a lot of room, especially when he had to skirt one of the trees. So, he was not terribly surprised when, as he crossed to drop his now-empty coffee cup and cookie wrapper in a trash can, he bumped a man going the other way. He quickly apologized.

What he didn't expect was the shout that rose from behind him a second later: "Oy, you! Stop right there!"

CHAPTER SIX

WYLIE'S FIRST INSTINCT, BORN FROM HIS EARLY YEARS, WAS TO GO completely still. Of course, that had worked a lot better when he'd been clad in only his fur and was hoping to blend into the equally white snow all around him!

"I said stop!" the shouter continued in a deep, strong voice, which puzzled Wylie further. He *had* stopped! What was the man on about?

Heavy footsteps thudded on the sidewalk—someone his own size or perhaps even bigger, from the sound of it!

Wylie glanced behind him. And stared.

Because what he saw simply made no sense.

First off, the pounding was coming from a small figure he quickly recognized as the boy street artist. How was he making such a racket when he was so small and slight?

Second, the boy was running away from Wylie, not toward him.

Third, he was not the only one running.

A man was fleeing, or trying to—despite the differences in their size, the boy quickly caught up with him. He looked familiar, and after a second, Wylie realized it was the same guy he'd just bumped into over by the trash can. Maybe he'd been littering? If so, they were really strict about that around here!

"Hand it over!" the boy demanded, and the deep voice proved to be his as well. The man resisted—and the boy grabbed him by the front of his jacket and hoisted him up into the air like an empty sack until his feet dangled off the ground, kicking uselessly. "I said hand it over!"

The man fumbled something out of a pocket, which the boy accepted before tossing his captive aside like so much trash. Evidently, the impact had not been severe, however, because a second later, the man stumbled back to his feet and hurried off, limping slightly. The other people around quickly turned away, acting as if they hadn't seen any of that but giving both of the figures involved a wide berth.

And the boy had now turned and was heading toward Wylie instead.

"Here you go," the little youngster said as he reached Wylie. He was holding out—Wylie's wallet. "I saw him nick it. Can't be having that, not on my watch."

"Oh." Wylie accepted the wallet back. It didn't have much in it, really—his driver's license and fishing license, a single twenty-dollar bill for emergencies, an old silver coin he'd found in a fish a few years back and had thought was neat—but still, he appreciated the gesture. "Thanks."

Up close, he quickly revised his impression of his savior. The "boy" was older than he thought, definitely an adult, albeit a small one. His face was clean-shaven and did have a boyish look, which was only added to by the long reddish-blond hair that flowed free from his cap, but his gray eyes were older and far too worldly to be those of a youth.

The cap drew Wylie's attention next. It was sort of a newsboy style, he'd guess, rounded in back and peaked in front, and it was a bright, vivid red that looked almost wet, it was so glossy. Otherwise, the boy—man—wore jeans, a T-shirt, a hoodie, and a lined denim jacket.

And the biggest boots Wylie had ever seen.

They looked like ski boots, those big, puffy things that resembled an entire layer of bubble wrap—Wylie had seen those advertised before and occasionally on tourists passing through town. Only these had a dull metallic sheen to them—not bright like chrome, more like old, heavy iron or lead, something like that. Were they actually made of metal? That and their size would explain the tremendous footsteps, at least!

The little man was examining him right back. "So, what're you, exactly?" he asked, tilting his head to the side and leaning back to peer up at Wylie properly. "Sasquatch? Ogre? Troll?"

"What?" Wylie frowned, shaking his head and wondering if he'd heard correctly. "I—don't know what you mean."

In response, his interrogator winked at him. "Oh, sure you do," he said with a grin. "Come on, lad. No need to be bashful—you're among friends here. I'm just curious, is all."

Suddenly very aware of the other people around—who were clearly listening in on the conversation even as they pretended not to be—Wylie held up his hands, the wallet still enfolded in one, and backed away. "No, sorry, I think there's been some mistake. Thanks again, but I need to—I've got to go."

And he turned and ran.

He wasn't entirely sure where he was going, of course. He didn't know this city at all. But he had to get away from this odd little man with his even odder questions.

Sasquatch? As if! But who here in this metropolis even believed in such things?

Wylie had on occasion encountered adults able to see him for what he was, of course, or at least enough to make them realize he wasn't quite normal. Not quite human. "Second Sight," a cousin had explained once when he was young, and they'd heard about a woman who'd seen another of their kin, seen them clearly. "Not many have it, and those who do, most don't realize what it is. But the few who do, they're dangerous. Steer clear if you can."

Well, that was exactly what he aimed to do now!

So, he ran, shoving past people with muttered apologies, squeezing through groups and small crowds, turning down streets at random, rushing across them to the honks of cars and the screech of brakes, until his heart hammered in his chest and his breath came in great, rasping gasps. Then he finally skidded to a halt, ducking around a building to shelter in the alley beside it, where he could lean over, resting his hands on his knees as he struggled to breathe again.

But at least he'd lost that stranger.

"You're pretty fast on your feet for such a big fella," a voice called from above, and Wylie straightened, peering up.

At the red-capped man, who dangled from a nearby fire escape.

"How?" he managed as the man grasped the railing and flipped forward, dropping gracefully to the ground.

"Parkour," the stranger replied. "A lot faster going over buildings than around 'em." He eyed the alley they were in. "Ah, gotcha—a more private place for such talk, am I right? No worries, man. I hear ya. Shoulda been more circumspect, you're right. My bad." He shrugged. "Anyway, Knox Adair's the name. Red Cap, obv. And you are?" And he held out his hand.

Wylie accepted the proffered handshake purely on reflex, which is also why he answered, "Wylie Kang. Uh" — he faltered under the other's steady gaze but finally mumbled — "Yeti."

"For real?" The man's — Knox's — eyes widened. "Nice! Never met one of you lot before. New to the city, then?"

Wylie nodded, his brain still dazed by this strange turn of events. "Got in last night. You — sorry, did you say 'Red Cap'?"

"Yep." Knox pulled off the cap and twirled it on his finger before setting it jauntily back atop his head. "You know, Red Caps? Goblins from the English-Scottish border? Short, strong, big iron boots, caps dipped in the blood of their enemies?" He must have seen Wylie's horrified expression because he let out a laugh that sounded far too light and cheerful for such a gruesome description. "Naw, no blood here, mate, don't worry. Oil paint, dontcha know? Gift of the gods, that is — never truly dries out. Amazing stuff."

"I —" Wylie didn't even know what to say to that. On some level, he'd known there were other supernaturals in the world. After all, his father had talked about Hunters as going after all of them, not just Yeti. And some of the shows he'd watched over the years, they'd featured such creatures — vampires and werewolves, mostly, but here and there a few others, like Goblins or Ghouls or Bigfoots. Plus, of course, he'd seen those movies with the elves and dwarves and orcs and so on.

He'd just never thought any of it was real. Not truly. He'd figured they were just stories, myths, tall tales, and the like. After all, the only creatures he'd ever seen that weren't human or regular animals were, well, other Yeti. But evidently, that was just another result of his sheltered lifestyle.

"So, you live here? In the city?" he asked now. He'd expected to see all kinds of new sights here, of course. But another supernatural hadn't been one of them!

"You betcha," Knox replied. He flung his arms wide, and Wylie noted that the little man's hands were dusted with bright colors, presumably from his art. "Welcome to the Twin Cities! Best place in the whole world! What's your pleasure? Music? Art? Food? Sports? Ladies? Gents? We got it all!"

"I —" Wylie frowned. "I'm just — I just need a place to lay low for a bit," he admitted slowly, not used to explaining himself to others. "To hide out and be safe."

"Safe? From what? Big strong guy like you, what're you afraid of, huh?" Knox elbowed him in the side. "Is it a jealous ex? I've had plenty of those, let me tell you! That ain't fun, can't blame you for running from something like that!"

"No, no, nothing like that." Wylie shook his head. "Look, I should really— thanks again. About the wallet. I don't want any trouble. Just looking to keep to myself for a bit." He turned and started out of the alley, his heart rate almost back to normal now despite the strangeness of this conversation.

"Oh. Hey, yeah, no worries. If you're sure." From the lack of footsteps, Knox wasn't following, for which Wylie was grateful. "You change your mind and need a local guide, though," the little man—Goblin?—called after him, "you know where to find me! That picture ain't gonna finish itself!"

Wylie held up a hand in a vague wave, acknowledging the offer, as he stepped back onto the main sidewalk and quickly marched away, trying once more to lose himself in the crowd.

He didn't look back.

CHAPTER SEVEN

MINNEAPOLIS, AS IT TURNED OUT, WAS HUGE. IT STOOD TALLER AND stretched farther than Wylie had ever imagined. After leaving the strange little Red Cap behind, he walked for hours until the sun had not only risen to sit high above him, beating down on him with its merciless rays, but then had fallen as well, until it was once more hidden behind the buildings that loomed up everywhere, and streaks of night began to stretch across the sky. He had vague images of neighborhoods he passed through, neat little houses at one point and clumped-together apartment buildings at another, and both gleaming skyscrapers and squat and grungy warehouses in between.

And the people! So many people, everywhere he turned! Some stared as he brushed past, but most barely glanced up from phones or friends. Wylie saw plenty of men and women in nice suits beneath their heavy coats, but there were also plenty of others in jeans or heavy canvas work pants or leggings or skirts, with hair ranging from missing to short and neat to shaggy to long and flowing. Most of the faces he passed were paler than his, but some were darker, too, and he saw people whose coloring and features suggested far different backgrounds from those he'd known in Embarrass.

But the one Wylie kept coming back to, in his mind, was a little man with a bright red cap.

He still couldn't seem to wrap his brain around that. A part of him knew he was being ridiculous—after all, he was a creature of legend, of folklore, so why couldn't he accept that there were others out in the world as well? And, intellectually, he could.

He just hadn't expected to ever meet one. And especially not on the streets of the big city!

"And he saw me," Wylie realized, his feet coming to a stop only because he had apparently run out of road somewhere along the way. Instead, he found himself staring out over a wide expanse of water, but one that ended in buildings on the far side even as it stretched to the horizon side to side.

He had reached the Mississippi.

It is beautiful, he thought, gazing out over the waters, which flowed past, dark and glistening under the fading sun and rising moon. So different from the lake back home. Heikkila was more than big enough for him but he could see shore to shore in every direction, and the surface was mostly placid. The Mississippi, by contrast, never stopped moving. It seemed as if the waters must stretch on forever, and although it looked smooth from here, he knew those currents ran swift and deep. Were he to enter them, the water would sweep him away like just another piece of flotsam caught in its inexorable grasp.

It was perhaps the most amazing thing he'd ever seen.

A smooth, pale shape arced across it, and he turned in that direction, following the bank around until he found himself beneath the stone bridge, shaded by its bulk. It soared high over even his head, yet it looked slender, almost flimsy, as it spanned the river. He'd driven over it this morning, or another like it, yet he had barely noticed.

What else hadn't he seen properly?

Which brought him back to his earlier thought. The Red Cap — Knox, he remembered — had seen him. *Really* seen him. Seen him as a Yeti, not some big, hairy guy. And he suspected he'd seen the Goblin as he truly was, as well.

Was that because they were both supernaturals? He had no idea.

"Hey." The voice was deep, so deep he felt it in his bones, and it seemed to shake the ground as well, though it was not loud. "You mind?"

Wylie glanced behind him — and stared.

Because there at the bridge's base lay a pile of trash, old clothes and bags and broken boxes and other refuse.

And rising out of the garbage was the biggest creature he had ever seen.

When Wylie had left his family behind, he had still been young, not yet full-grown. His father had been a giant to him then, at least a foot taller than he was and a third wider. He was fairly certain he'd caught up to him by now, maybe even passed the older Yeti in size.

This creature made him feel small again.

It was not a man, that much was certain. Not just from its size but also its shape — the arms were too long, the head too big, the shoulders too slumped, the eyes too large even for that head. And its skin was gray and brown, mottled, and looked so similar to the stone behind it in texture Wylie at first thought the creature had come out of the rock itself. There was a smell to it, too, but not of trash. It smelled... dusty and dry, like powdered stone or old mud.

"Sorry," he said automatically, taking a step away.

"Eh, it's fine," the creature rumbled, taking a single step that covered half the distance between them. "Just blocking my view, s'all." Its eyes were focused past Wylie, at the same scene he had been admiring, and a dreamy smile crossed its wide face. "Nice, right?"

"Yeah," Wylie agreed, looking out over the water and the bridge and the moon again himself.

"Real nice."

The creature's eyes cut his way for an instant and blinked, long and slow. "You're not a Troll, are you?" it asked.

"Me? No." For the second time that day, Wylie found himself saying something he never had before. "I'm a Yeti."

"Huh. Well, you can't have this bridge — this one's mine." The creature raised a hand nearly as big as Wylie's whole torso, though it didn't seem threatening so much as just hinting at the potential for a threat. Nonetheless, he got the message loud and clear.

"No worries," he promised quickly, backtracking a few more steps. "All yours. I was just admiring the view."

"Right, then." The Troll lowered his hand and went back to watching the sunset, and Wylie quickly retreated, shaking his head. So, first Goblins and now Trolls? What was going on around here?

Leaving the water behind, he headed in what he thought might be the direction of his pickup. But he wasn't really sure, and nothing looked familiar, plus so much of it looked the same, at least insofar as it was all big and busy and bewildering. Finally, he gave up and stopped a woman walking past.

"Excuse me," he started, sighing as she cringed slightly, eyes widening behind cat-eye glasses at the sight of him looming over her. "Could you tell me how to get to the parking lot on" — he thought back to the little slip he'd left on his truck's dash — "Thirteenth Ave?"

"It's about a mile that way," she answered, waving a hand behind her and to the right, seemingly reassured at the banality of his question. "Head down this street until you hit Eleventh, then take a left and go to Second. Right turn again, and follow it around to Thirteenth."

"Thank you." He didn't smile—he'd learned that the sight of his teeth didn't usually sit well with others—but dipped his head, and she did smile a little at that. Then he moved on, relieved that he had been going more or less in the right direction.

Unfortunately, he must have heard her wrong, or she'd been a little confused herself. He walked another ten minutes, then fifteen, seeing fewer and fewer people as it grew dark and cold, but saw no sign of any street called Eleventh. He did see a South Fourth Street and turned onto that, hoping the numbers would grow larger than smaller. He was relieved when the next block was South Fifth and kept going. But after successfully crossing Sixth, Seventh, and Eighth, he hit... East Fourteenth? That stopped him dead, and he stared around him, confused.

There wasn't another soul in sight, but Wylie was excited to suddenly notice a handsome little park beside him. The trees were taller than most he'd seen in the city so far, towering three, four times his height, and some of them had trunks thick enough he might not be able to wrap his arms around them. Snow still covered the grass, which he'd expected, but past a few feet, the walkway slanting through the space vanished as well, disappearing under the snow and ice as if it had never been. He stepped off the sidewalk, his boots crunching on the white beneath as he ventured past the first row of trees, taking shelter and comfort beneath their big, broad branches. At least this felt a little more like home—if he didn't look too hard, didn't glance back over his shoulder where the street was visible beyond these boughs, he could pretend he was safely out of the city and back in the woods once more!

A branch snapped nearby, startling him out of his reverie, and he looked around—to discover that he was no longer alone.

"What have we here?" The approaching figure called, the voice high and almost shrill. "Big man a little lost?" Whoever it was, their footsteps were light enough to make no sound across the snow and left no prints.

"Must be," another replied, equally sharp in tone. "Otherwise, he'd know not to be hogging our trees."

"Yeah, clear off, big man," a third said. "These are our trees. Get your own."

Wylie could make them out now, four of them, all about the same size and no bigger than Knox, though without his oversized footwear. That explained how they could walk so softly—none of them was much bigger than a large child. They all wore matching jackets, black leather with chains looped around the arms, and their bare heads gleamed slightly in the bits of moonlight filtering down through the trees.

And their ears—their ears were long and pointed. As were their noses.

"This here's Green Goblin turf," the fourth said, speaking for the first time, and he was now close enough for Wylie to see the flash of sharp little teeth. "Get lost afore we make an example of you."

Wylie frowned. "No need to get testy," he replied, straightening. "I was just resting a minute."

"Yeah? Rest somewhere else," the first one snapped. Something clicked in his hand as a shining blade appeared there. "Or you'll be leaving—in pieces."

"Don't push me," Wylie replied sharply, his frayed temper danger-ously close to snapping. "I said I was going."

"Too slow," one of them retorted, and lunged forward, a similar knife in his hand—

—and Wylie caught him by the wrist and around the waist, lifting the startled Goblin—because what else could he be, really?—completely off the ground and hurling him at his equally surprised friends.

No one ever expected someone Wylie's size to move so fast.

The four of them all tumbled to the snowy ground, leather-clad limbs tangled up together, and Wylie took the opportunity to exit the park at full speed, his footsteps sounding as he transitioned from soft snow to hard concrete. He darted across the wide street and back the way he'd come, ducking right at the first available corner in case the creatures decided to chase him. He was still trying to make sense of this latest encounter.

Had he really just had a run-in with an honest-to-goodness street gang, just like in the old shows?

Only, this gang had been made up entirely of actual Goblins!

What was with this city?

Turning left at the next block, he ran full-out for a bit, putting some distance between himself and those trees, just to be safe. He almost laughed when the street sign proclaimed he was now on Thirteen Avenue South. Just like that!

Except the road turned a few blocks later and became South Fifth Street instead. Sigh.

That took him to Eleventh, though. At last!

And that woman—she'd told him to follow Eleventh to Second. The street he was on now, he realized now that he felt safe enough to slow down again, was Eleventh Avenue. The others he'd crossed, those had all been streets. So maybe streets ran one way and avenues another? If he headed back up, then, to Fourth where he'd been at first, maybe—he almost wept for joy when the street after that proved to be Third. Yes! Past that was a bigger street, South Washington, but he kept going, and after that came Second. Finally! That curved around and became Thirteenth, just as she'd promised, and there, waiting in the lot like an old, faithful friend, was his faded green pickup.

Wylie almost collapsed in relief when he finally unlocked the door and slid into the cracked old seat he'd long since worn into his shape.

He drove back to the motel and was more than a little surprised when he unlocked the door to his room and found his TV and recliner still right where he left them and his bag up in the closet, seemingly undisturbed. Considering the day he'd had, he'd half expected to find the room empty, or missing entirely, or turned into glass, or chocolate, or who knew what.

Clearly, he thought as he ate more of the food Kyra had packed for him and sipped the other water bottle, slowly recovering from the events of the day, *I'm going to have to get a better idea of what this city is all about if I expect to survive here for even another day or two.*

Fortunately, he knew someone he suspected could provide him with some answers. And first thing tomorrow, he'd go find him again.

Plus, he could get another cup of that coffee while he was at it.

CHAPTER EIGHT

THE NEXT MORNING, WYLIE ROSE BRIGHT AND EARLY. HE HADN'T SLEPT well at all, and his whole body ached like he'd been working too hard—or like he'd slept in his recliner two nights in a row. Of course, his dreams probably hadn't helped any. In them, he'd been back home at his cabin, or at least in the woods nearby—and he'd been running. Because someone had been chasing him. Someone with a big knife in one hand and a big gun in the other. The Hunter. And although he was bigger and stronger by far, Wylie had known that he'd be a dead Yeti the second he stopped and dared to face her. He'd woken from that one gasping and soaked in sweat, and it had taken a while to fall back asleep afterward.

But for now, the sun was up, and so was he. He already knew there was no way he'd be able to go back to sleep at this point, so he might as well get on with his day.

After showering as best he could, getting dressed, locking up, and paying for yet another night at the motel—that was starting to seriously eat into the money from the can!—he climbed into his truck and headed for the same parking lot as yesterday, which he was happy to say he found without any trouble. From there, he did his best to retrace his steps after the coffee and was pleased when it only took a few wrong turns before he spotted the trees, the bus stop—and the street art just beyond.

As he'd hoped, a small figure in a bright red cap was already hard at work, adding to his chalk landscape. For a moment, Wylie just hung back and watched Knox work. His motions were quick, smooth, never jerky, but with long pauses in between—he would stand back, staring at his art for several long moments, then suddenly dart forward and add a hill here, a tower there, a shadow across a bridge over that way. Wylie had to admit that, while it wasn't something he'd ever really considered before, he kind of liked it.

After watching for a bit, though, he began to feel a trifle awkward, standing around staring like that. Besides, he'd come for a reason. So, he cleared his throat during the next pause. That made the Red Cap glance up, but if surprised, at least he didn't look annoyed by the interruption. Far from it, he smiled the second he spotted Wylie.

"Hey! Back again, huh? Thought you might be!" Knox approached, dusting his hands off on his jeans before offering his right. Wylie shook it. "It was Wylie, right?"

"Yeah." Wylie looked around. It was early. There weren't too many people waiting at the bus stop, but the few there watched the exchange with open curiosity. "Uh, could we talk a bit, maybe?" he asked, feeling silly. "Want a coffee?" He glanced back the way he'd come — he'd already passed the blue truck on the way here and could practically feel the pull of its iced coffee calling to him. "I'm buying," he added.

"Never touch the stuff," Knox replied but tipped his cap up with a yellow-stained finger. "Still, never turn down a cuppa. Come on." And he strode off, leading the way with confident strides. Wylie followed, feeling bigger and more oafish than ever.

"What about your artwork?" Wylie asked as he hurried to catch up. He'd have worried about someone ruining the work, himself.

But his companion just shrugged. "It's a public work, out on the street for all to see — and step on," he pointed out. "It gets ruined, no problem, just move on to the next site." He grinned. "The impermanence of art is half the fun of creating it."

Wylie mulled that one over, but after a minute, he gave it up for lost. Nope, he didn't get that one at all.

"Ah, I thought this was where you meant!" Knox exclaimed happily as, a few minutes later — far faster than Wylie had covered the distance either day — the truck came into view. "Nice! They do a good brew here, that's certain — and their scones are killer. Hello, ladies!" he called, sidling into line. The girls behind the truck's counter looked up, saw him, and giggled, the one by the register waving quickly. "Denise and Daphne," Knox explained in a low voice. "Sisters, not twins. Denise is studying veterinary medicine. Daphne's a cellist and a baker. She's the one who makes the scones and cookies and whatnot, though it's their grandma's recipes."

Wylie stared at his short companion. "How do you know all that?" he asked as they inched forward.

Knox shrugged. "I stop by here from time to time," he admitted. "Or, rather, by them—they move in the afternoon, different spots throughout the week. All part of the food truck biz."

"There's a business for this?" Wylie frowned, not sure if the small man was pulling his leg.

But the Red Cap just laughed. "Where're you from, anyway?" he asked. "'Cause it sure ain't around here!"

"Embarrass," Wylie answered, wishing his pockets were big enough for him to bury his hands in them—and maybe hide his face, too.

"That a place or a mood?" Knox asked, grinning.

"It's a town, yeah. Up north a ways."

"Gotcha. Never been here before, eh?"

That made Wylie laugh. "Is it that obvious?"

Knox shot him a look, his mouth quirking a smile. "Just a bit, yeah. But hey, no worries, man. Everybody's gotta have a first time, right? And you're here now. Morning, Denise," he declared, turning around, and it was only then that Wylie realized they'd already reached the front of the line. "I'll have one of those delectable blueberry scones, please, and a large black tea, milk, no sugar. And my companion here will have"—he glanced behind him expectantly.

"Large iced coffee, black, and a chocolate chip cookie," Wylie filled in. "Please."

"You got it." The girl rang all of that up. "Twenty even." She smiled down at Knox. "Got any new works up?"

"As a matter of fact, I'm just putting the finishing touches on my latest masterpiece, only a few blocks over from here," the Goblin replied with an easy grin. "Corner of Fourth and Tenth. Can't miss it."

Meanwhile, Wylie had been digging in his pocket and came up with a crumpled twenty, which he handed over. He slid out of the way after that while Knox continued to chat, though he'd somehow effortlessly transferred his attention to the other girl while the first went back to taking orders. A few minutes later, the second sister—Daphne, Wylie remembered—handed them each a cup and then offered a bag, which Knox snagged.

"Come on, let's find a good place to sit out of the cold," the Red Cap suggested after waving goodbye and stepping away from the truck altogether. He shivered, and eyed Wylie, one eyebrow raised. "Though I suppose you don't mind much, do ya?"

Wylie shrugged. "I like the cold, actually." It blew down from the northwest today, with hints of an impending storm around the edges, like a tinge of smokiness on salted meat.

"Course you do," Knox muttered. "An' if I had an all-over fur coat like yours, I'd probably like it, too." But he didn't sound or look truly annoyed, and a moment later, he was happily exclaiming about something else instead, pointing out an old lamp post they were just passing by and admiring its "classic lines." They went a few blocks, turning more than once, and Wylie was completely lost by the time his guide stopped and tugged open a glass door. "Here we are!"

"Here" proved to be a building, but not like any Wylie had ever seen before. The interior was all grey stone, floor and side walls and even ceiling, but that ceiling rose high above, and the front and back walls were glass. Along one side, planters separated an area with little groupings of chairs and tables. "It's a public atrium," Knox explained as he selected an unoccupied cluster and dropped down onto one of the chairs, though he was careful to set his tea and the bag on the table first. "Open for anyone to use. Great place to have lunch and people-watch."

Wylie sat more gingerly and was pleasantly surprised to discover that the chair was made of metal and only creaked a little beneath him. "The whole place is like this?" he asked, taking a sip of his coffee. Ah, that was good!

"Naw, just this part of the lobby," his companion replied. "There's offices above. Lots of buildings downtown have spots like this—brightens up the place a bit, plus it's good PR."

Wylie nodded, even though he had no idea what the little man was talking about. But Knox was opening the bag and handing over a large cookie, twin to the one from yesterday, and for a few minutes, they just nibbled and sipped. A few people did walk by, most of them in suits and similar attire, and more passed outside. It did seem a good place to sit and watch.

Finally, though, Wylie's curiosity could wait no longer. "I met—" he started, then trailed off. "Yesterday, I wound up by the river," he tried again. "Under a bridge. There was a—"

"Oh, ho!" Knox exclaimed, cutting him off with a hoot. "Under a bridge—I can guess! Which one?" He laughed at Wylie's expression. "Mean or mellow?"

"Uh—mellow," Wylie replied. "Wait, there's more than one?"

His companion snorted at that. "Well, duh! Each bridge has at least one! You were lucky—sounds like you met Sven. He's cool. For a Troll, anyways. Some of his cousins, they're not anyone you want to piss off."

"Right." Wylie shook his head. "And last night, there was this park, all covered in snow, and these guys with green skin and pointed ears and teeth and—" He stopped because Knox was already nodding.

"The Green Goblins," the Red Cap finished. "Nasty bunch, that. You must've been up by Elliot Park. There's always some of 'em hanging around there, harassing folks. The south end of it's fine, playgrounds and shit, and there's North Central University right there, but the north edge, that's their turf. They don't even let the city workers in there to clean. That's why the footpaths on that side don't get cleared properly." He eyed Wylie. "Surprised you got away without any cuts."

"There were only four of them," Wylie said with a shrug. "Can't be all that much trouble."

Knox laughed. "Oh, man, you're too much!" he said after he'd recovered. "Dude, there's like fifty of those punks, usually cruisin' town in this manky old van! You got lucky!"

"Fifty?" Wylie gulped. They hadn't been so tough, but you didn't have to be when you could swarm somebody. Ten or twenty and he'd have been overwhelmed, most like. Fifty? He wouldn't stand a chance!

Which brought them around to the real reason for this visit. "Just how many of you are there here?" he asked.

"How many of 'you'?" His guide repeated. "Don't you mean 'how many of *us*'? You're one too, pal—not like there's a whole lot of Yetis among the mundanes, huh?"

Wylie hung his head. "You're right," he agreed quietly. "Sorry. I'm not used to—I didn't even know any of you existed before yesterday!"

"Seriously? How'd you manage that?" Knox sipped his tea. "Grew up under a rock?"

"More like under an avalanche," Wylie said. "Way out in the snow, where most people won't go."

"Huh." Knox shook his head. "Can't even imagine. Sorry." He sat back, tugging his cap off and twirling it on one finger again. "How many supernaturals here in the Twin Cities? Dunno. Couple hundred? Couple thousand? Somewhere between the two."

Wylie stared at him, his mind desperately trying to process this information—and failing miserably. A couple hundred supernaturals?

He'd never even known there were any! How could there be so many? "All Goblins?" he asked before realizing he already knew the answer to that question.

Sure enough, Knox shook his head. "Naw, we've got all kinds," he replied. "Lots of goblinoids, though. We're probably the most common, though there's plenty of variety even amongst us. Like those street toughs you met last night, they're German. Me, I'm Scotch-English."

"And you can see each other — *we* can see each other," Wylie asked next. "The way someone with the Sight could. Or little kids."

"Yeah," the Red Cap said. "Whatever it is that makes folks not see the real us — their brains refusing to process or our natures protecting us or something else entirely — we don't have it. We see each other proper, every time." He frowned. "You've really never met another supernatural before now?" Wylie shook his head, surprised when his new friend laughed and slapped a hand down on the table. "Then I know exactly where to take you! Come on!" And, popping the last of his scone into his mouth and following it down by tossing back the final bit of his tea, the little Goblin rose to his feet.

Wylie started to protest but stopped. He'd specifically sought Knox out to get his help in understanding this strange new place he found himself in. So, if the Goblin thought he should go somewhere and meet someone, who was he to say no? Finishing his iced coffee and the rest of his cookie — that was a breakfast he could certainly get used to! — he stood as well.

"Okay," he agreed. "Lead on."

He just hoped he wouldn't regret it.

CHAPTER NINE

WYLIE FROWNED DOWN AT THE GOBLIN BY HIS SIDE. "IS FOOD ALL YOU ever think about?" he asked.

"What? No, of course not!" Knox protested. "I think about lots of other things besides food! Like beer! And tea! And cake!"

"Cake is food!" Wylie rubbed a hand over his face. "And we just ate!"

"That? That was just a warm-up," his guide protested. "Besides, we're not here for the food. Or not *just* for the food. Come on." And he sauntered across the floor, threading his way between people, eyes fixed on his destination.

Wylie sighed. He'd been intrigued when they'd approached, crossing the street toward what he'd initially thought was a collection of tan stone buildings but then realized was, in fact, a single building with many different levels to it, like it had been built out of mismatched blocks.

"Midtown Global Market," he'd read on the yellow awnings over every first-floor window. He didn't know what that meant, but it certainly sounded interesting.

Stepping through the front door had been an experience. The inside was enormous, stretching off in every direction so far that Wylie could not see another side. It also soared high overhead, the ceiling partially obscured by a tangle of pipes and metal frames that crisscrossed beneath it, lights hanging from those at seemingly random intervals. The floor was plain concrete and divided into wide aisles, each as wide as a regular road. And on either side of those aisles — and sometimes in the middle — were pallets of goods for sale, or stalls set up selling things, or whole restaurants. They ranged from gleaming and modern to shabby and primitive, and Wylie saw all sorts of items for sale, clothes and flags and toys and electronics and fresh produce and groceries. The air was filled with a complete mix of competing smells, sweet and savory and salty and sharp and acrid and plastic and chemical and flowery and herbal, and he couldn't even tell what, so much so that his nose itched and his eyes watered just from trying to make sense of it all.

And some of the stalls, he quickly noticed, sold food as well—but these weren't restaurants. They didn't have seats and tables and waiters. They just had a window with one or more people behind it serving something that smelled amazing. More like the coffee truck than the Roadside Diner.

It was toward one of those very stalls that Knox led them and toward which he was marching right now.

Wylie hurried after him. "Boa Comida," the sign above it read, and the woman behind the counter looked friendly enough as she chatted with a customer. She was wide and sturdy, with skin the color of bronze and her hair covered in a colorful head scarf.

"Mama Rheda!" Knox bellowed, and the woman paused her conversation to glance his way. Then a broad smile swept across her face, lighting her eyes.

"Knox Adair!" she shouted back, laughing. "An' aren't you a sight for sore eyes? Where have you been hiding, my friend? No time to stop in and see me no more? Don't like my cooking all of a sudden?" Her words had a rolling quality to them, almost musical in their cadence, and her accent was clearly not local.

"Now, Mama, you know that couldn't possibly be true," Knox replied, stepping up to the window and gesturing for Wylie to join him. "I've just been busy. You know how it is—art can't wait."

"Hmph." She studied Wylie beyond him, though her smile was still there. "And who might this be?"

"This is Wylie Kang," Knox told her. The previous customer had taken his food and moved away, which was good since Knox leaned in and said in a whisper not much softer than his usual volume, "He's a Yeti. Just came into town. I'm showing him around a bit."

"Oh?" Mama extended a hand. "Well, it's nice to meet you, Wylie," she told him. Her hand, when he took it, was warm and dry. "Welcome to the Twin Cities. Now, what can I get you, boys?"

"Two orders of stew and two Cokes, please," Knox answered. He pulled off his cap, felt around in the band, and then, with an "Aha!" pulled a folded bill free. It proved to be a twenty, and he handed it over to Mama with an elaborate flourish. "Keep the change, Mama."

"Don't mind if I do," she said, chuckling as she made the money disappear. Then she turned—and Wylie blinked, stiffening slightly as the scarf across the back of her head tightened like something had just moved behind it.

And then it growled at him.

It was a deep, low noise, barely audible over the general ruckus of such a large space filled with so many people, but Wylie was sure he had not imagined it or the movement. He glanced over at Knox, who winked. Perhaps there *was* something here besides the food, after all!

Mama apparently hadn't noticed the exchange. She was busy scooping two large helpings of rice into a pair of deep bowls. She followed that by spooning something thick and red onto it from a big, bubbling pot. The bowls she set on the counter, along with a pair of Coke cans she pulled from underneath. "There you go. Enjoy."

"We will," Knox promised. Wylie nodded as he accepted his bowl, drink, and spoon. It sure smelled good! Spicy, which wasn't something he did much, and hot, which he also didn't go in for, but the scent of chicken and some kind of herbs and vegetables had his mouth watering, so he was willing to give it a chance.

Wylie turned around—and almost dropped his bowl, stumbling back a step as he found someone in his face. Literally. A pair of wide, red eyes—their pupils actually tomato-red—stared into his own yellow ones from only inches away and not much lower than his own. They belonged to a very large woman, as it turned out. She was broadly built, with long dark hair in a pair of thick braids, and might have been mistaken for a raven-tressed Valkyrie if not for the pointed ears, those red eyes, what looked like horns poking up from under her hair, and the fact that her lower canines thrust up past her upper lip as a pair of tusks. That, and her skin was decidedly on the blue side.

"And who the hell're you?" she demanded, her breath hot on his face and oddly minty.

"Relax, Brea," Knox declared from somewhere nearby—Wylie couldn't see him with this newcomer filling up his view. "Wylie's cool. He's with me."

"Yeah? And how long've you known him?" This Brea snapped, not backing away at all. Wylie met her gaze and blinked.

"Excuse me," he said, keeping his own voice slow and calm. "But this is a bit hot, and I don't want to spill any. Would you mind?" He hefted the bowl up a little higher, catching her eye with it, and then carefully slid around her.

There were several places nearby where counters and tall stools waited, and Knox had already headed for one such. Wylie followed, feeling the heat of Brea's glare on his back as he went. "What's her deal?" he asked as he joined his friend, though he didn't even try the flimsy-looking stool—he was more than tall enough to be fine just standing at the counter instead.

"Eh, don't worry about it," Knox replied, already spooning what was evidently stew into his mouth. "She's like that with everyone. You get used to it." He raised his Coke in salute. "Eat!"

Wylie did so, taking a cautious first sip. Wow! The flavors hit him like a punch, hot and spicy and rich and somehow soothing. There were big chunks of chicken, and he saw pieces of tomato and onion as well, plus whole cloves of garlic, but there was also a strange, creamy flavor he didn't recognize. All in all, though, it was delicious, and he happily consumed the entire serving, even scraping the spoon along the sides to make sure he hadn't missed any.

"Told you," Knox said, laughing as he watched. "*Muamba de galinha*. It's a chicken stew from Angola. That's where Mama Rheda's from. It's made with red palm oil. That's what gives it that color."

"She's from Angola?" Wylie wasn't even sure where that was, though he knew it was outside the U.S. "And what's with the head scarf?" He kept his voice low since they were still in plain sight of the stall itself.

"She's a Kishi," his friend explained, just as quietly for once. "They've got two faces. The one you see in front—and another in back. That one's a lot less friendly. Don't let it bite you, whatever you do."

Two faces? Wylie shook his head. "And her?" he asked, for Brea was standing at the stall, arms crossed, talking to Mama while glaring at them.

"Ogress," Knox replied. "Couldn't you tell?" That did seem to make sense, but it was just another supernatural to add to the list. "Hey, where'd you say you were staying?" he asked next.

Wylie hadn't, but he answered anyway. "A motel. The U-Turn. Out by the highway."

"A pox on that!" his friend stated. "Those places'll bleed ya dry! That's the other reason I wanted you to meet Mama—come on." Collecting their empty bowls and used spoons, he headed back over, ignoring the scowl Brea directed their way. "Hey, Mama, Wylie needs a place to stay," the Red Cap announced when he was within a few feet of the stall again. "You got any rooms open?"

The food-stall operator considered for a second. "A few, yeah," she answered finally. "On the top floor. But they ain't got no heat." She looked at Wylie and smiled. "I'm guessing that may not be a problem, though?"

He smiled back. "No, cold is fine, thanks. Better, even. And the stew was amazing. Thank you."

That got a laugh from her. "Oh, I like you!" she proclaimed. "Yes, you need a room, I give you one! Two hundred a month. Phone is up to you, but I got everything else. You have a car?" He nodded. "That's fine, there's parking in back. You come back by here in a few hours, after the lunch rush, I bring you over and we get you settled. Okay?"

Wylie nodded again. There was something about Mama Rheda he liked, second face or no. And even if he was only here another week, two hundred dollars would wind up saving him money—and probably give him a lot more privacy. "Okay. Thank you."

Brea was still standing there, thick arms folded over her chest, and she scowled at him. "I live there too," she stated, narrowing her eyes in what was no doubt meant to be intimidating. "So, you'd better not cause any trouble."

"No trouble," Wylie promised, though she didn't scare him any. She was probably used to being the biggest kid on the block, but, well, Wylie was even bigger. "Guess I'll be seeing you—neighbor." He wasn't sure why he said it, except that she was annoying him with her attitude. What had he done to deserve such a hostile response? He'd just ordered lunch! But it was funny to watch her face scrunch up even more, her skin darkening to a deeper shade of blue, and her tusks jutting up almost to her nose. He had to fight to keep a straight face as he tipped his hat to Mama Rheda and quickly backed away to where Knox was already waiting across the aisle.

"Dude!" the little man said in a rush once they'd walked a few stalls away. "Talk about baiting the bear! Be careful. She'll take your head off!" He giggled, though. "Still, it was funny. I've never seen her turn that shade before—she was practically cobalt!"

"Yeah. The world's biggest Smurf." Wylie chuckled as well. He hoped that little jab wouldn't come back and bite him too badly and knew it probably hadn't been wise—after all, he was new here, and she seemed like a bit of a big shot—but he hadn't been able to resist.

And it really *had* been a good color on her.

CHAPTER TEN

KNOX SHOOK HIS HEAD AND WHISTLED, A THIN, HIGH SOUND MORE LIKE the keening of the winter wind than any sort of music. "You were paying to stay here?" he asked, studying the motel's exterior as they pulled up. "They shoulda been paying *you!*"

Wylie shrugged, shutting off the engine. "Most places wanted a credit card," he mumbled, pushing his door open and sliding from the truck. He'd have come back on his own, but the Red Cap insisted on accompanying him.

"I can guide you to Mama's after, save you the trouble of getting lost," the little Goblin had insisted. "'Sides, seems a nice day for a ride, and I don't exactly get into cars a whole lot."

Wylie hadn't quite followed that, but maybe he'd just meant he didn't own one himself? Did people in the city not need them? With everything so close together, he supposed they could just walk from place to place instead. He was happy to walk about, too, provided he didn't draw too many stares or bump into too many things—or people. But there was something about a good drive, with the windows down, the wind blowing in your hair, the road flying by beneath your wheels, the engine rumbling ahead of you—it was magical.

Driving with someone else in the car, though, had proven to be a little different. He'd actually never done that before, not since taking the test for his license all those years ago. He'd felt a bit nervous at first, just like back then, but Knox had proven to be an easygoing passenger. And a talkative one. "Sorry, guess I run off at the mouth a bit," he'd said at one point, laughing at himself. "Never was too good at silence—my old ma used to say if there was a gap in the conversation, I'd be sure to fill it."

Wylie had nodded since it hadn't really seemed to require a response. Nor had most of the talking that followed. In fact, once he learned to just let it wash over him, like some strange new type of background noise, he'd found it a lot easier to deal with and had started to relax a little again.

Anyway, they were here now. "I'm in that one," he said, indicating the last door. "Come on."

As they approached the door, he heard noises. At first, he thought someone had broken into his room or the manager had rented it out by mistake. But then he realized the sounds were coming from the room next door instead. It sounded like the same two voices as last time, too.

"What's going on in there?" Knox asked, gesturing toward the source of the sounds.

"No idea," Wylie replied with a shrug. "None of my business." Unlocking his door, he stepped into the room, leaving it open for Knox to follow. Everything looked undisturbed still, and it only took him a minute to haul out his gym bag, tackle box, and fishing rods, plus the remnants of Kyra's food packet. Then he grabbed the recliner.

"Need a hand with that?" his companion asked, but Wylie shook his head. He carried the big chair out and set it carefully into the truck bed before going back for the TV.

"Yeah, I can see why you wouldn't wanna leave those," Knox admitted. "Nice." He peered around the room. "Anything else?" But his gaze was drawn to the wall, from which noises were still emanating. Shouts—and something else. A dull thud.

Like someone hitting someone else.

"Right, that's enough of that," the little man muttered and stomped outside. Wylie hurried after, but only so he could lay the TV gently down and strap both it and the recliner into place. Behind him, he heard a banging, loud and sharp, and cringed even as he turned, knowing what he was about to see.

Sure enough, Knox was pounding on the door next door.

"Open up!" the Red Cap shouted. "Now!" Between his voice and the strength of his knocking, anyone would have thought he was Wylie's size—or bigger.

The shouting had stopped when he'd started, and there was nothing but silence from behind the door now. Finally, something clicked, and the door creaked open the tiniest sliver. "What?" a voice demanded. Male. Belligerent, judging by the tone.

"Motel security," Knox declared immediately. "We been getting complaints. Open up."

"Sorry, we'll keep it down," came the quick reply. Then the door slammed shut in his face.

Wylie took a step toward his new friend. "We should go," he urged. "Come on." He'd drop by the front office, hand over the key, get his deposit back, and they'd be out of here. No trouble.

But Knox was scowling—not at him but at the door that had nearly bruised his nose. "Close the door on me, will you?" he snapped, his face darkening. "We'll just see about that!"

And, rearing back, he kicked the door hard with one of his over-sized iron boots.

The flimsy barrier flung open, eliciting one shout and one shriek from within. "Hands where I can see 'em!" the Goblin demanded, stomping inside. Wylie moved a little closer, peering in, and saw a room much like his own. A man was glaring down at Knox—big enough by human standards, though a little thick in the middle, with buzzed-short brown hair and a thick beard—and a woman, smaller and slight, was cowering in the corner. Even from here, Wylie could smell the thick, sour scent of cheap beer and the sharper tang of equally cheap whiskey wafting from the room.

"You ain't no motel security!" The man bellowed, sneering down at Knox. "Get outta here, runt, before I teach you a lesson!"

"Yeah?" The room was small enough that two steps put Knox right in front of the man. "What lesson's that, how to hit women? No thanks. Try me instead." He grinned. "I dare ya."

The man didn't bother to reply to that, not really. Instead, he just grunted, spat a curse word or two, and swung his leg, meaning to punt the little Red Cap aside like a stray dog.

Only Knox caught the approaching foot with one hand and yanked. The man toppled with a squawk like a startled bird.

"I oughta pound you flatter than paper," Knox told him, leaning down and grabbing the man by the chin, forcing him to look up at the scowling Goblin. "But I'm gonna let you off with a warning. This time. Don't touch her again, or I'll be back. Understand?" He tugged the man's chin up and down, forcing him to nod. "Good boy."

Then the Red Cap let go, turning and marching away like he hadn't just taken down a man twice his size. "Ready to go?" he asked Wylie, heading around to the truck's passenger side and climbing in. "Come on, time's a-wasting."

Wylie stared at him a minute, then at the room, before sighing and hopping back into the truck. After that little scene, he definitely didn't want to stick around here any longer than he had to!

He'd expected Mama Rheda's to be a big old house where she rented rooms — there were a few places in Embarrass that he knew did stuff like that to make ends meet, usually letting them to weekend hunters and fishermen. So, Wylie was surprised when the building Knox directed him to proved to be a massive brick building that occupied its own city block and rose a good eight stories from the ground.

"Mama Rheda's been here a while," Knox explained as he pointed around the block, where a small parking lot was tucked in behind. "She bought this place from the city. Previous owner'd gone bankrupt and lost it. It was pretty wrecked, but she fixed it all up and has been renting it out ever since. She lives on the first floor." There was a large loading bay in back, and Mama herself stood there, waiting — Knox had pulled out a sleek little cell phone and called her once they'd left the motel, and she'd agreed to meet them here instead of at her stall.

"You find it okay?" she asked once they'd parked and stepped out. "Good. You got a lot of stuff?" Her eyes went to the back of his truck. "No, I guess not. Come on, we bring that all in, then go up." She hopped down easily — seeing her out from behind the counter, Wylie now saw that the Kishi was not much taller than Knox — and took his gym bag from him before he could protest, hefting the big bag easily as she swiveled around and climbed the concrete steps back up to the dock after.

Wylie saw there wasn't any point in arguing, so he handed Knox the tackle box, fishing rods, and food bag, then went to the back, unbuckled the tarp, and lifted the recliner out, hefting it over to the dock before going back for his TV. He rested that on top of the recliner and then leaped up beside them. Mama had already opened a wide door into the building and disappeared inside, with Knox right behind her.

Going in after them with the TV tucked under his arm, Wylie found himself in a large, empty loading bay — empty except for them, his stuff, and a row of washers and dryers against the far wall. "You use 'em any time you need," Mama told him. "That's what they for."

He nodded and followed her over to a large elevator with only a rough wooden frame barring it. A freight elevator—he'd seen them in movies enough times to know. There was plenty of space there for all of them plus his things, even once he'd gone back out to grab the recliner, and soon they were all rumbling their way up to the eighth floor.

"Not many up here," Mama explained as the elevator creaked and groaned on its slow ascent. "Too cold for most." When it shuddered to a stop, she lifted the matching wood-slatted door out of the way and stepped out, leading them down a wide hall. The floor was wood, old and worn, but it was solid beneath Wylie's feet, and the walls were freshly painted, the ceiling high, and the light adequate.

At the far end, she inserted a key into the big, heavy door, which was graced with a large cursive A upon its front, then turned it, pushing the door open in front of her. "Here we go."

The room she showed them into was big, Wylie saw at once. The ceiling was high enough that his fingertips could just graze it when he stretched up, held aloft by thick iron beams spaced evenly down the center of the room and bracing thick wooden beams overhead. The outer wall was rough brick broken up by large windows, and to one side, a door led into a smaller room, which she told him had a bathroom through it. The big room's far side was taken up by a long countertop, a big old farm sink centered on it, with a stove at one end and a fridge at the other. A small table and a pair of chairs stood nearby, and a short but sturdy-looking cabinet stood against the other wall. The main room alone was easily twice the size of his cabin, and although that thought brought with it a sudden burst of homesickness, Wylie also couldn't help but be impressed with the place. He instantly loved the rough, rustic feel of it.

"You like?" Mama asked, and he nodded, his eyes drawn to the windows. He could see the city spread out before him and the river beyond it—and past that, another city, like this one's older, more stately twin. St. Paul. He hadn't even thought to explore there yet!

"I don't got no bed big enough for you," she said. Wylie started to tell her that was fine, he was used to that, when she continued, "so I figure this will work." She gestured at something in the bedroom, which Wylie had barely glanced at before. Now he obediently went and took a closer look.

What he saw took him a second to understand. At first, it looked like the biggest bed he'd ever seen, but then he realized it wasn't, not exactly. It was two beds, both on the small side, but set up side by side to create one much larger one and made up with sheets and a small stack of blankets and a veritable mountain of pillows.

"They're full-size beds," she told him proudly. "A little over four feet wide. But tied together—"

Eight feet and more. Even longer than he was. Wylie sat on the edge and then carefully lay down, scooting back until he stretched entirely atop the paired mattresses. For the first time *ever*, he could stretch out completely and still be on a bed! It was amazing!

"Good." She nodded, but he could see she was pleased with his reaction to her handiwork. "I didn't get a chance to raise the showerhead yet, but I will, or if you're handy and wanna replace it yourself, go right ahead. You got first month's rent?"

Climbing back to his feet, Wylie fetched out his coffee can and extracted two hundred. He handed that over, and Mama traded him a set of four keys for it. "Front door, back door, your door, mailbox key," she explained, lifting each one in turn. "You get locked out, you call me or come find me, I let you in, make more sets, but you pay for 'em, hear?" Then she laughed and patted him on the cheek. "Good. You get settled in. Welcome." And with that, she headed for the door.

"So?" Knox asked once she'd gone. "Whaddya think? Not too shabby, huh?"

Wylie nodded, busily throwing open all the windows to let in the cool, refreshing afternoon breeze. Even with them open, he could barely hear the traffic outside. He was high enough up that it was just a dull, distant murmur. He'd already spied a set of outlets on the wall that led to the bedroom and, even better, a television cable. Now he set the TV atop the cabinet and plugged it in, dragging his recliner over to face the set and then settling into the comfortable seat with a happy sigh.

Yes, this would definitely do.

CHAPTER ELEVEN

WYLIE WOULD HAVE BEEN CONTENT TO JUST SIT THERE, WATCH SOME TV, eat his remaining leftovers, and call it a day.

He quickly discovered that Knox was not so easily satisfied, especially not with solitude or inactivity.

"Come on, man," the little Red Cap insisted, latching onto one of Wylie's arms and struggling to haul him from his chair. "We gotta go celebrate! I'm thinking pizza. You like pizza?"

Wyle shrugged, shifting to try peering around the smaller man. He'd found the oldies station, and *Bewitched* was on. He loved that show.

Knox planted himself squarely in Wylie's field of view, fists on his hips like he was spoiling for a fight. "You don't like pizza? What's wrong with pizza?" Then a sly look slid over his face. "You ever had pizza? They get that up there in the frozen north?"

"I've had pizza," Wylie retorted. "Embarrass isn't the boonies, you know. We've got a Domino's." He'd never been all that impressed, though, to be honest. The pizzas he'd tried had been a bit small and not terribly exciting, flavor-wise. Roadside had better food by far.

His guest snorted. "Domino's? That's not real pizza, man! We're definitely getting you a proper pie!" Doffing his cap, he felt around the inside rim and produced a folded green paper, which proved to be another bill, this one a fifty. "Grub's on me!" Knox declared triumphantly. "Come on!"

Wylie considered kicking the Red Cap out. After all, he'd literally just moved into this place—shouldn't he have time to enjoy it, as well as explore it a little? But he could already tell there was no changing Knox's mind once the little man had it made up, and he didn't want to alienate his local guide when he had a feeling he'd still need help finding his way around the city. So, he shut off the TV with a heavy, almost tortured sigh and let himself be dragged to his feet.

"Fine," he grumbled. "Where're we going? He glanced out the window. "It's not even dark yet," he complained. "And we only had lunch a few hours ago. What've you got, a hollow leg? Or you storing all that food there under your cap?"

He worried after he'd said it that his comment might come across as insulting, but Knox laughed. "Naw, I can always eat," he replied, rubbing his belly. "Big guy like you, I'd've figured you'd be able to keep up with me and then some. 'Sides, place we're going, it's a solid walk. You'll see, you'll be ready to eat by the time we get there."

Wylie wasn't entirely sure of that but let himself be led out of the apartment anyway. He remembered to stop and lock the door as they left—another thing he wasn't used to—then followed Knox down the hall toward the elevator. They didn't take it, however. Instead, Knox pushed open a door beside it, a heavy metal door with no window and with an "Exit" sign lit above it. Wylie was pleased to see stairs beyond, good solid concrete ones that wouldn't protest under even his weight. He'd be happy to never risk that elevator again if he didn't have to!

"Sure we shouldn't drive?" he asked as they traipsed down the stairs. Ahead of him, Knox shook his head.

"Naw, you'd have to find parking and all, and besides, nice night for a walk," came the reply. "Plus, this way you'll get to see the city more. Can't do that as easy when you're concentrating on driving, am I right?"

That much was certainly true, and Wylie didn't object to a little exercise, so he didn't argue further. Instead, once they'd reached the first floor and slipped back out through the loading bay, he let Knox take the lead and contented himself with looking around as they headed in what he estimated to be a true westerly direction.

"We're in East Phillips now," his guide explained, slipping easily around people and occasionally nodding to passers-by. "Most diverse neighborhood in Minneapolis—and the most supernaturals. Easier to blend in here and all that." He waved a hand behind them. "Mississippi's that way. Most streets're numbered—streets go east-west, and the numbers increase as you go south, avenues are north-south, and numbers get higher as you head west."

Wylie nodded. That would've been good to know the other night! Now that he did finding his way around would be a lot easier.

"We're headed to Lyndale," the Red Cap continued. "Bit more upscale than here, more fancy. Not a lot of our kind living over there. We tend to stand out a bit too much from all the yuppies. Good food, though. You'll see."

Wylie did see. The streets hereabout were a lot like those he'd seen before, when he'd first met Knox, though perhaps a bit more built up, with more buildings a bit closer together and a lot more little shops and restaurants on the ground floor. The people were just as varied, and every now and again, he saw someone he thought might not be completely human — too tall or too short, too thin or too broad, hair an odd shade or skin a funny hue, eyes a bit different. Though that could just be a big-city thing, maybe?

But as they walked, he saw less and less of that. More and more of the men wore, if not full suits, nice slacks and nice shirts and nice leather jackets. More and more of the women wore nice dresses or nice skirts or nice, flowy pants. With every block, Wylie felt more and more out of place in his jeans and plaid shirt and baseball cap. Still, Knox was dressed similarly, and he didn't appear put out at all, so Wylie figured he'd trust his guide on this one.

Knox had been right about one thing already — the sun began to go down, and the more they walked, the more Wylie's stomach hinted that it would not, in fact, object to another meal. Preferably, sometime in the near future. He was almost relieved when the Red Cap announced, "And here we are!"

Wylie studied the place before them. It was a single-story building, long and low, with a brick exterior pierced by big picture windows that let him see the tables and chairs and booths inside. A strange sort of porch stood out front, the roof nothing more than open beams, but those and the garbage cans filled with plants that were lined up beneath its edge formed an outdoors seating area, currently empty. Knox was already tugging open the front doors. "Welcome to Pizza Lucé Uptown," he declared, bowing and ushering Wylie inside. Directly ahead was a counter, and Wylie's stomach growled at the smells rising from behind it, but Knox steered them left instead, where a young woman waited. "Meeting friends," the Red Cap explained, peering past her. "Ah, there we go!" And he stepped around the girl, directing Wylie with a hand on his elbow. "Come on, some folks I want you to meet."

"What?" Wylie frowned, even as he let himself be led through the place, which was already half-full, toward a boisterous group in the back. He hadn't realized they'd be meeting anyone! When had Knox arranged that? And who were these people? More supernaturals? He was already regretting letting himself be talked into this and wondering if there was some way he could beg off, just grab a slice to go, and head back to his new place. By that point, however, they'd already stopped before the booth in question, and the three people there were watching him expectantly.

"Yo," Knox said, sliding into the booth on one side as the two women there cursed him through warm smiles and slid over. "Gang, this is my new buddy Wylie, only got into town a day or two ago. I'm showing him around. Wylie, this is Jeannie, Swift, and Dougie Dog."

"It's just Doug," the guy on the other side corrected, shaking his head, but he held out his hand as he slid back into the corner, making room. "Good to meet you, Wylie. Have a seat. We only just ordered, but we'll get Guy back around to take your order."

"Thanks." Wylie accepted both the handshake and the offer, though he was careful to settle slowly onto the bench seat so that it could distribute his weight. All three of them looked similar enough to be related, he noticed, with an almost golden sheen to their skin and dark blonde eyebrows, plus dark eyes, long, broad noses, and slightly pointed ears. So, probably not fully human. That might make this a little easier.

Sure enough, no sooner had he eased himself fully onto the seat than one of the women leaned forward. "Okay, gotta ask," she said, her voice low enough to not carry beyond their table. "Sasquatch?"

"Yeti," he answered, still finding it strange to admit that out loud. Nor had he expected the look on her face, which was wondering, almost awed.

"Seriously? Whoa! Heard of you, never met one," she admitted. "Cool." Her hair was buzzed short on the sides, little more than dark fuzz, but the rest was long and the same shade as her brows. Her flannel shirt was open over some sort of band T-shirt.

"Very cool," the other woman agreed with a grin. "Frozen, even." And she proceeded to launch into an off-key rendition of the lead song from that movie, which even Wylie recognized. Fortunately, she was laughing too hard to continue past the first few lines, but she didn't seem to be mocking him, so he decided he didn't mind. Her hair was also short on the sides but had been spiked up down the middle, where it was dyed a deep purple. The punk look from the hair and the array of studs and rings down both ears was offset by glitter over her eyes and even on her lips. Her outfit, too, was more what Wylie would have thought of as glam rather than punk, shiny and shimmery rather than torn. Interesting.

A waiter approached, and the way the others all joked with him made it clear they were all regulars here. "What'll it be, fellas?" he asked Knox and Wylie, and Wylie gestured for the Red Cap to take the lead there.

"We'll keep it simple for your first time here," Knox assured him. "Extra-large pepperoni pie and a pitcher of beer, plus waters." The waiter—Guy, Doug had called him—nodded, marked it down, and promptly retreated, though he was back a moment later with two large glasses of water and a basket of breadsticks. Wylie's stomach rumbled loudly at the sight and scent of the latter, making his new companions laugh, but it didn't seem mean or judgmental. Then they were all digging into the breadsticks, talking about other things, and he forgot to be embarrassed.

It was probably, Wylie decided later, the single most interesting meal he'd had since the very first time he'd scared off some campers and gotten to feast on their left-behind hot dogs and hamburgers, his first-ever human food. Knox's three friends were all very nice and clearly had known each other and him a long time, considering how often they joked about shared past events or made what Wylie guessed were in-jokes. They were Kobolds, he found out, a German supernatural, sort of like a Goblin. They were also artists, like Knox, though Jeannie said she did mainly sculpture, and Swift did mobiles, while Doug focused primarily on painting. He worked for an auto-refinisher, the latter explained, doing custom paint jobs on cars, which was how he financed his art on the side. Swift worked at a crafts store.

"It's my sis here who's the respectable one," she joked, nudging Jeannie. Ah, so they *were* related. "That's why she looks so clean-cut." Which she certainly did next to the other two, since Doug's hair was buzzed down to mere fuzz, rings and studs sprouted from his ears, brows, lip, and nose, and a bunch of tattoos covered his muscled arms and chest. Other than the shaved sides, Jeannie looked completely normal, and Wylie suspected she could cover those if she let her hair down instead of pulling it back the way it was now. "Tell him what you do," Swift urged, already laughing. She seemed to laugh a lot.

"I teach art at a daycare," Jeannie revealed, elbowing her sister right back. "Nothing wrong with that. Besides, I like kids." She sighed. "It does cut into my studio time, of course. But that's just the way it goes. Only Knox manages to do this full-time," she added with a clear touch of envy to her voice. "Not sure how, entirely, but he always comes up with enough cash to get by."

The Red Cap shrugged good-naturedly. "Just gifted that way," he replied, which earned him an elbowing and a smack to the back of his head, both of which he accepted with a grin.

The food was a revelation when it arrived. "Not exactly Domino's, huh?" Swift teased, Knox having told them all about Wylie's woefully inadequate previous pizza experience, and all Wylie could do was shake his head. The pizza Guy set before them was twice as thick, for one thing, the bread golden brown in places along its rim. The cheese was thick too and still molten hot, and the pepperonis were big thick slices strewn artfully about. The smell alone was enough to make his mouth water, and when he extracted a gooey slice and shoved the tip into his mouth, biting down on hot, fresh cheese and tangy sauce and spicy pepperoni—he couldn't help but groan in pleasure.

"Yeah, I'd say he liked it," Swift said, smirking. She was the most playful of the three, Wylie was getting. Jeannie was the most serious, though that wasn't saying a whole lot, while Doug was the laid-back one of the bunch. Wylie quickly found himself relaxing around the four of them in a way he couldn't remember doing since he'd first left his family. He didn't have to pretend to be something he wasn't here. He didn't even have to talk much because these four were always more than happy to fill in any awkward silences.

At one point, after finishing two big slices and an entire pitcher of beer, Wylie decided to slow down a little. He leaned back, looking around the room. The place had filled up now, and most of the booths and tables were filled with groups like theirs, people sitting and laughing and talking over pizza or pasta or big sandwiches. At one booth across the room, however, he noticed a single person sitting alone. And with a start, he realized he recognized her. It was the tall, ethereal woman he'd seen the other day, the one who had walked by him when he'd first been wandering the streets.

"Who's that?" he asked, gesturing, and the four paused their conversation to look.

"Oh, her." The disdain in Jeannie's voice spoke volumes. "That's Sinead."

"Don't bother, man," Doug advised. "She's too good for the likes of us."

"Really?" Wylie frowned, studying the woman. She was bent forward over her table, but her plate had been pushed to one side. Instead, he saw that she had a book in her hands and was clearly absorbed in its contents. "She one of us?"

"She'd never admit it, but yeah," Swift put in. "She's a Banshee." When Wylie shook his head, the Kobold explained, "Irish, I think? Wails at the dead? They're in movies and stuff, man!"

"Huh." Wylie had never seen any, but the concept sounded vaguely familiar. "She doesn't like people much?"

"No, total snob," Knox agreed. "Won't talk to anyone. Don't worry about it."

Wylie nodded, but he kept going back to his previous encounter with her. If she was really that full of herself, why had she looked away like that? Still, she was clearly content with her book, and he wasn't about to disturb her.

The rest of the evening passed surprisingly quickly, and before he knew it, Wylie was trailing Knox back to his apartment. "You good from here?" the Red Cap asked once Mama Rheda's building came into sight.

"Yeah, I got it," Wylie replied. "Thanks. This was fun." And he meant it. He couldn't remember when he'd enjoyed himself so much.

"Good deal. Hey, I'm back on the picture tomorrow, but stop on by. Maybe around lunchtime?"

Wylie nodded and watched as the little Goblin turned to go. *Is this what it is like having a friend,* he wondered. If so, he thought maybe he kind of liked it.

With that thought warming him as much as the pizza and beer, he trudged the rest of the way to the apartment, up eight flights of stairs. By the time he'd unlocked the door and stepped back inside, he was so tired he barely managed to wash up before kicking off his shoes, shedding his shirt and jeans, and collapsing on his bed.

CHAPTER TWELVE

WAKING UP THE NEXT MORNING WAS SURPRISINGLY PLEASANT. WYLIE stirred, shifting about on his bed, and slowly awoke to the fact that no part of him was currently not on the bed in question, which was a novelty—his feet were still supported, his back was flat, one arm was flung over his head, yet all of him fit. Huh. The mattress was firm enough to hold him yet soft enough to sink into, and a clear advantage of the strange construction was that there were not one but two cross-bars to help hold things up in the middle—as a result, the bed barely groaned at all beneath his weight.

Meanwhile, the early morning sunlight was slanting in through the tall windows, the sun too low to be in his face but high enough that its beams lit up the ceiling and slowly eased their way down the far wall. If he focused, Wylie could hear the sound of cars outside, but it was distant, just a background rumble. Up here in his room, everything was still and quiet, the sunbeams catching on the air to create a cascade of dancing, glittering motes swirling lazily above his head.

For a few minutes, he just lay there, enjoying it.

As he did, the previous night's dreams began filtering into his conscious mind. He'd been prowling through the woods again, though he hadn't recognized the area itself. But he'd come across more hunters or campers or fishermen, people minding their own business—and had once again torn them to shreds. Just thinking back to those fleeting and mercifully fading images made Wylie shudder, disturbing his recent contentment. Why would he be dreaming about such things? Maybe it was just because he was in unfamiliar settings, so his mind was working through its anxieties? Whatever the reason, he hoped he wouldn't have any more of them. The idea of killing anyone made him sick to his stomach. Still, they were just dreams and laying here, relaxing, he was slowly able to recapture the calm he'd woken within.

Finally, he roused himself. Rising to his feet, he lumbered into the bathroom. It was bigger than it really needed to be, but he certainly wasn't complaining—there was enough space that he could sit on the toilet and not have his knees brushing the wall before him, which was another strange new experience, and the shower was a simple glass box but wide enough for him to stand within without having to basically hug himself tight. The showerhead was a little low, but he knew how to fix that—he'd just need to get to a hardware store at some point.

Once he was cleaned up, Wylie grabbed a clean shirt—blue plaid today, nice and cheery—and tugged that on, along with his jeans. Then he checked his coffee can. It was still there, of course, but its contents looked sadly depleted. Between what he'd paid for the motel room those nights and now what he'd given Mama Rheda, he didn't have a whole lot left. Of course, he wasn't sure how long he was staying, but if possible, it would be better to refill the can a bit.

That was a good question, and he leaned against the wall in the main room, gazing absently out the windows as he considered it. He'd initially fled Embarrass to avoid that Hunter, but surely she'd given up and moved on by now? Then again, maybe not—he'd seen regular hunters settle into a blind for several days or more while waiting for some particular type of game to appear. And hers was *very* particular. Could she have set up outside his cabin or even within it? He couldn't discount the possibility. So, best to stay put at least a few more days to be safe.

Besides which, bad dreams aside, he was actually starting to like being here. He'd never expected that—the city had always been just this big thing looming far off in the distance, a scary story he knew to steer clear of. But now that he was here, with all these people and places and sights and smells and foods, he found it fascinating.

Especially since, for the first time since leaving his family, it wasn't just him and humans. Knox and Jeannie and Mama and the others might not be Yetis, but they were still supernaturals, which meant he wasn't alone.

That was definitely something he wanted to explore a bit more.

"Right, then," he decided, pushing off from the wall. "Time to go make some money."

Only, he acknowledged as he shoved a few bills into his pocket for food and then went and stuffed his feet into his boots, he had no idea how to do that here. Could he fish in the Mississippi? If he did, would he be able to sell those fish somewhere? Where?

Maybe Knox would know.

Grabbing a baseball cap from his bag and sticking it atop his head, Wylie headed for the door, remembering to check his pocket for his keys right before he pulled it open—

—to find someone standing right outside it.

Or, more accurately, leaning against the wall directly opposite. Muscular arms crossed, head down, long dark hair tugged back neatly out of the way, red eyes fixed on him the second he pulled the barrier aside.

"What do you want?" Brea asked, lifting her head but not moving otherwise. Her skin was once more that pale, cool blue it had been when he'd first met her.

"Shouldn't that be my line?" Wylie asked, stepping out and closing the door behind him. He made a point of locking it. "Seeing as how you're lurking outside my door?"

"I want to know who you are and what you want here," the Ogress replied, straightening and taking a step toward him. "This is my city, and I don't like surprises."

Wylie frowned, glancing her up and down. "Y'know, I'm not up on local politics or anything," he remarked slowly, "but I'm pretty sure I'd remember if the mayor was a six-foot-plus, blue-skinned Ogress." He was a little surprised at himself for talking back like this—normally, he avoided confrontation like the plague. Then again, normally, he was dealing with irate humans and couldn't risk them finding out about him. That wasn't an issue here.

Still, no point in making things worse. "Look," he continued, holding up his hands to indicate a truce, "my name's Wylie Kang. I'm a Yeti. I've been living up north, little town called Embarrass. I came down here for a bit to see how the other half lives. That's it. I'm not looking for trouble."

"You'd better not be," Brea snapped, moving even closer to glare at him. "Because if you think you can cause problems here, think again. I'm watching you, Wylie Kang. One wrong move—"

Okay, that was about enough of that. "And what?" Wylie shot back, straightening to his full height. She was tall, but he was taller and broader. "I told you I don't want trouble," he said, his voice dropping a bit into a deep rumble. "But that doesn't mean I'm gonna let you, or anybody, push me around, either. You really think you could take me if I decided you were a problem?" He grinned, showing her his teeth. "Think again." Then he forced himself to relax, slump a bit, and tamp down his grin. "Now, if you'll excuse me, I need to find a way to earn some money."

Brea continued to stare at him a moment, not moving, her face still close enough that her tusks nearly brushed his beard. But finally, grudgingly, she backed up a pace. "Try the docks," she said, so quietly he almost didn't hear her. "They always need workers."

"Yeah? Thanks." He was surprised by the suggestion, or more accurately by its source, but he wasn't about to look a gift horse in the mouth. Instead, he just nodded to her and headed for the stairs.

He could feel her watching him the whole way down the hall.

There was just one problem with taking Brea's advice, Wylie realized as he stepped outside, stopping just beyond the back door to let the cool, crisp morning air wash over him. He wasn't entirely sure where or how to find the docks. He pondered that for a minute, trying to figure out if there was somewhere he could go or someone he could ask about it—he was sure Knox would know, but he didn't want to disturb the Red Cap while he was working, and besides, he didn't want to be solely dependent upon the Goblin for help.

As he was thinking about this, the door behind him clicked. Wylie spun about, thinking it might be Brea keeping tabs on him and was surprised to find someone else entirely stepping through. It was the tall, slim, lovely white-haired woman he'd seen the night before. Sinead, Knox's friends had said her name was. She had her head down and was about to bump into him when he coughed to get her attention. Startled, she stopped just in time, head coming up and eyes widening in surprise to find someone standing there blocking her path.

Up close, she was even more stunning than he'd realized, her face a perfect heart shape, her eyes large and luminous, their irises a bright, vivid blue. Her hair was long and pure white, and her skin was pale as well, though closer to ivory in shade. "Oh!" she whispered, backing up a pace, and Wylie was surprised to hear her voice, for it was far raspier than he would have expected.

"Sorry," he said, retreating as well. "Didn't mean to startle you. I was trying to figure out where I'm headed, and, well, you were about to bump into me." He patted his chest and chuckled. "Wouldn't have done me any harm, but I didn't want to knock you down."

"Thanks." The word came out as a hoarse whisper, and she ducked her head, letting her hair fall over her face and obscure her features. "Sorry. I wasn't looking."

"No worries." He held out his hand. "I'm Wylie. I'm new here."

For a second, she seemed to shrink in on herself, but then she nodded. "Sinead."

"Nice to meet you." Was that a touch of a smile on her pale pink lips? It was hard to tell under all that hair! "Say, you wouldn't happen to know where the docks are, would you?" he asked suddenly. "I'm looking for work, and Brea suggested I try there."

"Brea did?" He wondered if she smoked heavily or if her voice was naturally that rough. Maybe it was a—what had they said she was again?—Banshee thing. "They're south of here," she said finally. "By the airport. Follow Highway 55. You can't miss it." Then, as if appalled that she'd said so much, she hugged herself and quickly stepped around him, making to hurry off the loading dock and away.

"Thanks!" Wylie called after her. "See you around?" But she was already darting around the corner. He watched her go, that long hair flowing behind her like a banner streaming in the wind. Odd. She hadn't seemed standoffish, though, or arrogant. Just shy.

Well, it looked like she lived here too, so he'd probably run into her again. Maybe she'd get more comfortable talking to him over time.

Meanwhile, he now had a direction, thanks to her. And it sounded like he'd be better off driving this time, so he hopped down and headed for his truck.

As Sinead had promised, the port area proved easy enough to find. Ten minutes later, Wylie was parking in a large lot and looking about. He'd been around water most of his life, of course, but that had been rivers and lakes up north, where you only occasionally saw another soul, and there wasn't anything more built-up than the occasional hunter's cabin.

This was very, very different.

The waterfront was crowded with buildings, for one thing. Most of them low-lying, blocky places with metal siding and few windows but massive loading doors. Warehouses, he gathered, peering into the few that were open and seeing boxes and shipping containers stacked high inside, matching the mounds and piles between those buildings and the river itself.

And in between those two were people. Lots and lots of people.

Though he'd probably seen as many walking around the city the other day, Wylie was struck by the difference in pace and focus here. These people all had jobs to do, and they were all busy doing them and quickly. No one dawdled, no one chatted with friends or checked their phones — all he saw were people carrying things, people directing other people, people conferring with one another over clipboards or tablets.

It certainly seemed like a place where everyone worked, and that was probably a good sign.

The next question was, how did he find work here himself? Who could he ask? He stopped, making sure he was off to one side so as not to block anyone's path, and studied the scene. Maybe one of the people with clipboards? They looked to be in charge.

As he was deliberating, a pair of men walked past, each one hefting one end of a big, heavy plastic shipping container. One of them stumbled, his heel catching on a crack in the concrete, and the container's handle slipped out of his grip. His partner tried to compensate but couldn't, losing his hold. The first man cried out, falling over, the heavy box about to land atop him.

Wylie reacted without thinking. Lunging forward, he got his hand under the container and heaved upward, practically flipping the big shape into the air. Then he stepped forward, planted his feet, and caught it with a loud grunt as it tumbled back down.

"Damn!" The second man was at his side a second later. "Thanks, man! That was close! Leo, you okay?"

"Yeah, fine," the first guy replied, picking himself up and dusting himself off. "Thanks, dude. Saved my ass." He shook his head. "I'd've been flat as a pancake, you hadn't stepped in."

"No problem." Wylie held still while the two grabbed the handles again, then slowly lowered his arm, letting them take the weight once more. "I'm actually looking for work. You guys hiring?"

"Hell, yeah!" the first man said. "Talk to Ted. He's the one there with the yellow hardhat." He nodded. "I'm Leo, and that's Hiro. Good luck, man." Then the two of them were on their way once more.

Looking where he'd indicated, Wylie spotted a man heading his way. Tall, skinny, yellow hardhat, clipboard—he guessed this was Ted. "Hey," the man said, coming to a halt in front of him. "I saw what just happened. Thanks. Ted McCall, Twin Cities Transfer Co."

"Wylie Kang," Wylie replied, accepting the hand Ted offered. "I'm actually looking for work."

"You okay with hauling stuff?" Ted asked. "Cause if so, you're hired. Eight hours a day, five days a week. Pays twenty an hour."

Wylie nodded, quickly running the numbers in his head. That was eight hundred a week! He'd have the coffee can refilled in no time!

"Great!" Ted clapped him on the back. "Let's get your paperwork filled out and put you to work!" He led the way toward the warehouse—which Wylie now noted displayed the company's name in big letters on the side—and Wylie followed behind.

Things were definitely looking up. And to think, he had Brea to thank for it!

CHAPTER THIRTEEN

THE WORK PROVED EASY ENOUGH, THOUGH CERTAINLY STRENUOUS—
Wylie was used to sitting still for long periods or roaming the forests
unencumbered, so lugging heavy boxes and containers for hours on
end quickly took a toll. Despite his strength, he was more than
happy to stop and catch his breath when a whistle blew, and Ted
called, "That's lunch!" Wylie sighed and pulled off his cap to wipe
the sweat from his brow. Who knew that manual labor could be so
exhausting?

"Hey, Wylie!" It was Leo, standing with Hiro and a few others
Wylie had seen and nodded to throughout the morning. "You bring
food?" Wylie shook his head. "Come on, then!"

Surprised but pleased at the invitation, Wylie hurried across the
floor to catch up.

"It's Thursday," Leo explained as they filed out of the warehouse
and onto the docks, a big, dark-skinned man taking the lead. "Which
means it's Gumbo Day!"

"Gumbo Day?" Wylie wasn't sure what that meant but didn't mind
finding out, especially since the others all looked excited about it.

He got his answer a few minutes later when they cut across a large
yard filled with containers, slipped through a gate in the tall chain-link
fence surrounding the whole place, and crossed a street to get in a
line mostly made up of men in similarly casual work attire. Their
destination, Wylie saw over the others' heads, was a truck pulled up
along the curb right by the corner. It was painted a deep, rich red, and
his nose twitched as it picked up some very enticing smells rising
from the vehicle. *Spices and tomatoes,* he thought, *and maybe seafood?
Chicken? Both?*

"We get different food trucks around here on different days," Leo told him as they waited, inching forward bit by bit. "Thursdays, it's The Cajun Dream. Best Gumbo in the North."

When their little group finally reached the front, Wylie saw that the truck's menu consisted of only four things: gumbo, jambalaya, po boys, and cornbread. He didn't know what those first three were, exactly, but he followed the others' lead and got a large gumbo when it was his turn, along with a water. He received a big quart container that was warm to the touch, a tinfoil-wrapped square, and a water bottle.

He'd been the last in line, so once he had his food, they retraced their steps, stopping short of re-entering the warehouse to take shelter alongside it instead, perching on stacks of empty pallets set off to the side there. "This is Jay, Mateo, and Danny. Guys, this is Wylie. Just started today and already saved my ass."

"Join the club," one of the others—Mateo?—quipped, extending his hand. "Good to meetcha, Wylie. Welcome to the chain gang."

They all said hello, and Wylie returned the greetings. He'd rarely had anyone be as welcoming before, and as far as he could tell, his new friends were all fully human. Though interestingly, not all alike—Jay was clearly African-American, Mateo, he suspected, was Hispanic, and Hiro looked Asian. Leo and Danny were both white, but Leo had red hair and freckles while Danny had dark eyes and darker hair. That made them a more mixed group than most Wylie had seen in the Twin Cities thus far, but nobody seemed to care, nor did they treat him any differently from each other.

Gumbo proved to be a rich, thick soup filled with rice, shrimp, chicken, celery, and some vegetables and herbs he didn't recognize. It was amazing, and even though he didn't normally care for hot food, Wylie could hardly complain about how it warmed him inside. The tinfoil held two large squares of cornbread, and following the others' example, he dunked those in the gumbo, soaking the soft, mealy, sweet bread until it was almost ready to fall apart before quickly stuffing it into his mouth. He was glad there had been several napkins provided along with the food because he wound up having to wipe his beard clean more than once, much to everyone else's amusement.

"Yeah, might want to ditch the Mountain Man look," Hiro said with a laugh. "Saves a lot of time on cleanup." His round face was perfectly smooth, and any hair he did have was hidden beneath a bright red do-rag.

Wylie smiled back because he could tell Hiro didn't mean anything by it. The men tossed far sharper barbs back and forth throughout lunch, but none of it seemed to be for real. He'd heard similar things last night from Knox and his friends. Strange how people behaved.

Still, it was a pleasant break, and when Ted blew the whistle again, and they all filed back inside, Wylie was smiling.

The rest of the day passed quickly, with a few brief pauses amid the heavy labor, and before he knew it, Wylie heard the whistle once more. "Quitting time!" Ted announced to a chorus of cheers, whistles, and applause. "See you all first thing in the morning!" The overseer glanced about, and his eyes quickly landed on Wylie. "Wylie, good first day!"

Wylie nodded, holding up a hand. "Thanks." Leo and the others crowded around to pat him on the back and shoulders or offer high-fives.

"We're gonna go grab a beer," Leo told him. "You coming?" The others were already gathering their things. Most of the workers had taken off by now or were standing around talking in ones and twos, but clearly, the five Wylie had fallen in with were an established group.

"Can't," he replied, shaking his head. "Sorry. Need to catch up with another friend." He felt bad about not meeting Knox for lunch, but of course, last night, he'd had no idea any of this would happen. "Another time, though, definitely." He meant it, too, unlike all the times Ray had invited him to hang out after the diner closed, and he'd always begged off. But things felt different here.

"Sure, no worries." If Leo was offended, he certainly didn't act it. "See you in the morning, man." And, with waves of goodbye, the group headed for the door.

A part of Wylie wanted to run after them, to tell them he'd changed his mind. But that wouldn't be fair to Knox, who was probably wondering what'd happened to him this afternoon. As Wylie exited, making for where he'd left his pickup, he hoped the little Red Cap wouldn't be too angry about being stood up.

"Yo, what's the word, big man?" Knox greeted him, glancing up from his street art. The piece had filled in considerably since just yesterday, Wylie saw, with a good deal more detail everywhere. In fact, to his eye, it looked completely finished, though he fully admitted he wasn't exactly an expert when it came to art.

"Hey," Wylie replied, arms folded over his chest. He'd found the Goblin standing back, admiring his handiwork, and once again had been forced to cough loudly to get his attention. "Sorry about lunch today."

"Hm?" That made the smaller man pause and peer up at the sky, where the sun was just starting to set. "Oh, yeah. We were gonna grab lunch. Crap. Sorry, man—got caught up in the work. But whaddya think? Looks good, right?"

"Absolutely." And it did—Wylie had never seen anything so fanciful before, and yet the detail and clarity almost made it look real, like a photo rather than a chalk drawing. "It's amazing."

"Thanks." Knox grinned, absently wiping his hands on his jeans and leaving colored streaks. "She's all done, too. Man, I'm starving!" He rubbed his belly, putting a slash of pale purple across his shirt in the process. "I'm thinking Juicy Lucys. You in?"

Wylie nodded, though yet again, he had no idea what that meant. Still, so far, Knox had not steered him wrong!

"Great! Blue Door it is!" He pulled out his phone. "I'll let the gang know, and then we can head over. You drive or walk?"

"Drive." Wylie hadn't been quite sure how far it was from here to Mama Rheda's, and of course, he'd already been several hours late— not that Knox seemed to notice or care—so he'd driven straight here instead. The parking lot here was starting to feel like a second home! Though he'd been sorry to see that the Caffeine Burst had already been gone for the day. Maybe tomorrow he could swing by on his way to work.

Work. That was such a strange new concept for him! He was dying to tell Knox all about it. Which was strange, in and of itself. When was the last time he'd had someone to talk to about such things? Never, really—when he'd been young, there hadn't been anything to talk about, his family had known everything about him anyway, and since then, he'd kept to himself to stay safe.

Wylie wondered how he'd even start. How did people have conversations with one another? He really wasn't sure.

Knox had been tapping something on his phone as Wylie thought, and now tucked the device away. "Why don't we drive back to Mama's, drop the truck off, and then we can walk from there?"

"Sure."

As they set out, Knox solved Wylie's silent dilemma. "So, how's the apartment?" the Red Cap asked. "Sleep okay? And tell me you haven't been holed up in there all day!"

Wylie laughed, relieved at being provided such an easy opening. "No, not at all. In fact..."

"Blue Door" was actually the Blue Door Pub, as it turned out. It was in Longfellow, Knox told him, which was just below Phillips and to the right, on the other side of Highway 55, though the pub was down almost at the bottom of the neighborhood. "Hey, I took this road this morning," Wylie commented as they crossed over the highway. "Sinead told me about it."

"Sinead?" His companion twisted about to look back at him since, as usual, Knox was leading the way. "You actually talked to her? And she talked back?"

"Yep." Wylie smiled, thinking back on the encounter. "She was nice, actually. I think — I think she's just shy."

"Uh-huh." It was clear Knox didn't believe him, but Wylie let the matter drop. For now.

"Here we go," the Red Cap said at last. The area around them had flattened out and spread as well, the buildings becoming lower and smaller and more spaced out, with most of them looking like small one-story homes. The building in front of them didn't look much bigger than its neighbors, but it was closer to the street, lacking any sort of front lawn. Windows took up the entire front and much of the side beneath a dark blue awning. The door itself was a much brighter shade of blue, and up above the awning were the words "Home of the Blucy." Wylie had no idea what that meant but suspected he was about to find out.

The inside was considerably darker and homier than the place from last night, with wood paneling and a tin ceiling. A long bar took up one whole side, with an enormous mirror on the wall behind it. The rest of the restaurant was tables and booths, and Wylie quickly spotted Jeannie, Swift, and Doug at one of them. "There they are," he said, pointing the trio out to Knox.

"Ha, helps having a tall guy around from time to time," the little man said, grinning as he made a beeline for them. "Hey. kids, guess what?" he exclaimed upon reaching the table, with Wylie right behind. "Wylie's buying—he got himself a job!"

That was greeted by cheers from the three already seated and a good-natured groan from Wylie. "I haven't even been paid yet!" he reminded his friend, squeezing into the booth with the others—this one was a corner booth, so there was more space for them to spread out. "But once I do, sure."

"Fair enough," Jeannie agreed, and Swift grinned and added, "We'll hold you to that." Then they wanted to know all about the job. All three expressed surprise that Brea had been the one to suggest it to him and utter shock that Sinead had taken the time to tell him how to get there. "Directions from the Ice Queen herself," Swift muttered. "Will wonders never cease?"

Wylie started to defend her but stopped himself. He didn't really know Sinead yet, after all. Maybe she'd just been nice to him because he was new in town? Then again, if she was as stuck-up as they all said, why would that have mattered to her?

The arrival of their waitress put a stop to his musings, at least for the time being. Instead, he finally studied the menu before going with something called an "Ergy Burgy Blucy"—it had "sharp white cheddar, house pickles, house aioli, lingonberry jam, and creamy beef gravy," apparently—and an order of cheese curds. Plus, a pitcher of beer.

The rest of the night was much like the previous one, filled with good food—"Blucy" was evidently another name for a "Juicy Lucy," or a cheeseburger where the cheese was melted inside the beef instead of being laid across the top, and his was excellent, juicy and well-seasoned—and lots of talking and laughing. Again, Wylie let the others do most of the speaking, but he chimed in occasionally and even made the others crack up a time or two. That felt good, and by the time he got home, his face was sore from smiling so much. Of course, the rest of him was sore for different reasons, and he was only too happy to wash up and collapse on his bed once more. But it had been a good day, and he liked that he already had a plan for tomorrow. This would be his first day here where he wasn't just floundering about, trying to figure out what to do next, and he looked forward to it.

CHAPTER FOURTEEN

THE NEXT DAY WAS FRIDAY. WYLIE WAS STILL HAVING TROUBLE wrapping his brain around the idea of "going to work," something he'd heard a thousand times on TV but had never experienced himself, so he decided against stopping by the Coffee Burst on his way to make sure he could get there on time. Fortunately, he spotted a similar truck near where he parked, and though the iced coffee wasn't quite as good, it was still tasty and did an excellent job waking him up.

Friday was apparently Sub Day for the boys, and at lunch time they delighted in introducing Wylie to the Yellow Submarine, a big, bright yellow truck that offered up all kinds of sandwiches. Wylie went with roast beef and cheddar, with lettuce, tomato, and horseradish, and had to admit that both the sandwich and the side of seasoned curly fries were excellent.

The work seemed less strenuous somehow. Maybe that was because Wylie was already starting to get used to it or because he knew what to expect now. Or it could have been because he could share a joke or chat for a minute with the other guys in between or even while hauling loads. Whatever the reason, when Ted blew the whistle to mark the end of the workday, Wylie found that he wasn't as exhausted as he had been the day before.

Plus, there was the fact that it was Friday, and evidently, that was Pay Day.

"It's only the two days, of course," Ted told him as the foreman handed over an envelope with Wylie's name on the front. "But still, you're off to a great start. Glad you're here, man."

Wylie accepted the envelope and the praise, the former eagerly and the latter awkwardly. He waited until Ted had moved on to the next few guys before glancing inside—and staring at the single sheet of folded paper within. What the heck was this?

Pulling it out, he saw that the bottom portion was a different shade and had a perforation along the top so it could be separated from the rest. Ah, it was a check. He'd seen plenty of those on TV, of course.

The only problem was, he didn't exactly have a bank account. So, what the hell did he do with it?

The guys saved him again. "Need to cash it?" Mateo asked him, appearing at his side. "Come on." He led the way outside to where the others were already lined up by a small booth affixed to the front of the warehouse. Wylie had half-noticed it before, but now he saw that there was a big sign over the counter in front. "Checks Cashed! No Fee!"

"The company's gotta pay us by check for bookkeeping and all that," Mateo explained as they joined the others. "But some of us don't have bank accounts or just don't wanna deal with the hassle. Regular check-cashing places, they charge you an arm and a leg. So Twin Cities Transfer set up its own version, just for us. Only cashes checks from them, but there's a set twenty-buck fee. And since it's technically off their property, they can get away with it." He shrugged. "Works for us, right?"

Wylie had to agree. When it was his turn up at the counter, he copied what he'd seen Mateo do right in front of him, separating the check from the rest of the page, signing it on the back, and handing it over. The man in the booth nodded, ran it through some kind of machine he had there, and then added the check to a stack before opening a drawer, pulling out several bills, putting them in another machine, and then sticking them in an envelope which he slid back across. "Have a good day," he said. He'd barely even glanced up through the process.

Still, Wylie muttered, "Thanks, you too," as he took the envelope and moved out of the line before glancing inside. Fifteen twenty-dollar bills were nestled within. Yes!

"You'll wanna set some aside for taxes later," Jay advised as he joined them where most of the workers had gathered a little ways away. "That's the one drawback to getting paid in cash. They don't take anything out for us. We've gotta do that ourselves." Wylie just nodded, pretending he knew what his friend was talking about. He'd seen references to taxes on various shows, but of course, he wasn't an actual U.S. citizen, or at least not one with a birth certificate and a social security number. Well, he'd worry about that later—assuming he was even still in town when taxes came due. For now, it was enough to know that, just from working two days, he had enough to cover next month's rent and then some. A full week's work next week, and he'd easily have the coffee can back up to full.

A muttered curse distracted him from his musings, and he glanced over to see Leo scowling at someone on the other side of the clustered group. Following his friend's gaze, Wylie saw a fellow he'd seen around the past two days but hadn't spoken with at all. "Problem?" he asked softly, and Leo cursed again.

"It's Friday, so RT's doing his usual shakedown," he explained, practically spitting out the words. His face began to flush as dark as his hair. "I'm sick of it!"

"Don't, man," Hiro warned, resting a hand on Leo's shoulder. "Remember what happened to Bobby."

"Bobby's a friend of ours, used to work with us," Mateo told Wylie quietly, turning his back on the room so the man across the way wouldn't see. "He told RT no one time. Next thing we knew, he had two broken hands. Couldn't work anymore, obviously. He refused to say who did it, but we all knew." The glare he shot over his shoulder could have turned solid stone to ash.

Wylie frowned, studying the man in question. He was big, over six feet, with the kind of build that said when he wasn't working, he was working out. Dusky skin, bald head, dark goatee, and the tight black T-shirt he wore showed off tattoos covering much of his arms, neck, and possibly upper chest. He was going from worker to worker, and as Wylie watched, each one handed over a wad of cash. Then he was standing in front of their little group.

"Guys," he announced, a smile on his lips but his dark eyes hard and cold. "It's Friday, which means it's dues time. Pay up." He clearly assumed that everyone would do exactly that without question, and a few of the others were already reaching into their pay envelopes.

Wylie had just earned this money, though. He wasn't so eager to hand it over to someone, especially for no reason. "Dues for what?" he asked.

RT seemed to notice him for the first time, and his smile grew strained as he tipped his head back to meet Wylie's gaze. "Hey there, big fella. Name's RT. I'm the local union rep, and I'm collecting dues. It's a hundred bucks a week per member."

"I didn't agree to join any union," Wylie replied. "I'll pass."

Now the smile dropped away. "Not really an option, my man. This is a closed shop, see. If you're not union, you don't work."

"Oh?" Wylie folded his arms over his chest. "Ted didn't say anything about that when he hired me yesterday. Let me ask." He turned toward where the foreman was still on the other side of the wide doorway, going over something on his clipboard with a few of the people who worked in the warehouse's office area, but paused as a hand clamped down on his shoulder.

"Let's not bother management with stuff like this," RT suggested, but his voice was low and cold. "This is strictly for union guys, not suits. You get that, right? So, let's not start any trouble here." He squeezed, his grip tightening.

Wylie smiled. "Oh, it's no trouble." Then he peeled the man's hand off him like it was a wet leaf that'd just blown onto his shirt. "But I won't be paying any dues. And neither will anyone else." He straightened and glared down at RT from a full head taller. "Got it?"

For the first time, the big man's confidence seemed to falter. "Sure, sure," he said quickly, backing up a pace. He turned as if to go—and then spun around fast, his fist flying toward Wylie's face.

But Wylie had been expecting that. He'd grown up reading predators and prey, anticipating attack and defense. Besides which, he'd watched a lot of television. He didn't bother to duck, though. Instead, he caught RT's hand in his own, his fingers completely engulfing the man's fist.

And then it was his turn to squeeze.

"All right, all right!" RT yelped, his knees starting to buckle from the pain. "No dues!"

Wylie released him, and the man found his feet again, massaging his injured hand. "You're gonna regret that," he warned before stomping off.

"Not half as much as you will!" Leo hooted, slapping Wylie on the back. "Damn, that was awesome, man!" the lanky redhead crowed. "Now you *gotta* come out for a drink with us! I'm buying!"

Wylie grinned. "How could I turn down an offer like that?"

They went to a bar a few blocks away, a dark, cozy little place whose proprietor clearly knew the guys. Wylie stuck around for one beer, then begged off, saying he had promised other friends he'd meet them for dinner. Which was actually true, since the night before, he'd agreed to meet Knox and the Kobolds at Pizza Lucé again. "Next time, I'll stay longer," he promised as he stood to go amid protests. "I promise. Catch you all Monday."

He was humming to himself as he headed out. So many times, he'd watched scenes where people gathered with friends for a drink after work, and now he was the one actually doing that! It was like living in some sort of weird dream.

But he found that he liked it.

The others were already seated when he reached the restaurant, in the same booth as before. And they weren't the only familiar faces in the restaurant.

"Hey," Wylie said, stopping first by the booth across the way. Sinead glanced up, startled, and he held up his hands. "Sorry, didn't mean to scare you. I just wanted to say thanks. For the directions the other day? They were perfect."

"Oh." As before, her voice was so low he had to strain to hear, and again she shifted, so her hair fell forward and covered her face from view. "You're welcome."

He nodded. "Cool. Well, I won't keep you from your book" — he waved a hand toward where she held it propped up against the table's edge. "I just wanted to say thanks. See you around, I guess." Turning away, he headed over to his friends, but he thought he heard a whispered "See ya" behind him.

"Still chipping away at the Ice Queen, huh?" Swift asked when he joined them. "Gotta admire your persistence."

Wylie ignored that but deliberately sat next to her and hip-checked the snarky little artist hard enough to send her sprawling into her sister, producing a pair of outraged Kobold squawks and chuckles from Knox and Doug. "So, guess who got paid today?" he said, changing the subject by pulling some of the bills from his envelope and laying them on the table. "Dinner's on me!"

That made the girls' grumbling turn to cheers, and soon they were all chatting and joking again.

"What's up with the hat, man?" Doug asked after they'd placed their orders and were noshing on breadsticks. "You trying to get into fights or something?"

With a frown, Wylie plucked his cap off his head and studied it. He'd picked a navy-blue check for his shirt today and had gone with a blue hat to match. "Sorry?" The hat only had two letters on it, an "N" and a "Y," both in orange and superimposed one atop the other. "What's wrong with it?"

"What's wrong with it?" Doug echoed. "Are you kidding? You're wearing a Mets cap in Twins territory! I mean, it's not a Yankees cap, thank God, but it's close!"

"Oh. Sorry." Wylie shook his head. "I didn't realize. Should I put it away?"

"Naw, don't worry about it," Swift told him, and Knox nodded.

"Yeah, Dougie Dog's just messing with ya," the Red Cap promised. "But you really didn't know? So, you're not actually a Mets fan? I was wondering—you had a different cap the other day, right? Who's your team, then?"

Wylie picked at a breadstick. "No idea," he admitted. "I've only ever seen any of them play on TV."

That had all four of his friends slapping the table and leaning forward. "You've never been to a real live game?" Swift asked. "Dude, we gotta fix that, stat!"

"You said it," Knox agreed, his phone already in his hand. "Hold that thought." He tapped the screen, scrolled a bit, then tapped again. "Aha!" he said. "Perfect! They're playing at home tomorrow, against the Orioles! Five tickets, coming up!"

Wylie glanced at the others. "You can do that?" he asked, aware that he sounded slightly awed—because he was. "Just call up and get tickets to a game like that?"

"Well, Knox can," Jeannie clarified, shaking her head. "Couldn't tell you how, exactly, but somehow he always manages."

Sure enough, a second later, the Red Cap tucked his phone away and reached for his beer, a big smile on his face. "All set," he told them. "Five seats for tomorrow's game. One pm, Target Field." He grinned at Wylie and raised his glass. "You're gonna love it."

Wylie grinned back, clinking his glass to his friend's in salute. "I can't wait," he said and meant every word.

CHAPTER FIFTEEN

WYLIE WAS CAREFUL TO PUT ON A BLUE, RED, AND WHITE-CHECKED SHIRT the next morning to match his Twins cap. He whistled as he headed downstairs and was pleased to see Knox waiting for him on the loading dock—they'd arranged to meet the others at the stadium. His excitement dimmed a bit, however, as he took in the Red Cap's frown.

"What's going on?" he asked, and the little Goblin *harrumph*ed, tucking away the phone he'd just had to his ear when Wylie emerged.

"Dougie Dog canceled on us," Knox answered. "Rush job came in. Boss needs him, yada-yada-yada." He sighed. "Well, the four of us'll just have ta have fun without him. Maybe I can scalp his ticket or something." Shaking his head, he hopped down onto the asphalt parking lot. "You ready to go?" He'd explained the night before that they'd be taking the light rail instead of driving because apparently, trying to park for a game was murder.

"Sure thing," Wylie replied. He stepped down but only took a step when he heard the door creak behind him. A quick glance showed a now-familiar pale, willowy figure—and suddenly, he had a crazy idea.

"Okay if I invite someone else along?" he asked Knox quickly, hunching over and keeping his voice low. The Red Cap eyed him suspiciously, one eyebrow shooting up, but nodded.

"Yeah, sure, why not?" the little street artist agreed. "The more, the merrier."

"Cool." With that, Wylie straightened, turning toward the stairs— just as a certain Banshee stepped off them. "Hey, Sinead," he called, and she froze, glancing up at him in surprise. "You busy?"

She studied him, eyes wide, but after a second, she shrugged, the motion barely perceptible. She wore something like a hooded poncho, he saw, in a pale, almost pearly gray, though she had the hood down so her hair could flow free. Beneath that, she had on dark gray leggings and high, sturdy boots. The bag at her side probably held the book she'd been reading, he thought, or perhaps a new one if she'd finished that one. Which meant he was most likely interrupting her plans for the day. Still, he'd gotten up the courage to start—might as well finish.

"It's just"—Wylie shuffled his feet. How did people do this sort of thing? It looked so easy on TV! "We're gonna go to a baseball game," he explained. "My first ever. And we've got an extra ticket. Would you— do you wanna go? With us?" He felt flushed all over, and his palms were sweaty. He could practically feel Knox snickering behind him and Sinead searching for a way out. What had he been thinking?

She didn't actually move, though. Just stared at him a second. Then she asked softly, "Why?"

"Why?" He blinked. "Why go to a game? I dunno. It looks like fun. Why go with us? Well, why not? We're neighbors, right? And you helped me out the other day." He grinned, forgetting that his teeth often scared people half to death. "What do you say?"

There was a pause, and then her chin dipped and rose, just the once, barely an inch. "Okay." The word was little more than a breath, but Wylie heard it anyway.

"Yeah? Great!" He clapped his hands together, and this time he was sure he saw a smile touch her lips. "Come on! Oh, do you know Knox? Knox, this is Sinead."

To his credit, the little Red Cap didn't stay stunned for long. "Never met for reals, but I've seen you around, 'course," he said, waving. "Nice to have you along. Now come on, kids, we gotta go catch the train."

"I've never been on a train," Wylie confided in Sinead as they followed the little Goblin onto the sidewalk and down the block. "That probably sounds dumb, huh?"

She shook her head, sending her hair streaming about her. "No," she said, slightly more audible than before. "Brave," When he tilted his head, she must have read his confusion because she explained, "trying new things."

"Oh. Huh. Yeah, I guess." He smiled. "That sounds a lot better than 'dumb' so let's go with that." There was that smile again, just a flicker of it, but Wylie knew he'd seen it. Nice.

Knox led them across an enormously wide street that looked like a highway except that it ran through the city. "Hiawatha Avenue," the signs said, though Wylie saw another marker as they crossed, indicating this was the same Highway 55 Sinead had directed him to the other day. "Look, it's your street," he told her. That earned him a little snort. Once across that, they turned left, following Minnehaha up to East Franklin. Then back a block to a blocked-off stretch of concrete with a low platform on either side and two sets of rails running between them: a train station.

"We gotta grab you a Go-To card," Knox said, heading across the tracks to the platform on the far side. Wylie and Sinead followed him up onto it and then along it to a row of strange machines, upright like small vending machines but with a touchscreen set in the upper half and a compartment just below that. When Knox frowned at it, Sinead slid past him and, without a word, tapped her way through several screens in rapid succession. Wylie was watching closely enough that, when she glanced back, he handed her a ten-dollar bill, which she accepted and slid into a slot along the side. The machine then spit something out into the compartment. She scooped that up and handed it to Wylie. It looked like a credit card, except it was all blue and yellow and said "Go To" on the front in white.

"Thanks," he told her. She nodded, but before she could reply, there was a loud rushing sound as a train pulled into the station. Wylie wanted to cover his ears, the screech of its brakes was so loud, but his friends barely reacted, so he forced himself not to do more than wince a little. The train was long and white, with a broad blue stripe down its center around the windows and yellow at the front and back. Its doors hissed open, and Knox hurried the two of them inside, elbowing his way through the crowd that was disembarking. Sinead followed, and Wylie brought up the rear. He was worried about hurting anyone, and he barely made it on before the doors slid shut again.

"Dude, you gotta be more aggressive," Knox told him as the train lurched into motion again. "Otherwise, you won't get nowhere."

Wylie shrugged. That was easy to say when you weren't liable to break bones if you pushed! Case in point, the train's sudden motion had startled him, throwing him off-balance, and he'd grabbed hold of a nearby metal pole — and had crumpled it like a thin cardboard tube. Crap. Trying not to think about that too much, he studied their surroundings instead.

It was a bit low-ceilinged, of course — he had to hunch over, and he'd had to seriously duck to pass through the door without bashing his

forehead. There were rows of seats up and down, two sets of two on either side of a center aisle, and all facing toward the center. He wasn't sure he could squeeze into any of those. They looked really narrow, with barely enough room for a normal person's knees. Fortunately, there was a metal rail running overhead on both sides, with loops hanging from it. Those led to matching uprights around the doors, and there was more space to stand here, too. Besides, Knox couldn't reach the overhead poles, so the three of them clustered by the door instead. Wylie smiled, watching the streets whiz past outside. This was so cool!

The train stopped several times, and they had to shuffle to the side to let people on and off. A few grumbled at them for blocking the way, but most took one look at Wylie and decided to keep their complaints to themselves. Finally, the announcer stated, "Target Field Station, last stop!"

"Okay, stick close," Knox warned as they began to slow. "This crowd'll eat you up otherwise."

"Hungry crowd," Wylie remarked, and beside him, Sinead smiled.

Then the train screeched to a halt, the doors slid open, and everyone began pushing and shoving their way out.

Wylie deliberately did not push—he never even raised his hands from his sides. But he did use his bulk to carve a path, nudging others aside as he went. Knox was already out in front, his ever-present red cap making him easy to find, and Sinead stuck to Wylie like a pale shadow. It proved to be a short walk from the station across to the stadium, not even a full block, and Knox called back, "look for the Will Call booth. That's what we want. It's in the Time Life Lobby."

There were signs everywhere, so it was easy enough to spot the escalator down to the lobby, and from there, the words "Will Call" over a group of booths to one side of the long row. Wylie pointed them out and then saw something else not far from their destination—a flash of purple hair. "I see Jeannie and Swift!" he said.

"Nice. You two go get them. I'll grab the tickets," Knox instructed and split off, disappearing into the crowd of people milling about and mixing with those lining up.

Wylie smiled at Sinead. "Come on. You'll like them." And he plowed a path toward the two waiting Kobolds.

Both girls broke into big smiles when they saw Wylie—and then those smiles froze on their faces as they spotted the slender woman behind him. "Uh, hi," Jeannie said as the four of them met up—she and her sister had been standing off to the side by the wall, next to a large metal sculpture of a dog with one paw resting on a ball, which was a great spot because the statue forced the crowd to flow around them. "I'm Jeannie." She was wearing one of those long, padded winter coats, the kind that looked all puffy but was actually really lightweight and yet still really warm. At least, that's what the commercials always said.

"This is Sinead," Wylie told her. "And that's Jeannie's sister, Swift. Doug couldn't make it," he explained. "So, I invited Sinead to join us."

"Yeah, Dougie told us," Swift confirmed. Her heavy leather motorcycle jacket was decked out with various chains and pins and looked pretty sharp, though Wylie suspected Jeannie's coat was the warmer one. "About him not being here, I mean." She eyed the Banshee. "So, you a big Twins fan?" The way she said it, with a twist to her lips, suggested she already knew the answer.

Which was why they were all surprised when Sinead set her hands on her hips. "Donaldson's good," she replied in her rasp, "and Kepler's solid. I think Cruz is starting to slip a little, but I like Hill over Berrios and Buxton's underrated." She tossed her hair back, raising her chin, and they could all see her smirk clearly for a change.

For a second, no one moved. *This was a mistake*, Wylie thought sadly, his heart beating like a drum. *Now they'll just think she really is as stuck-up as they claimed before.*

Then Swift laughed. "Not bad, girly-girl," the colorful Kobold declared, stepping forward and slinging an arm around the much taller Banshee's shoulders. "Not bad at all." Jeannie nodded as well, and Sinead's smirk widened—into a real smile, the first Wylie had seen on her. Then she was laughing, too. Not a giggle, and not raspy at all, but a full-out laugh, deep and warm. It spread around the four of them, and Wylie found himself laughing too, as was Jeannie.

They were all still chuckling when Knox joined them. "What'd I miss?" the little Red Cap asked, holding out four tickets.

"Just talking ballers," Swift replied, and she and Sinead giggled again. That made Wylie feel good—there was no question that the two Kobolds had accepted her now.

"Right." Knox clearly didn't believe her, but he shrugged as he passed out the tickets. "We're over this way. Let's go."

They turned—and Wylie gasped. He couldn't help it. "You've got a tail!" He blurted out, hand flying to his mouth immediately after the words leaped forth. But he couldn't help it. Because when Swift had turned, there, jutting from the back of her jeans just below her jacket and just above her rear, was a long golden tail.

She just looked back at him and winked. "That's right," she agreed, grinning. "What, you never seen a girl with a tail before?" And she flicked it at him, exactly like a cat would.

Wylie shook his head and trailed after as Swift took off after Knox, her arm falling from Sinead's shoulders to link arms with her instead. Jeannie patted Wylie sympathetically on the arm as she fell in beside him. "She's just messing with you," the calmer sister promised. "But yes, we have them. Nobody else sees them, of course." She smiled up at him. "Just like nobody sees"—and she wiggled her fingers at his face and then his claws—"all that."

"Right. Sorry." He felt silly. "I just—you all are the first other supernaturals I ever met, you know? I had no idea Kobolds had tails."

She nodded. "Well, now you know." But her smile was kind, and by the time they found the right gate and stepped through, Wylie felt better.

He had to stop there, however, because what he saw before him blew him away.

He'd watched games before, of course. And his TV was pretty big. But that experience didn't hold a candle to this one.

The field stretched out before him, a beautiful expanse of smooth, silky-looking green, perfect and pristine, the lines deeply etched in warm brown, the plates tidy white shapes accentuating each corner. On either side, the stands rose, row upon row, towering up and back, yet the sky loomed overhead, so large he couldn't possibly feel closed in even with so many people about. And the people! The noise of the crowd filled even such a large open space, creating a dull roar that lifted him up, carrying him on a wave of excitement that just made his pulse race.

"This is amazing," he whispered.

"Wait until you see them play." The voice was quiet beside him but clear, and it took him a second to realize it hadn't been Jeannie who'd said that or even Swift.

It had been Sinead. And she was still smiling.

"Come on," she said and pointed to where the others were already climbing the steps between rows. Wylie nodded and followed obediently after her. The walkway was barely wide enough for him to stand, and he was glad they had seats at the end of their row because there was no way he could fit to walk between them! As it was, he groaned a little, squeezing his butt down between the armrests and onto the hard plastic seat, and his knees were practically in his face.

"Stick them out in the aisle once people stop moving around," Sinead suggested. She'd taken the seat next to him, Swift on her other side, and when he glanced her way, the wind flung her long hair in his face, blinding him for a second. She looked mortified, but he just laughed it off. "Sorry."

"Girl, you need help," Swift stated, but not meanly. "Jeannie?"

"On it." Somehow, Jeannie hopped up onto her seat and then over its back, gliding forward to then crouch behind the startled Banshee. Her hand had dipped into her pocket and emerged with something small and round, a thin circle of some kind, and her other produced a brush. "Hold still." With quick, strong strokes, she brushed out Sinead's hair, gathered it in her hands—the brush dropping into her lap and the circle held between her teeth—and then slid the circle onto the bunched hair to craft a quick, rough but serviceable ponytail. "Done," she proclaimed, rising to her feet once more, brush in hand.

"Advantage of working with kids," Swift explained as her sister returned to her seat. "Fastest ponytailer in the North."

Sinead just nodded, one hand going to her head to gently pat the hair there and then to feel the ponytail. "Thanks." She smiled, and now there was no hair to hide behind.

She didn't seem to mind.

"Damn, girl," Swift muttered. "Blind us, why dontcha? Might need to get you a hat, 'fore you got guys falling all over themselves for a five-mile radius."

The way Sinead laughed and pinked told Wylie she didn't believe the Kobold for a second. But Swift was absolutely right. With her hair back and her delicate features on display, Sinead looked like a model. Or a movie star.

"You can borrow mine if you want," he offered, but Swift wrinkled her nose.

"That's sweet of you to offer, dude," she said, "but I think a trip to the gift shop might be in order. And the concessions stand."

"Oh, hell yes!" Knox exclaimed from the far end of their little group. "Sausages on a stick!" They all laughed at that, but the little Red Cap was already on his feet. "Who wants?"

Wylie nodded but didn't get up. "Okay if I stay here?" he asked instead, pulling out some cash and offering it to Knox. "Less likely to trample people that way."

"Sure, no worries," his friend declared, taking the money. "You hold down the fort. I'll grab the grub."

"We'll come along," Swift said, hopping up as well. "Hop to it, Sinead." And she hauled the Banshee to her feet.

Sinead glanced at her feet first, then at Wylie. He could read the question there and smiled. "Go on," he told her. "Somebody's gotta keep Swift out of trouble."

"Good luck with that," Jeannie remarked, but Swift just thumbed her nose at her sister. She and Sinead were laughing as they followed Knox back down the steps and soon disappeared through the little tunnel onto the main walkway beyond.

"Okay," Jeannie said once the others had gone. "You were right. She's nice. Not stuck-up at all. Just shy as all get-out." Wylie nodded, and she studied him. "How'd you see that when we didn't?" she asked seriously. "We've been around her for years and never even thought to ask. You've been here days, and you've got her laughing and smiling and talking to people."

Wylie shrugged, scratching his cheek. "Dunno," he said truthfully. "Maybe just because I'm new, so I didn't know any better?"

"Maybe," Jeannie agreed. "Well, anyway, you did a good thing, inviting her." She leaned back, resting her head on the top of her chair. "I'm really glad Knox met you, Wylie."

"Me too," he replied, feeling like his face might split from smiling so wide. "Me too."

CHAPTER SIXTEEN

BY THE TIME THE OTHERS GOT BACK, THE GAME WAS STARTING. KNOX returned first, carrying what looked almost like a strange meat bouquet, a veritable forest of sticks rising from his clenched fist, each one topped with a long, thick, blackened sausage. Wylie could smell them from several steps away, and his stomach was already growling in response when Knox made it to their row. "No worries, big man," the little Goblin said with a laugh, passing him several sticks. "I got you covered. And there's more." He hoisted one of those carboard drink holders in his other hand, each of its six sections crammed with a big plastic cup. "Beer to go with it. And"—setting the drinks down on the empty seat at Wylie's side, he revealed a plastic bag dangling from his wrist, then reached into that to pull out and hand over a deeply angled paper dish filled with familiar golden-brown nuggets—"cheese curds to top things off."

"Nice." Wylie accepted the cheese curds and one of the beers. "Thanks," he told his friend as Knox gave Jeannie a similar set and then took some for himself, leaving the remainder between them for their missing duo. He bit into one of the sausages, enjoying the way the skin resisted a second before parting and squirting juices into his mouth. Ah, that was good!

Just then, Swift and Sinead reappeared on the stairs. They were chatting away as they climbed and looked to be completely comfortable together now. "Ta-da!" Swift announced as they rejoined the group, adopting a salesgirl pose and waving her hands to display the Banshee, who smiled but couldn't help looking away still. "Whaddya think?"

"Looks great," Wylie said, which was the truth. Sinead now sported a Twins cap, but unlike his own, which was dark blue save for the white-limned red "M," hers was a soft gray that almost perfectly matched her poncho and had an interlocked "T" and "C" in white. She also wore a pair of sunglasses which, judging by the thick purple frames, he suspected were actually Swift's, but the combo certainly worked on her. He hauled himself out of his seat to let them slide past, then helped hold the food and drinks until the girls could get settled and take their share. Once that was done, he squeezed back into the chair and continued munching away.

They watched the first pitch, and then the game started in earnest. Wylie quickly discovered that Sinead had not been faking her knowledge of the sport or the team as she began muttering under her breath, exhorting players to do better — and cursing them when they messed up. "What was that all about?" he asked when he saw the pitcher gesturing and saw Sinead shake her head.

"He's calling for a different pitch," she told him. "He wants the curveball, but this guy eats those for breakfast. He should know that." Sure enough, the Oriole at-bat cracked the next pitch solidly toward the fence, scoring two bases off the hit.

"You really know your stuff," Wylie said, and Sinead smiled. Which was a lot easier to see now when she couldn't hide behind her hair.

"Yeah, not bad for a princess," Swift remarked from her other side, but her tone made it clear she was teasing. And then she shrieked because Sinead had just tossed a cheese curd at her, the fried treat smacking the Kobold squarely on the cheek.

"Keep it down," someone said, and Wylie identified the speaker as the man sitting in front of him. "Trying to watch the game here." He looked young, with dark hair curling beneath his baseball cap and a beard that was barely more than pencil lines along his jaw.

"Watch with your eyes, not your ears," Swift retorted. That earned her a glare from the man. He was sitting with a woman, though she was clearly trying to ignore the banter behind her.

The next batter also got on base, and Sinead bared her teeth. "Stop throwing easy pitches!" she called in what would have been a speaking voice for anyone else, but Wylie suspected was as close to shouting as she got. "Man up!"

"Hey!" The guy scowled at her. "Pipe down!"

"Mind your own business!" Swift snapped back. "Game's out there, not back here."

"I know, so shut up so I can watch it!"

"Hey," Wylie cut in. "No need for that."

That brought the man's attention to him. "You wanna make something of it, pal?" he demanded, popping to his feet and turning around to glare directly at Wylie. "Come on, then—let's go!"

Wylie raised an eyebrow. Then, slowly, he drew his legs in front of him and began to lever himself up from his seat.

And up.

And up.

He watched the man's eyes go wide as he continued to rise. The guy gulped, his cheeks going dark. Wylie still wasn't standing upright when the man said, "You know what, forget it—you're not worth it. Come on, Suzie." And, grabbing his date's arm, he all but dragged her down the steps to claim a pair of empty seats a few rows down.

"Oh, yeah," Swift called after him. "Totally not worth it. That's why you ran like a little girl!" She held up a hand to Wylie. "High five, dude!"

He slapped his hand gently against hers, though he actually felt a bit embarrassed about the whole thing. Still, at least that guy wouldn't cause them problems anymore.

And there was an added bonus. Once he was seated again, rather than angling his legs back out into the aisle, he lifted his feet up and over the chair in front of him. He was able to set them on the chair seat and let out a sigh. This was a lot more comfortable!

Sinead eyed him speculatively. "Should just buy two seats back-to-back next time," she suggested. "Save time."

Wylie nodded, but all he really heard was "next time." Did that mean she was thinking of doing this with them again?

Cool.

They were into the bottom of the fourth when Swift turned to the Banshee beside her. "So," she said, "spill." Even behind the dark glasses, Wylie could see Sinead's eyebrow arch. "We don't know a thing about you. Like, whaddya you do for a living?"

Sinead smiled and raised her chin. "What do you think I do?" she asked. She'd been growing steadily more vocal as the game went on, speaking a little more loudly and showing a bit more sass. Which Wylie thought was awesome.

"Hm." The purple-haired Kobold tapped her lower lip, giving that some thought. "Dog groomer!" she declared at last. "That way, you don't have to talk to people!"

"Except the pet owners," Jeannie pointed out, smacking her sister lightly on the arm.

"Race car driver," Knox offered from the end. "Out on the track, just you and the car."

"IT," was Swift's next guess. It was clear from the gleam in her eye that she was enjoying this game. "No talking, only typing."

"Professional mime," Knox countered. "Talking's actually detrimental." He glanced at Wylie. "What do you think, big man?"

Wylie considered. "Book reviewer," he said finally. "You're always reading, and you can just write up your reviews and send them in." He wasn't sure that was a real job, but it sounded good.

Sinead just laughed at them all. "Cold, so cold," she said, shaking her head.

"Well, we'll just see for ourselves," Jeannie announced. Reaching across her sister, she grabbed one of Sinead's hands in her own and began examining it, fingers and palm, knuckles and nails.

"She's really good at this," Swift told the Banshee. "She's like the job whisperer."

"Just observant," Jeannie replied, still performing her inspection. "Huh. Wouldn't have guessed that one."

"What?" her sister demanded. "Talk!"

"Mechanic," came the diagnosis as Jeannie let Sinead's hand go. "Am I right?"

Now it was the Banshee's turn to stare. "How did you know?" she asked. "My hands are clean!"

Jeannie smiled. "Still have hints of engine grease caught in the folds around your knuckles and at the edges of your nails," she explained. "Just like the clay on mine." She held up her own hand for comparison, but Wylie couldn't see a thing besides gold-hued flesh.

"So, you're a gearhead?" Knox asked. "Cool. And hey, race-car driver wasn't that far off!"

"How'd you get into that?" Wylie wanted to know. "If it's okay to ask." He didn't want her to feel like they were all ganging up on her.

But Sinead didn't seem upset. "My dad's a mechanic," she explained. "I grew up around cars, learned how to work on them from him. When I was old enough, I started helping out around the shop." She shrugged. "I like cars. They make sense to me."

Wylie nodded. "That's cool." She definitely wasn't anything like what he'd thought or what the others had suggested. But in a good way.

They all stood for the seventh-inning stretch, and even with the advantage of the extra chair, Wylie was glad to move a little, even if it was just shuffling from foot to foot. Still, he was having a great time.

"You don't realize how loud it is," he said to Sinead once they were seated again. "On TV, you hear the crowd, but it's so muted, just a faint rumble. Here, the sound's all around you." He looked about, seeing people everywhere—people talking, laughing, arguing, eating, drinking, shouting. But unlike on the streets, everyone here was at least partially focused on the same thing—the game in front of them.

Sinead opened her mouth to reply—and burst into song instead. It was the strangest thing. Wylie had almost gotten used to her rasp, and to her deep, throaty laugh, but this was something else entirely. It was high and clear but sharp, less sweet than haunting, and it was also surprisingly loud, especially coming from someone who seemed to exist in a whisper. The others all turned, staring, and behind her sunglasses, Sinead's eyes were wide as well.

Wide—and terrified.

She clapped both hands over her mouth, but still the song emerged, if it could even be called that. There was no melody, no words, just this odd, eerie undulating wave of sound sweeping over them.

Then she leaped up and, hurdling Wylie's legs, charged down the steps and out of sight.

Wylie was on his feet in an instant, pounding after her. "Sinead!" He ducked through the tunnel and skidded to a stop, looking this way and that before catching a flicker of motion to his right. "Wait!" His boots pounded on the concrete of the walkway as he ran after her, his long legs eating up the distance, that song still floating from her lips and echoing all around him. Finally, he was close enough to lay a hand on her shoulder. "Stop!" he pleaded. "Please?"

She did, panting, and the cry faded now that she was no longer producing it. Her head was down, hair shrouding her, and when she tugged off the sunglasses, Wylie saw tears dripping down her face.

"Hey," he said. "It's okay."

Wylie didn't have much experience with human contact. He'd barely spoken to anyone more than a few minutes in all the years since he'd left home and certainly didn't touch anyone beyond the occasional handshake or fist bump. But some instinct overtook him, and he held out his arms—only to have Sinead barrel into them, burying her face against his shirt, her tears soaking the fabric. Carefully, he patted her on the back, and slowly her sobbing ebbed.

"Sorry," she whispered, detaching herself and stepping back a pace before wiping at her eyes and her nose.

"No problem. You okay?" She nodded, digging a tissue from her purse. "So, what was that all about?"

Rather than answer, she turned away, and at first, Wylie thought she was avoiding the question. Then he realized her attention was focused on something farther along the walkway ahead of them. A pair of EMTs were carrying someone out on a stretcher.

Someone under a sheet.

Then he got it. "Oh." What was it Doug had said about Banshees? "Wails at the dead." And someone had just died.

"Yeah." She leaned against the wall behind them. "Awesome, huh?" She blew her nose. "Just who everyone wants to be around—the girl whose song means you're gonna die."

"I didn't die," Wylie told her, tapping his chest. "I'm fine. So're Swift and Jeannie and Knox."

That made her frown. "I guess so," she admitted. "Maybe you hear me because you're supernaturals too? Before, it's only been the... the people who're about to die." She shook her head again. "Sorry I ruined your first game." And she turned to go.

Wylie stepped in front of her. "You didn't ruin anything," he insisted. "First off, this isn't your fault or even a fault. It's just who you are, right? Second, I've been having a great time. Third"—he grinned—"we've still got two whole innings to go. And we're up four to two!"

She studied his face, particularly his eyes, as if trying to read his thoughts. Then, slowly, a tentative smirk touched her lips. "Only if Pineda can hold it together long enough," she replied. "Or if they break down and bring Dobnak in to close."

"Guess we'll just have to go back and see, huh?" he suggested and held his breath until she nodded.

Then they turned and walked back together. Neither of them said anything on the way to the others, but Wylie figured that was okay. There was enough noise filling the stadium around them anyway.

CHAPTER SEVENTEEN

THE RISING SUN THE NEXT MORNING FOUND WYLIE STILL IN BED. HE WAS awake, of course—he always seemed to drift upward out of sleep with the dawn—but saw no reason to get moving just yet. Instead, he lay back, enjoying the ability to stretch out comfortably, hands behind his head, and thought back to the previous day.

It had been a good one. Sinead had been embarrassed, of course, when they'd returned to the others, but his three friends had been quick to assure her that it hadn't been a problem for them. Strange, yes. Eerie, sure. But that was all.

"If you were hoping we'd be scared of you now or something, you're gonna have to try harder than that," Knox had told her, and though it hadn't gotten her to laugh, Sinead had smiled, some of the tension visibly fading from her hunched shoulders and furrowed brow. Then Swift had teased Knox about being scared of fireflies, of all things, and a few minutes later, they were all settled back down and watching the rest of the game.

Afterward, they'd found a local bar—Knox seemed to know places everywhere in the city—and had gotten beers and mozzarella sticks and garlic bread and talked about the game and random topics. Sinead had finally relaxed fully, and when they all traipsed back to the train to head back down toward East Phillips—Knox and Swift and Jeannie all lived somewhere in the vicinity, it seemed—the Banshee had been happily arguing with Swift over pitchers and ganging up with Jeannie to counter Knox's claims about pinch hitters and their use on a team. Wylie had only understood maybe half of what they were all saying— even though he'd watched games on TV, he'd never really known more than just the bare basics—but he'd enjoyed listening to them all.

He stretched — and frowned. Why did his arms and legs ache when all he'd done yesterday was sit on his butt for hours on end? Maybe it was the dreams. He'd been back in the woods yet again, running and hunting. He didn't recall if it had gone beyond that, but he sure felt like he'd been loping through forests throughout the night. And, although it was fading now with the warm sunlight, he thought there'd been a touch of something dark and gloomy clinging to his thoughts when he'd first awakened. If there was anything he didn't love about being here so far, it was these bad dreams.

Dragging himself upright and setting his feet on the ground, he hauled himself up and staggered toward the bathroom. A good hot shower would help, both to wake him up and ease his sore muscles — not to mention chase away the last of whatever that somberness was. Of course, he could only manage to shower from the neck down without getting down on his knees.

That was his first priority for the day.

Once he'd cleaned up and thrown on jeans and a shirt — white, black, and gray checks today — he tromped out into the main room. He was starting to get hungry, but a glance in the fridge confirmed that there wasn't much help to be had there. He'd finished off the last of his leftovers the other day and had yet to go shopping. Another item for today's to-do list.

With a sigh, Wylie grabbed his boots from where he'd kicked them off by the front door, returning to his recliner to put them on. Then, sticking his Twins cap back on his head and scooping up his keys — after checking to make sure the rest of the money from yesterday was in his pocket — he stepped out the door, locking it behind him.

It was a nice day out, clear and cool, and Wylie took a deep breath once he was back on the loading dock. Perfect day for a stroll, really. Nor did he have anywhere else he had to be besides shopping. Knox had said something about having to take care of some things today, Swift had to work, Jeannie'd said she needed to prep materials for tomorrow and then was planning to do some sculpting, and Sinead was apparently spending the day with her dad.

Funny how I've already started mentally including her in my new group of friends, Wylie thought, smiling. But when they'd all discussed their plans on the train and had agreed to meet up for dinner tomorrow night instead, she hadn't seemed to mind. And when the two of them had made it back here, having split off from the others after the train station, she'd actually given him a quick hug.

"Thanks for today," she'd said. "Really."

He was glad she'd darted up the stairs after that, so she wouldn't turn back and see him standing there grinning like an idiot.

Anyway. Wylie glanced around, frowning as he studied the parking lot and what he could see of the streets beyond. He knew where he was, more or less, and thought he could possibly retrace his steps to the train station. But what he needed right now was a hardware store and then a grocery. There had to be stuff like that near here, right? What he'd spied in the neighborhood had been lots of little shops and restaurants and stores mixed in with apartment buildings like this one.

He just didn't know exactly which way to go.

Well, he wasn't in any rush. Time to wander a bit and see if he could figure it out.

His first few tries turned out to be wrong, leading him away from the neighborhood and into one that was decidedly more businesslike, first, and then into one that was clearly more residential. At least he'd happened across a food truck and bought a few sticks of grilled chicken to sate his hunger. But eventually, Wylie found his way to a small hardware store. He had to duck to get through the door, and turn sideways to fit down the narrow aisles between old, wobbly shelves that were crammed full of bins and boxes and packages with all manner of nuts and bolts and screws and tools and other parts.

"Help you find something?" a voice asked.

Wylie contorted himself to peer down at a little, older gentleman who'd appeared practically under his feet. He was nearly bald, with just wisps of white hair clinging to a scalp the color of old polished wood. Small wire-frame glasses perched on his nose, but his eyes were bright and his smile friendly.

"Yeah," Wylie admitted. "I need a shower extension, the kind that lets you raise the head higher."

"I'd imagine so," the little man agreed, chuckling. "You're about two aisles off, though. Follow me." And he threaded his way down the aisle and around the corner, with Wylie trying not to knock into too much as he pursued. Sure enough, two aisles over, the man stopped and indicated one shelf, where Wylie saw exactly what he needed.

"There you are," the man said. "Anything else?" His tone was relaxed, not like he was trying to get rid of Wylie quickly—he'd certainly encountered that enough times to know what it sounded like. This guy was just trying to be helpful. And succeeding.

Wylie considered the question. "Adhesive hooks," he said finally. "Strong enough to hold a hat." He'd actually have preferred to get ones that screwed in but wasn't sure how Mama would feel about him putting holes in her walls. Stick-on ones would work for now.

"Ah, yes—back over here." The little man took off again, forcing Wylie to turn around and go back the other way, then around a different corner. But this time, when they stopped, they were right in front of several different kinds of adhesive hooks and clamps and loops and so on. Wylie found a pack of twenty hooks that looked perfect. He also spotted tools and collected a hammer, wrench, and screwdriver, the kind with multiple heads.

"That should do it for now," he said, hefting his finds. "Thanks."

"Happy to help." This time their route led back toward the front, where the man slipped behind the counter. There must have been a stool there because suddenly he grew six inches, allowing him easier access to the register. "That will be forty," he said, ringing up the items.

Wylie handed over the cash and let the man take his purchases from him and drop them into a plastic bag. "Thanks," he said, accepting it back. "Oh, do you know a decent grocery store?"

"Of course," the man replied. "You want the Durdur. It's on East Lake, about three blocks from here." He pointed. "Just head out and take a right at the corner. You can't miss it."

"Cool. Thanks." Wylie headed out the door, the bag in his hand. One down, one to go.

Locating the place did indeed prove easy—it was a single-story whitewashed building with a big sign over the door saying "Durdur Bakery and Grocery, Inc." Inside, the aisles were actually wide enough for Wylie to walk down easily, and though the pegboard shelves and gray tile floor weren't fancy, it did seem to have a lot of food available. Wylie had never heard of some of the things he found, and there were plenty whose labels didn't appear to be in English, but though small, the fresh produce section was self-explanatory, as were areas like meat and dairy. Grabbing one of the small, bright orange plastic carts, Wylie wheeled his way down aisle after aisle, plucking things from the shelves as he passed. Mainly, he stuck with dry goods like cereal and crackers and chips and cookies, canned items like soup and beans, and easy choices like deli meat, sliced cheese, and bread. He also picked up a six-pack of soda, another of beer, and one of bottled water. That should hold him for a little while, especially if he kept meeting the others at places for dinner.

He was almost to the cashiers when he spotted an aisle of cleaning and laundry supplies. That might come in handy. A quick jaunt through it netted Wylie some laundry detergent, a package of kitchen sponges, a hand towel, paper towels, dish soap, a mop, a bucket, and spray cleaner. Now he was all set.

Once he found his way back to his apartment, Wylie put away the groceries. Nice to have a fridge that wasn't completely bare! Then he shucked his boots and shirt and got to work. The place was clean, of course—even having only met her twice so far, he wouldn't have expected anything else from Mama Rheda. Still, it had probably been sitting vacant for a while. No harm going over it once more. So, he mopped the floors, wiped down the entire kitchen area, and scrubbed the sink, then cleaned the bathroom, including the toilet and the shower.

That done, he retrieved his hardware purchases. The old shower-head came off easily enough. It was just screwed onto the pipe. Taking out the pipe itself was only slightly harder—he had to unscrew the plate over it first, then just screw the pipe out of the wall. The new extension screwed in there instead, with a plate to fit over that, and the shower-head mounted on top of the adjustable arm. Wylie had it done in twenty minutes and nodded in satisfaction when he was through. The arm was long enough that he could actually fit under the showerhead without having to duck, which was perfect. He hadn't even been able to do that in his cabin. The roof there hadn't been tall enough. Here, that wasn't a problem.

Then he broke out the package of hooks. He hadn't thought to get a tape measure or a ruler, much less a level, but found a ball of twine under the kitchen sink. That would work. Attaching one of the adhesive hooks to the wall at eye level right by the door, he walked to the corner and put another at the same height. Then he tied the twine from one to the other, making sure it was taut. Now he had an even line to work with. Starting at the door again, Wylie used the cardboard back from the showerhead packaging to measure out evenly spaced spots along the twine, marking each by scratching an X with his nail. Then he placed a hook in each spot.

When they were all up, he untied the twine, then fetched his caps. They all fit and made a nice, colorful display across the wall. Plus, it'd be easier for him to select one each morning.

By the time he'd finished everything, it was starting to get dark. Wylie was also feeling a bit hungry again. He put together a sandwich from his newly acquired groceries and paired that with a bag of chips and a soda. Then he plunked himself down in his recliner and switched on the TV. He was certainly enjoying hanging out with Knox and the others, and with Leo and the guys at work, but it also felt good to just kick back by himself and watch some of his shows tonight. Wylie smiled as he took a big bite of his sandwich and watched the opening credits of the original *MacGyver*.

For now, this was all he needed.

CHAPTER EIGHTEEN

WYLIE WAS FEELING GOOD WHEN HE STROLLED INTO WORK THE NEXT morning. He'd slept solidly, for one thing—no strange dreams that night, or if so, at least he hadn't remembered them. Then he'd been able, for the first time ever, to take a shower without having to slouch or crouch or hunch or stoop, the water pouring down over his head instead of having to splash it up to his face. Plus, he'd left himself enough time to pick up an iced coffee after parking his truck.

Leo and Mateo were already there when he arrived and greeted him with waves. But Leo didn't stop whatever he was saying to Mateo, not even when Wylie joined them.

" — terrible, from what I heard," the redhead was telling his friend. "Like wild dogs or something."

"What's this?" Wylie asked, sipping his coffee. Ah, that hit the spot!

"Pair of kids camping up near Duluth," Mateo answered. "Got cut up pretty bad Saturday night. Rangers found 'em this morning."

"Not cut up," Leo corrected. "Torn to shreds! Barely enough of 'em left to identify!" He shivered. "I wouldn't like to meet whatever did that!"

Wylie frowned. "Duluth?" He remembered seeing that name on one of the signs on his way down from Embarrass.

"Yeah, not actually in the city or anything," Mateo clarified. "There's a state park up that way, Savannah something or other. That's where it happened, they're saying. Bear, they think." He shook his head. "Poor kids."

"Yeah, poor kids." Hiro and Jay showed up, distracting them from the gruesome conversation, but Wylie couldn't quite shake the news.

Something had torn apart some campers just north of here the other night. Or maybe some*body*, like whoever — or whatever — had killed those campers out by Embarrass? That didn't sound good. Especially the fact that whoever it was, they were near him once again.

And then there was the fact that they'd said it'd been Saturday night.

The same night he'd had those awful dreams again. Like the ones he'd had back at the cabin — right before Roy'd mentioned some campers turning up dead.

But how did that make any sense?

Fortunately, Ted blew the whistle, forcing Wylie to quickly down the rest of his coffee. He set aside both the empty cup and his concerns and focused on hauling goods in from the docks. A big shipment had apparently just come in, and there wasn't even time to pause long enough to chat for the first few hours.

Wylie didn't mind at all.

By the end of the day, he was dog-tired. Every muscle ached, and he groaned as he sat on a crate, resting his hands on his knees. Wow. How was it he hurt as much now as he had the first day he'd done this? Wasn't this kind of thing supposed to get easier with repetition? Then again, he'd probably carried twice as much today as he had Thursday or Friday, so that might have something to do with it. Other than the hour for lunch — tacos today — and a few short breathers, they'd been working nonstop from that first whistle.

The others were leaning or sprawling nearby, so at least Wylie knew it wasn't just him. "You were a beast, man," Danny called, shaking his head at Wylie. "An absolute beast. Don't know how you do it."

"Man's got some skills," Jay agreed, leaning his head back against the warehouse's outer wall. "You keep this up, you're gonna make the rest of us look bad!"

Chuckles arose at that, but everyone was too tired to do much more than that. Wylie lowered his head to his chest and shut his eyes for a moment. He was supposed to be meeting the others at Pizza Lucé for dinner tonight but was strongly considering ditching them to go home and just stand under the shower instead.

A new sound intruded, cutting through the slow conversation. Footsteps. Heavy ones, heavy enough to make the ground shake slightly beneath his own feet and the crate he was resting on. Then, adding to that, came a slow, rhythmic slap. Clapping?

"Not bad, not bad," someone said from nearby. Wylie scowled as he recognized the speaker. It was RT. "Guess you earned today's pay for real. Too bad you'll be handing it all over to me. But them's the breaks, I guess."

Wylie opened his eyes and lifted his head — to find RT standing perhaps ten feet away, a smug smirk firmly anchored on his face. But it was the figure with the local bully that drew Wylie's gaze and caused his mouth to drop open in surprise.

RT was not a small man by any stretch. Well over six feet and heavily muscled. The man behind him was at least a full head taller, with shoulders significantly wider, and his arms and chest were massive, his dark olive skin standing out against his black muscle tee. Still, it was his visage that made Wylie stare.

The man's head was that of a bull, his skin shading to a mottled brown as it rose up his neck and onto his jaw. He had a wide, squared muzzle and small, narrowed eyes. And, to complete the look, massive horns jutted out to either side of his head — from beneath an unfamiliar blue and white baseball cap, no less.

"Oh, this is my buddy Darius," RT explained, jerking his thumb back toward the bull-headed man. "He's Roman."

Darius made a sound like a growl deep in his throat. "I am not from Rome," he corrected, his words heavy and slightly slurred, but his irritation evident nonetheless. "That is in Italy. I am from Crete!"

The guys had all been silent, staring at the enormous figure before them. But Leo clearly couldn't help himself as he piped up, "So, you're a... *cretin?*"

That led to a round of snickering, which only grew worse when Darius howled, "Cretan! The word is Cretan. Creet-ahn!"

"We got it. You're a cretin," Jay agreed, grinning. "But what's with the horned helmet routine, dude? Isn't that the Vikings?"

If it was possible for a bull's face to show sorrow and disappointment, his did. "You do not like my cap?" he asked, reaching up to touch its brim.

"Not a like or dislike," Hiro assured him, his face carefully blank. "Just trying to understand, yo. Vikings ain't from that part of the world, right? So, why the horns?"

"Maybe they were cretins too?" Danny suggested, his lips twitching.

"Right, right," Jay agreed. "Cretins unite!"

"Shut up!" Darius threw back his head and bellowed a deep, low scream of pure rage. Then, dropping his chin back down, he charged the startled Jay, head down so the top was aimed like a battering ram—and those horns glinted as their points drove toward Wylie's friend.

But Wylie got there first. Leaping to his feet, he planted himself between Jay and Darius, shoving his arm straight in front of him, his palm up—and the bull-headed man slammed directly into his hand, head-first.

And stopped cold, feet scraping along the floor, whereas Wylie's arm barely budged and his own boots remained firmly planted.

"Look, pal," Wylie told him, leaning in so he could keep his voice low enough that the others wouldn't hear. "You don't haveta do this, okay? Just walk away, and we'll forget the whole thing."

Darius retreated a pace, shaking his head to free it from Wylie's grip, and stood up straight, studying Wylie. "What are you?" he asked, his voice equally quiet.

"Yeti," Wylie answered. "You?"

The big man slapped his chest proudly. "Minotaur."

"Got it. Nice to meet you." Wylie sighed. "So, what's it gonna be, man? You gonna back off, or do things have to get ugly?"

"And?" Knox demanded, slamming his empty beer down on the table with a resounding thud. "What happened? What'd he do?"

The others all leaned in, impatient to hear as well. Wylie shook his head, doing his best to hide his grin. Finally, when he thought Knox might leap across the table and throttle him for taking so long with his reply, he said, "Oh, things got ugly. He did that weird howl thing again and charged—but straight at *me*, this time. Horns out."

He lifted both hands, more or less level. "So, I grabbed him by the horns, one in each hand. And then I did"—he twisted them suddenly as if he were wrenching a wheel—"this!"

Everyone at the table shuddered. "That can't have been fun for him," Sinead whispered, and the others laughed.

"No, probably not fun at all," Doug agreed drily. He'd been a little unsure of Sinead joining them at first since, of course, he'd missed the game yesterday, but had warmed to her almost immediately. It'd helped that she and Swift were bantering back and forth once more, but what had really cemented the deal was when Sinead had told him, "I hear you work on cars. Me too," and proceeded to good-naturedly grill him on his favorite makes and models before discussing engines and other parts Wylie only barely knew existed.

"Oh, it definitely wasn't," he agreed now. "He kinda squealed in pain. Then I punched him full in the face. That left him stunned for a second—he didn't say anything, didn't even make a sound, really, just sorta stood there blinking. Before toppling over." It had been like a tree being felled—the Minotaur had tipped back and had hit the floor with a thunderous report, landing hard enough that Wylie had actually felt sorry for him.

He'd had a lot less sympathy for RT, who had taken off running the second Darius collapsed. The big guy hadn't even spared a backward glance for his so-called "buddy."

The others laughed. "Nice," Swift said, raising her glass to Wylie so they could clink them together in a toast. "Guess those two'll think twice before they try shaking down anyone there again!"

"Let's hope," Wylie agreed. He laughed and smiled along with his friends as Knox started talking about a stray dog that'd taken a liking to him that morning and spent the entire rest of the day following him about, and leaned back, trying to let the calm, casual, friendly atmosphere of the bar and the company wash over him and take all his troubles away.

But in his mind, he kept going back to Rice Creek, wondering who had done that to those campers—and what they wanted here.

CHAPTER NINETEEN

WYLIE HAD JUST STROLLED INTO THE WAREHOUSE THE NEXT MORNING when Ted stuck his head out from his office. "Hey, Wylie!" he called. "Come see me a sec?"

Confused, Wylie glanced at his friends, but they all shrugged. "No idea, man," Leo told him. "Can't be about yesterday—that Darius dude isn't one of us, so if anybody's in the wrong on that, it's RT for dragging some outsider into all this."

"Probably just paperwork or something," Jay agreed. "No worries, man. You'll be fine." And he slapped Wylie on the shoulder.

Paperwork. Right. Wylie had filled that out last week, but maybe he hadn't put something down correctly? Ted hadn't sounded angry. So he nodded and headed over to the foreman's office.

It wasn't a big space—really just a windowed box set against the warehouse's side wall—and most of it was taken up by the filing cabinets lining the back wall and the desk placed in front of that, the latter's ends covered with folders and papers on one side and a computer screen on the other. Ted was seated behind his desk and gestured to one of the two chairs before it. "Come on in, Wylie," he said. "Take a seat." He still didn't sound angry, so Wylie sat carefully, balancing his weight on the flimsy chair and praying it held.

"You've been doing a great job," the foreman started, smiling at him. "Really appreciate having you on the team, and I know the guys all do, too. Nice to see you making friends, too—Leo and them are all good guys."

Wylie nodded, relaxing a little. "Thanks. Yeah, I really appreciate your hiring me, and I like working here." Which was absolutely true. He'd never thought that a job would be something he'd have, much less enjoy, but despite the physical exhaustion, he looked forward to coming in each day. And to be honest, even the manual effort was enjoyable—it was nice, after so many years being mostly sedentary, to put his muscles to work. Plus, there was something rewarding about doing a job where you could see a visible result, like hauling an entire pallet of boxes from one place to another.

"Glad to hear it," Ted told him. "So, there's just one little hiccup." He swiveled his computer screen around so Wylie could see it too and tapped a spot. Leaning in, Wylie saw that the monitor displayed a work application. His.

"I was inputting your info," the foreman explained, "and the system flagged your Social Security Number. Said it didn't match." He shook his head. "I double-checked it against your form to make sure I entered what you wrote down, which I did. So, I'm guessing you just messed up a digit. It happens. Sucks that you lost your card, too, or I'd just photocopy it directly. I will need the correct number, though. Otherwise, I can get in a heap of trouble for having you on-site and working without proper authorization."

"Oh. Right." In his head, Wylie was cursing up a storm. Of course, he hadn't even known what a social security number was until he'd gone for his hunting and fishing license. After all, he was a Yeti, born in the wild—it wasn't like they'd registered him for a birth certificate! He'd simply made up a number on the spot, and back in Embarrass, the examiner hadn't much cared and hadn't asked to see any proof—she'd written it down, taken his money, issued him the license, and that was that. When he'd realized he'd need a driver's license too, he'd used the same number, claiming he'd lost his social security card but reciting the number off his hunting license, and again it had gone through without a hitch. The advantages of being in a small, sleepy town, he guessed. Now he was in the big city, however, and apparently, they were a bit more thorough about this sort of thing.

"I'm guessing you haven't found your card yet," Ted said, no doubt seeing the concern on his face. "That's fine. Just get it to me when you can, okay? I can probably manage for this week, but I'll need it by Friday to get this filed properly for next week."

Wylie nodded and, seeing that there wasn't anything more to say, rose to his feet. "I'll get it for you," he promised, backing toward the door.

"Great, great." Ted pulled a face. "I hate this stuff too, believe me. But that's how it is these days. Gotta dot the I's and cross the T's. You understand." Then, glancing at the clock on the wall, the foreman stood as well, grabbing his clipboard from where it hung on a hook and his hard hat beside it. "Right, time to get moving." He followed Wylie out and blew the whistle to start the workday, but Wylie only half heard it. He spent the rest of the day lost in a daze, to the point where his friends teased him about sleeping on the job, but deep inside, he was in a panic.

What the hell was he going to do now?

That night, over dinner — they'd gone to a different place this time, a little restaurant called La Mejor Comida that proved to have Mexican food — Wylie told the others about this new problem. As he recounted the scene, Sinead shook her head.

"You don't have an SSN?" she asked in that husky voice of hers. Wylie had been pleased to note the night before that Knox had entered her number into his phone so he could include her in his texts about dinner plans and that Doug had done the same, showing that the Banshee really had become part of their little friend group. Swift and Jeannie, it seemed, had already exchanged numbers with her. Meanwhile, he didn't have a phone, though he was starting to think maybe he should get one, if only for that. "No, of course, you don't," Sinead immediately corrected herself. "Why would you?"

"You guys all do?" he asked, and his friends all nodded.

"Born and raised here in the Twin Cities," Sinead explained for herself. Which made sense, since he knew her dad was still here and owned the mechanics' shop where she worked. She'd mentioned the other day that he was actually a normal, but her mom had been a Banshee — evidently, those traits were passed from mother to daughter. She'd died when Sinead was young, leaving her to learn about her heritage and abilities the hard way when they'd manifested at puberty.

"We're from Cleveland," Swift added, gesturing at her and Jeannie. "Dougie's from here, though. That's how we wound up here — we wanted out of Ohio, needed someplace new, and our favorite cousin" — she leaned over to give him a quick one-armed hug, which he returned, grinning — "invited us up for a visit and a look around. Been here ever since."

Only Knox seemed to understand. "I wasn't born in the States," he replied, "so I didn't have one when I got here, either. But no worries, man. I've got a mate'll set you up proper. Let me make a call." And he started tapping into his phone.

"See, Knox's got this," Swift reassured him. "You'll be fine."

Wylie nodded, relieved. It did seem that Knox knew just about everybody. That was good. With that thought in mind, he relaxed enough to be able to enjoy his food. He'd had enchiladas and burritos before, of course, but the frozen kind didn't hold a candle to these masses of flour tortilla and beans and rice and chicken and cheese that sat before him now. Not even close!

He was still digging in, enjoying the way the jalapenos brought a flare of spice alongside the smooth creaminess of the guacamole and sour cream, when a shadow fell across their table. Glancing up, Wylie was surprised to see a certain blue-tinged Ogress scowling down at them—or, more precisely, at him.

"We need to talk," Brea declared, placing both hands on the table to lean in on him further. "Now."

Wylie frowned, but he wasn't about to let her ruin his meal or his time with his friends. "So, talk," he replied. Their booth was already packed tight, but there were tables beyond it, and he leaned to the side to reach out to the nearest and snag one of the chairs from it. "Pull up a chair."

"Not here," she replied. "Outside." And she turned and stomped away, shoving past tables and diners toward the exit.

"Better see what she wants," Jeannie suggested. "Brea's not known for her patience."

With a sigh, Wylie gulped down a quick swig of his beer and rose to his feet. "Right. Back in a few." And he set off after the Ogress, trying to be more careful than she had about bumping into people and things.

When he stepped outside, Wylie was surprised to find not one but two tall figures waiting for him under the restaurant's brightly striped awning. The first being Brea herself—and the second a tall, dark-skinned man with a squared face and wide horns.

Darius.

The Minotaur had his chin up defiantly, arms folded over his chest, but he didn't meet Wylie's gaze. Brea, on the other hand, glared daggers at him as he joined them. "I told you not to cause trouble," she started at once, hands on her hips. "And now I hear you've been beating up on people? That stops now!" she poked a finger at his chest.

Wylie felt his brows lowering and his lips pulling back to show his fangs as his own temper grew. "Excuse me?" he said, batting her hand away. "*I'm* beating up on people?"

"That's right," she snapped. "Darius told me all about it. He was hanging out by the docks, minding his own business, and you decided to throw your weight around and rough him up! I warned you, and you wouldn't listen—now I'm gonna have to teach you the error of your ways." Her whole body tensed, and her fists clenched.

"Okay, hold on a second," Wylie said, holding up both hands. He was fairly confident he could handle Brea if it came to that, but he'd rather it didn't. "That's not even remotely what happened. Darius was down by the docks, yes. And I did rough him up. But only because he was threatening my friends. He tried to impale one of them!"

"Your friends?" Brea had looked ready to launch herself at him, but now she paused, one eyebrow going up. "Those guys?" And she nodded toward the restaurant, where Knox and the others were presumably still at the booth. "What were they doing down there?"

Wylie shook his head. "Not them. My co-workers."

"Your... co-workers?" Now the ogress's eyes were wide. "You mean mundanes? Normals?" When Wylie nodded, she spun about—to get right up in Darius's face instead. "Explain," she hissed, and one hand shot out to clamp down on the Minotaur's shoulder, hard enough to make him wince.

"I was just doing a friend a favor," the Minotaur whined, grimacing at the pain from her grip. "I didn't mean anything by it, honest! I was just supposed to scare 'em a bit!"

"Scare them?" Wylie remarked drily. "Is that what you call charging Jay with your horns like you were gonna run him through?"

"He insulted my horns!" Darius declared angrily. "And my heritage!"

"No." Brea shook him by the shoulder, and Wylie revised his thoughts on who would win if he had to fight her. "You know better than that. We don't threaten mundanes. Not ever. And we definitely don't let them see what we really are. Got it?" The Minotaur nodded quickly, and she finally released him, to an audible sigh of relief. "Don't ever let me catch you doing anything like this again," she warned, her voice soft but her tone unmistakable. "Go." And Darius took off, fleeing as if for his life. Which maybe he was.

Wylie, on the other hand, waited, arms crossed. And after what seemed an eternity, Brea turned toward him and nodded once.

"Apparently, I had it wrong," she admitted grudgingly. "Sorry." Uttering that word looked like it physically hurt her.

"No worries," Wylie replied, willing to be magnanimous. "If I'd really done what you'd said, I'd have deserved it."

The look she gave him was frankly assessing, and at least she was no longer glowering. Maybe, just maybe, she was starting to change her mind about him. He hoped.

The door creaked behind them, and Wylie glanced over to see Knox stepping outside. "All good?" the little Red Cap asked and smiled when they both nodded. "Great. 'Cause I talked to Eli, and he said we can pop by now if we want. Shouldn't take too long, and the others'll hang here till we get back. We'll wanna go by your place first, though—you'll need some cash."

"You're taking him to see Eli?" Brea asked. "Why?" But she sounded less angry than genuinely curious, which was an improvement.

"My man needs some papers," Knox explained. "Gotta be all legit, right?"

The Ogress nodded. "Yeah, okay." She turned to Wylie and nodded. "Later." Then she spun on her heel and charged off down the street, as people leaped to get out of her way.

"I think she's starting to like you," Knox commented, nudging Wylie in the side. "Maybe Sinead's got a little competition, huh?"

"Shut up," Wylie replied, thwacking his friend on the back of the head—but lightly, just enough to knock his cap forward over his eyes. Still, he was grinning as they set off toward his apartment, less at the first part of that comment than the second.

CHAPTER TWENTY

THEIR ULTIMATE DESTINATION WAS ONLY A FEW BLOCKS FROM MAMA Rheda's, in a row of small shops. "There?" Wylie asked, glancing across the street at one of the few places still open along the block, its large neon sign stating, "24-hour Access" in big, burning bright letters.

"There," Knox agreed. Traffic was light at this hour, and he started immediately across the street, making straight for the cybercafé. Wylie followed—and was thus highly surprised when his friend turned about, tackling him just as he was stepping up onto the opposite curb.

"Back!" the Red Cap hissed, trying to drag Wylie away, but of course it was much like a small child attempting to move a mountain. Still, Wylie could see that Knox was serious about something, so he let himself be angled off to one side and then led quickly under the awning of another store one or two spaces over, a tailor's that had long since shut for the night.

"What the hell?" Wylie asked but was quickly shushed. The two of them were pressed up against the tailor's door, which was recessed in from the front windows and thus at least partially hid them from view. Why they were hiding, though, Wylie really couldn't say.

"Keep quiet," Knox instructed, a hint of pleading to his voice. "Please." Wylie had never heard the confident—one could even say cocky—little Goblin so desperate before, so he merely nodded and kept his mouth shut.

They waited there, tensely, peering out and about, until Wylie saw something move to their right. From the direction of the café. A figure stepped out, then another, then another. There were five in all, and they sauntered away as if they owned the entire neighborhood, crossing the street without bothering to look for cars and trusting any vehicles to brake well shy of their path. All five looked to be some manner of supernatural, Wylie thought, studying their backs—several had points to their ears or skin in strange shades. One was completely covered in short dark fur, while another sported a long, thin tail that forked at the end. All of them wore headbands and sashes in a deep, dark red.

"Okay," Knox said quietly once the quintet had strolled around the corner and out of view. "I think we're good."

"Who the hell are those guys?" Wylie asked. So far, he hadn't seen anyone his friend didn't know and get along with, but that had definitely been a fear reaction taking hold of him.

"The *Tori no kotei*," Knox replied, stepping out of their little alcove and resuming his trek to the café, though more slowly and cautiously than before. "Local street gang, mostly here in Phillips, but they like to roam, so you see them pop up all over the city. The name means 'Emperors of the street,' so not full of themselves at all." He actually shuddered a little. "Though with those guys, maybe they've got a right to be."

"They looked like they were all supernatural," Wylie said, following his friend. He'd already seen one gang like that, the Green Goblins, but they'd just seemed like pests, mostly. Not that size was always what mattered, but these guys had all been a whole lot bigger.

"Oh, they are," Knox agreed. "And every one of them is a bad-ass. But their leader, Takata, he's the worst. He's an Oni, a Japanese Ogre, basically." He shook his head. "Even Brea won't tangle with those guys—she might take out one or two, but there's way too many of them and only one of her."

They'd reached the café's front door, and Knox pushed it open, letting the electronic chime announce their presence. "Eli?" he called, leading the way inside. "You here? It's Knox."

"Yeah, come on back," a voice called, and Wylie jumped because it had sounded from right beside him. Then he realized a small speaker nestled up where the wall met the ceiling.

The café was a decent size, with tables and chairs arranged in front and a serving counter toward the back. All along the outer edges ran a tall built-in table ledge, with computers placed at intervals down its length, each one facing a stool. The glass-fronted counter displayed cookies, cakes, and pies, and behind it stood a soda fountain, a coffee maker, and a small cooler with bottled drinks. The whole place smelled faintly of coffee and chocolate and cinnamon. Only one or two others were in here, a girl at one of the café computers and a guy sitting at a table with his laptop, but Knox ignored them both, nodding to the woman behind the counter as he slipped past it down a narrow hall. Two doors on the right proved to be bathrooms, but it was the door at the far end they went through, entering a wide, dark office lit only by the glow of many screens, all of them arrayed around the single large desk and lighting up the person seated behind it. As opposed to the front room, the smell here was spicier, more like some kind of incense.

"Hey, man." The voice that reached them, the same from the speakers, was high and melodious, but the figure lounging behind the desk had a long, braided beard and a long, drooping mustache the same pale blonde as his long hair and thick eyebrows. His skin was pale as well, but his eyes were so dark they were black and seemed vaguely dreamy as he watched them approach. "Good thing you weren't a few minutes earlier," the relaxed figure informed them.

"We saw," Knox confirmed. "Figured we'd wait our turn."

"Smart, smart." Those dark eyes fell on Wylie. "You must be the friend Knox told me about. Eli." He offered his hand, and though he couldn't have been more than five and a half feet tall, his pale, slender fingers were as long as Wylie's, nearly wrapping around his palm.

"Wylie Kang." Not sure what to do next, Wylie glanced at Knox for help, but it was Eli who answered his silent question.

"You need an SSN, correct?" The strange man waved those long fingers. "Do you have any ID on you? And my fee, of course?"

"Oh. Yeah. Here." Wylie dug out his licenses and handed them over. Then he pulled out the envelope from last week's pay—it'd still had two hundred in it, and he'd added another three to that, which hadn't left a ton in the coffee can, but he'd figured if this worked, it'd be worth it.

Eli accepted the envelope and glanced inside. He quickly flicked through the bills before nodding and setting that aside to consider the cards instead. "Hm." He studied them both, then stroked the nearest screen, bringing it to life from the sliding, melting landscape it had been showing. Wylie wasn't sure how he'd done that since he hadn't used a keyboard or a mouse—a touchscreen, maybe? "Let's have a look." A few taps on the monitor—touchscreen, had to be—and a window appeared, some sort of database. "So, bad news, my friend," he said after a moment, studying the results on his screen. "I can see why the D.O.T. flagged you. That social's already been used—by a dead man." He swiveled the screen around so they could see it as well. "James Robert Stock," he read aloud, "born January third, nineteen-forty-seven. Died April sixth, two thousand sixteen." Those eyes fixed on Wylie again. "How'd you come by this particular number?"

Wylie shrugged. "I just made it up," he admitted. "There were nine boxes, I put down nine digits, and that was that."

"He's from up North," Knox explained. "Tiny little town."

"Ah. So, they probably never bothered to run the number properly," Eli agreed. "But down here? Different story." He frowned, though even that looked languid on him. "I could change the name, erase the death certificate, but if our Mister Stock had any family, widow, kids, that could muck with his death benefits, and that'd draw attention. Let's try something else instead." He stroked the screen again, running those long fingers along the side much the way someone might pet a cat, and the information changed. "No, that won't do, either — this one's still active." Another caress and another set of data appeared, only to be quickly dismissed as well. Yet again — and this time Eli smiled.

"Ah, here we are," he declared, displaying the screen as if it were a grand treasure just being unveiled. "Walter Craig, born August fifteenth, nineteen seventy-two — died August twenty-third, same year. Sad, but good for our purposes since he never used the number, and no one would remember it now."

He tapped, not on a keyboard — Wylie still hadn't seen one of those — but on the screen itself, and some of the details rewrote themselves as he watched, the birth year shifting to nineteen ninety-four, like on his driver's license, and the death details disappearing completely.

"Now we add a name change request, long since approved," Eli stated, his fingers almost seeming to draw on the display itself. "And, Voila! Walter Craig becomes Wylie Kang. You have a place in town?"

"He's at Mama Rheda's," Knox supplied. He'd perched himself on the far corner of the desk, behind one of the screens.

"Perfect. Apartment number?"

"Eight A," Wylie answered.

"Good. I've ordered a replacement card for you and expedited it, super-rush, couriered delivery and all. It's not even a twenty-four-hour turnaround on those. You should get it sometime tomorrow." He held out Wylie's two existing ID cards. "You might wanna adjust the birthdate on here to match, though," he suggested, waggling the driver's license. "Just to be safe."

Knox snatched the cards before Wylie could reclaim them, then tossed him the hunting license. "I'll take care of that," the Red Cap promised, tucking the other card away. He grinned at Wylie's confusion. "My art's more than just sidewalk chalk," he said with a wink. "Trust me, when I'm done, you'll never know it'd been changed. Meanwhile, once you get the new SSN card, you can tell your boss you found it, blame sloppy handwriting for the number being written down wrong, show him the card, and you're all set." He hopped down. "Thanks, Eli. You're a prince."

The man gave him a slow, sleepy smile. "I do my very best. Welcome to the Twin Cities, Wylie."

"Thanks." Wylie nodded. "And thanks for this."

"No worries." Those long fingers drifted upward, splaying out in a dreamy farewell, and Wylie took that as a sign to let himself back out into the hall. Knox was right behind him.

"He's a little spacy, but he's a good guy," the Red Cap explained as they retraced their steps down the hall, across the café floor, and outside.

Wylie waited until they were outside in the crisp night to ask, "So, what is he, exactly?" Because there was no way that man was strictly human!

"Hm? Oh, Eli's a Mara," Knox answered absently, scanning the street for cars. "Norse Goblin, sits on your chest and enters your dreams, feeds off 'em and your health." Wylie must have made a face because the Red Cap laughed. "Eli figured out he could enter computers just as easily, feed off the electricity, make the screens do whatever he wanted. Now he's got this nifty little café, and he hacks on the side."

"Got it." That at least sounded more pleasant than stealing people's health and dreams! But Wylie supposed it was a lot like Knox's cap— some of the old legends still held true, but the rest people figured out how to adapt. He'd done the same, in a way. After all, who'd ever heard of a Yeti with a job, a car, an apartment? Friends?

Speaking of which, Knox had just checked his phone, and now he grinned. "The others got tired of waiting, so they're finishing up dinner," he said. "Swift said you can owe her for yours, and they're getting what's left of yours and mine to go for us." Wylie knew his face had fallen because his friend laughed at him. "So, we're thinking dessert instead," the Red Cap added, patting him on the arm. "Whaddya say? You ready for the best ice cream sundae you've ever had?"

The rumble of Wylie's stomach, audible even over the noise of the street, was reply enough.

CHAPTER TWENTY-ONE

THE NEXT MORNING, WYLIE MADE A POINT OF STOPPING IN BEFORE THE whistle to let Ted know that he was still looking for his card, but he expected he'd find it soon. "Only so many places to look," he said, and the foreman nodded.

"Good thing you're not a packrat like me, then," Ted told him with a laugh. "If I had to hunt for old paperwork, it'd take me a month! And that's assuming my wife didn't throw it away during one of her periodic purges. Everything must go!" He smiled and clapped Wylie on the back as they both headed out of the office, his clipboard in hand. "No worries, Wylie. Thanks for letting me know, though."

"Sure thing." Wylie felt a little bit better about all that, though he knew he wouldn't fully relax until that new card showed up and he could get the rest of the paperwork squared away. As it was, the drive in had been a harrowing experience for him. Funny how just not having your license on you, knowing that if you got pulled over for even the slightest thing, you could wind up in jail, turned a routine commute into a hellride! Hopefully, Knox would get the card back to him tonight.

Or maybe it had just been his dreams that had him so spooked. He'd had them again last night, much like the previous ones—stalking prey through the woods, but the prey was human. And savagely dispatched.

Maybe what he really needed was to lay off all this rich, new food!

His friends were already gathered together, but there wasn't time to do much more than wave and exchange nods and fist bumps before Ted blew his whistle. They had a big shipment to unload today, plenty to keep them all busy, and even Wylie found he was too winded to have time for chit-chat throughout the morning.

Thus, it wasn't until they broke for lunch that he got to talk to the others. Or hear about what had taken place the day before.

"Couple more people turned up dead," Leo explained as they stood in line for a vividly red-orange truck called Nice Rice. "Up at Solana this time, near Mille Lacs Lake." He shook his head. "They're saying it's like a pack of wild dogs or a wild boar or something."

"A wild boar?" Danny snorted. "What're we, in Africa all of a sudden? This is Minnesota! Ain't no boars stupid enough to come up here — they'd be pigsicles in no time!"

"Maybe so, but that's what they're saying," Leo argued, his face flushing at being contradicted. That was one thing Wylie had already learned — the redhead tended to turn, well, red any time he got excited. Or annoyed. Or scared. Or embarrassed. Or just about anything else. "A boar, or dogs — or a bear. Whatever it was, it tore 'em all up real good. Ripped to bits, just like those kids before."

"So, what're they doing about it?" Jay asked without turning around. He was in the lead today and nearly up to the window. Looming over the others, Wylie could already see past them well enough to tell that the truck served only three options: chicken over rice, lamb over rice, or both of them together. At the same time, there seemed to be a variety of other items you could get included, like olives or corn or tomatoes or cheese, and a few different sauces, and he could smell the meat, with that distinctive smokey odor that came from grilling, and just a hint of seasoning. He was starting to salivate at the thought of it.

"What I hear," Leo answered, "they may start taking volunteers, forming up hunting parties, sending them out to try catching whatever kinda crazed critter it is."

"Good luck with that," Mateo offered. "First Savanna, now Solana? We're talking like fifty miles between the two, and, what, clear across the state? Even with a dozen parties, that could take 'em months to cover."

"Better that than anybody else gets hurt," Danny pointed out, and they all nodded.

Wylie felt a prickle of concern over the conversation but did his best to shake it off. Maybe it really was a wild boar, crazy as that sounded. Or a bear, which up here was a lot more likely. He'd run into more than a few of them when he was younger, even had a tussle with one in his teens. They could grow even bigger than him, and though they couldn't match a Yeti's strength, it had still been one hell of a fight. His fur had been all that'd kept him from getting some nasty scars from that bear's claws. In the end, he'd sent it packing, but if there was one loose in the area, it could certainly be causing all this mayhem.

But what if it wasn't a bear or a boar at all? What if it was something else—something like him, only worse?

Or not even merely like him, he admitted, facing for the first time a fear that had been slowly growing in the back of his mind the past few days. What if it *was* him? What if he hadn't been dreaming each time? What if he'd actually been out there, killing people? Like sleepwalking, but a thousand, million times worse?

For a moment, Wylie could barely breathe. The idea that he might have performed such savagery, even unconsciously, caused him to tremble, his vision blackening at the edges, his heart pounding so hard he was afraid it might burst.

Being a wild beast had been bad enough. He never wanted to go back to that. Being a vicious killer—he wasn't sure he could live with himself if that were the case.

His time at the window came, and Wylie had to push those thoughts away and force himself to concentrate on ordering. The sheer normality of that helped, as did the presence of his friends and even the strangers in line with them. *This* was reality, not that. Those were just awful, terrible dreams. They had to be.

Wylie focused on the present, on the sights and sounds and sensations of a nice, safe life. By the time they headed back to the warehouse, a stuffed-full takeaway container in his hands and a Coke tucked into his pocket, he'd managed to push his fears back down. Seated on one of the pallets again, he opened the container and got a face full of aromatic steam, the rice and chicken and other ingredients and sauce—he'd gone with white and green, at Hiro's suggestion—all mixing together to create something that smelled heavenly.

"It tastes as good as it smells," Jay assured him, grinning as Wylie's stomach rumbled audibly.

After his first bite, Wylie was quick to agree.

The rest of the mealtime conversation turned to other topics, like cars and sports, and Wylie had finally relaxed enough to tell the others how he'd gone to his first baseball game the other day. That led to talk about all going together some time, which he enthusiastically seconded.

An idea came to him of bringing his two groups of friends together, but Wylie bit it back before the words could tumble from his lips.

Would that really work? He wasn't completely sure. Both groups had welcomed him, which was something he'd never imagined possible. But would they be as accepting of each other? The artists on the one side and the dockworkers on the other — or, perhaps, more importantly, the supernaturals and the mundanes? Would they distrust each other on sight, as being from wholly different worlds, or would they be able to look past that in favor of finding mutual interests and all having fun at a game?

He wasn't sure. And, much as he loved the idea of being able to enjoy everyone's company at once, he figured he'd better consider it carefully — and probably see how Knox and the others felt about the notion — before suggesting it to the guys.

Besides, worse came to worst, he'd wind up attending sporting events with the two groups separately. He certainly wasn't going to object to more reasons to go to games!

When he pulled up at Mama Rheda's after work that evening, Knox was sitting on the edge of the loading bay, waiting for him. The Red Cap's legs dangled over the side as he spun his trademark cap lazily about on one finger.

"There he is," the Goblin declared, hopping up as Wylie parked and climbed out of the truck. "Man of the hour. And now" — he dipped his fingers into the front pocket of his jean jacket and fished something out, which he thrust forward — "totally legit."

It was Wylie's driver's license. He accepted it and studied the print in the apartment building's outdoor lights. He saw that the birthdate had been changed, but if he hadn't known, he never would have guessed. "Looks great," he told his friend, sticking it back into his wallet. "Thanks." Then, with Knox behind him, he headed inside to check his mailbox in the front hall. As he'd hoped, there was a large, brightly striped envelope from the federal government stuck into his box. Tearing it open, Wylie extracted a small, surprisingly flimsy little blue and white card with "Social Security" emblazoned in an arc across the top. Below that was his altered number and his name. *Strange that something so small and fragile could hold such power over me,* he thought as he gazed at it.

"Like I said," Knox commented, shattering Wylie's momentary reverie, "totally legit." He patted Wylie on the arm. "Now, let's go get some grub. Don't wanna keep Dougie-Dog and the girls waiting."

"Right." Wylie added the new card to his wallet, then followed his friend outside. "Where to tonight?" he asked as they jumped down to the parking lot and walked around to the street.

"Oh, someplace a little different tonight," Knox promised with a grin. "Ever have Mongolian barbeque before?" Wylie shook his head, and the little man laughed, rubbing his hands together. "Oh, you'll love it!"

That turned out to be true. They wound up at a place called Khan's, which was noisy and colorful and full of energy. The others were already there when Knox and Wylie arrived, and Sinead wasted no time showing him how it all worked, the Banshee taking it upon herself to guide him through the process.

"Take your bowl," she instructed, holding up the one she'd been handed after she'd paid. The large, heavy ceramic bowl looked even bigger in her hands. "So, first, you select your proteins," she continued, leading him over to a circular buffet table. Metal containers held chicken or beef or fish or shrimp, some with spices or marinades and some without. There were even a few "fake meat" options. "Take as much as you want, but don't overdo it because we're going to be adding a lot more," she warned, so Wylie restrained himself and only selected some beef and some shrimp for now.

Next, they moved to a similar table, only this one had other ingredients like sesame seeds and peppers and mushrooms. Again, they selected their choices, adding them to the bowl.

The next table held noodles of various lengths, ingredients, and consistencies. Wylie had no idea what the difference was between udon and soba and pad thai, so he copied Sinead and stuck with just one choice, ramen.

After that came the sauces. "You might want to go with one of their premade selections," his guide suggested, though she tossed bits and splashes from several containers onto hers. Still, Wylie figured he should listen to the expert here, so he chose something labeled "traditional blend." It smelled good, anyway!

When all that was done, they joined the line and waited their turn to approach a large circular area surrounded by a tall counter. At its center, two men stood before a massive flat-topped circular metal table of some sort. The heat from it was so intense Wylie winced, but the men seemed completely unaffected by the temperature. As he watched, one of them took a bowl off the counter, emptied its contents onto the table, and began to stir it with what looked like a long set of metal chopsticks. After a few minutes, he lifted the mass up, scooped it back into the bowl, and returned that to the counter, where its owner reclaimed it. Sinead set her bowl in an empty spot on the counter, and Wylie did the same. The freshly grilled food, when it came back to him, smelled amazing—salty and sweet and spicy all at once.

"And now we eat," Sinead told him, grinning as they threaded their way through the crowd toward the table their friends had claimed.

"Sounds good to me," Wylie agreed, following her.

"She didn't even tell you the best part yet," Knox called as they sat. "This place is all-you-can-eat, so after you finish that, you can go back up and do it all over again."

"Yep, and you can do it differently each time," Swift agreed. "Different sauces, different meats, different noodles... whatever you want."

Wylie grinned, all his earlier worries wiped clean away by this thrilling revelation. He was already planning what to try next.

CHAPTER TWENTY-TWO

"WATCH IT, FURBALL!"

Lost in thought, Wylie glanced up, startled and automatically freezing in place. He hadn't noticed the trio of toughs ahead, walking side by side and blocking his path. All three of them crowded around him, getting in his face.

"Sorry," he said reflexively. "Wasn't looking." Nobody else was around, which seemed strange. It wasn't late, but somehow the whole block was empty except for the four of them.

"Yeah?" The one on the left replied, leaning in, his nose almost touched Wylie's. They were almost the same height, though the stranger was nowhere near as broad. His gray and leathery skin made him look even thinner, almost cadaverous, but there was nothing anemic about his angry gaze. "Better start," he warned now, nearly spitting the words. "Otherwise, you might get hurt."

Wylie's initial surprise faded, slowly replaced by anger. "That sounds like a threat," he said quietly, straightening to look down at the gray man, even if only by a few inches. "I'm not fond of threats."

"You fond of your own hide?" The stranger on the other side asked. "Cause if not, we can help you with that. Make a nice fur rug, I'd bet." He cracked his knuckles loudly, showing off big, thick hands. Though not as tall as his friend, he was wider, with jet black skin, a smooth scalp, and ears that flared and were tined like bat wings.

The third figure growled at the remark and slapped the one who'd spoken. "Watch it with those cracks," he warned. He was shorter still, probably not much taller than Knox, but covered head to toe in dark, dense fur. His face had an odd cast, though Wylie couldn't quite place what was off there. *Something about the nose and jaw,* he thought.

It occurred to him that he'd seen someone like this just a day or two ago. Then he remembered where. They had been emerging from Eli's cybercafé. That street gang Knox had been worried about.

Which is when he realized these three were wearing those same dark red headbands and sashes.

"You're"—he tried to remember what Knox had called them—"Street Kings?"

"Emperors!" The bat-eared one snapped, shoving a fist up under Wylie's nose. "*Tori no kotei*, Emperors of the Street!"

"Right, that." Wylie frowned and took a step back. "Sorry. I wasn't trying to be funny."

"Yeah? You trying to get dead?" the first one said, advancing to stay right in Wylie's face. "That what you want? Cause we can oblige, furball!"

"I said knock it off with that crap!" their friend repeated. But Wylie wasn't paying attention to him anymore. He was focused on the gray man instead.

"You're going to want to back off," he said softly, baring his teeth. "Now." The gang member's eyes widened a little, and for a second, he seemed to go even paler under all that pallor. Then he stiffened.

"Don't miss with us, fu—jerkwad," he corrected at the last second, at a hiss from his friend. "We'll put you in the ground."

But Wylie'd had more than enough of this posturing. "Maybe so," he agreed calmly, with just a hint of a bite to his words. "If there's enough of you. But I'd take a bunch of you with me first." He growled low in his throat, a sound that rippled up out of him to echo off the buildings to either side and raised his hands, flexing and extending his fingers so his claws were in full evidence. "And you three? You'd go first."

For a moment, the gray man just stared at him, evidently stunned at the thought that anyone could have the audacity not to bow down or run screaming whenever they appeared. But then the furry one—werewolf, maybe?—grabbed his arm. "Let's go," he warned, and the other two nodded and backed away, eyeing Wylie carefully.

"This ain't over!" the gray man warned, and bat-wing nodded as they hurried off. "Nobody talks back to us and gets away with it!"

"Yeah, except apparently I just did," Wylie muttered. He watched them go, then continued on his way, shaking his head.

"Man," Knox commented when they met up two days later for lunch—it was Saturday, and there had been more of those awful, unsettling, bloody dreams, so Wylie had slept in a bit, then cleaned up and did some laundry. "You really shouldn't oughta have done that."

The others were all busy doing their own things, so it was just the two of them. They were at a tiny little restaurant Knox knew that he claimed served the best empanadas outside of Mexico, and Wylie had to admit that the tiny interior certainly smelled good, the air thick with the rich scent of fried dough and spiced meat.

"What's the big deal?" he asked now. The restaurant only had tiny bar tables and stools, so Knox perched on one of the latter as Wylie leaned against the wall, carefully lest he accidentally shatter the tiles there. "They were punks, that's all. Full of themselves and convinced they're so tough everybody's afraid of them." He shrugged. "I'm not."

"You should be," Knox insisted, scrubbing at his face with both hands. "Yeah, sure, you're a big guy, you can handle yourself and all that, you'd be okay against two or even three of 'em. But there's like two dozen in that gang. And a few of 'em, like Takata himself—well, I wouldn't wanna weigh your chances against him, that's all."

Wylie frowned. "He's really that bad?"

The Red Cap nodded quickly. "Worse," he said. "I hear he tore a guy in half once. Like, clean in half—grabbed one shoulder in each hand and just"—he gestured like he was ripping a sheet of paper in two.

"Huh." Was that even possible? Wylie wasn't sure. But what he did know was that his friend was clearly terrified—and not just for himself, but for Wylie. Which is why he said, "Okay, I'll steer clear of them from now on. Happy?"

"Ecstatic." Just then, the staff brought over a tray, weighed down with two large plates piled high with small, crescent-shaped objects all golden brown. "Or, I'm about to be," Knox added, forcibly changing the subject as he rubbed his hands together in evident glee. "That's what I'm talking about! Dig in!"

Wylie picked up one of the little pastries, sniffed, then popped the whole thing into his mouth. It instantly exploded, juice coating his tongue, rich and tangy and just a little bit hot, all of that balanced by the salty, grainy flavor of the grilled cornmeal shell. "Wow," he managed after he'd chewed and swallowed.

"I know, right?" Knox held up a shaker bottle of something green. "Try a squirt of this on it first. You'll thank me."

They ate in silence for a bit after that, enjoying the food, but at one point during the lull, Wylie heard something about "attacks" from back by the kitchen. It sounded like a TV was on, and he strained to listen.

His friend noticed his concentration and frowned, his face going unusually intent. Then he nodded. "Yeah, more of those," he agreed. "Damn. And at Rice Creek, too. That's practically on our doorstep."

"Rice Creek?" Wylie hadn't heard that name before.

"Eh, it's a park," Knox replied. "Maybe half an hour north. Hiking, fishing, biking, stuff like that." The little Red Cap shrugged. "Not really my scene, but I guess if you're into that, you can get it without having to go too far from home."

"Yeah. Nice." Wylie sighed, his appetite forgotten. "Hey, Knox, you ever worry?" he asked slowly, wrapping his hands over his knees beneath the table. "About hurting people, I mean? We're a lot stronger than most of them, right?" He sighed. "And we're..."

"What?" his friend asked. "Monsters?" He snorted. "Don't make me laugh. I mean, sure, my ancestors, they were terrors—no oil paint for *their* caps! But you know what? Most humans were just as bad, just as nasty. And there's always been a whole lot more a' them." He shrugged. "I'm not saying we couldn't cause trouble, mind. Think about what I was just telling you, with Takata. You're always gonna have a few bad eggs in any group, right? And yeah, we gotta be careful sometimes. But so what? So's anybody bigger and stronger. No big deal."

"I—yeah, I guess." Wylie wanted to tell him about the dreams, but it sounded insane, even to him. *Guess what, Knox? You know those murders? I dreamed about them, and the ones before them — but when they were happening, not afterward. And I'm starting to wonder if they weren't dreams at all. Any of them. If maybe that Hunter was right to come after me.* But that would mean explaining about the Hunter, too. And he was terrified that, if he did, his new friends would suddenly not want to risk being anywhere near him. Then he'd be all alone again, only way worse than before, because now he knew what it was like to *not* be alone all the time. How could he go back to living like that?

"Hey," Knox suddenly cut into his thoughts. "I clean forgot—how'd the ID thing go?"

"Oh, yeah, good," Wylie answered, shaking off the doldrums and releasing his hand to reach up and scoop up his soda, a big gulp of the sugary cola washing everything down and cleansing not only his palate but, at least temporarily, his mood. "Thanks." He'd brought the Social Security card in Thursday morning and handed it to Ted, who'd compared it to what he'd had on his computer.

"Huh," the foreman had muttered, glancing back and forth between the two. "Weird." Then he'd pulled out Wylie's original form to study against them. "Ah, yeah, guess I just read that digit wrong," Ted had said after a second.

"Sorry, that's probably my fault," Wylie had offered, just as Knox had suggested previously. "My handwriting's pretty bad, I know."

"Naw, no worries, man," Ted had assured him. "It's all good." He'd typed the new digit in, hit Enter, and then handed back the card. "All set," he'd promised. And it had turned out to be true.

"He told me when he was handing out our pay yesterday that it'd already gone through," Wylie recounted to his friend now. "So, yeah, all set. Thanks. I owe you one."

"Yeah?" Knox grinned. "Good. Because there's a place not far from here does a killer brownie, all crispy on the outside and gooey on the inside." Gobbling up the last of his empanadas, the Goblin hopped down from the stool. "And you're buying."

"Fair enough," Wylie agreed with a laugh, his friend's cheer washing over him and driving away the last of the fear. Downing his final morsel as well, and tossing back the last of his soda, he followed his friend out the door and into the mid-day sunlight. Good thing there was a brisk wind to offset that heat, or he'd be melting, but for now, walking in the brightness and warmth definitely felt like the right choice.

CHAPTER TWENTY-THREE

MONDAY WAS COLD AND CLEAR, WITH A CRISP BREEZE FROM TRUE NORTH, just the way Wylie liked it. He'd woken up the morning before feeling a little stiff, but not now—he felt good, awake and alert and rested as he got ready for work. Traffic seemed light, and he made it down to the docks in record time. He had his pick of parking spots in the lot, and only two people were ahead of him at the coffee truck. That meant he got his drink and still had time for a walk along the water, letting the cold coming off it ruffle his fur. Ah! That felt nice! As a result, he was in a good mood when he strolled in through the front gates toward the warehouse. He was even whistling.

Up ahead, he spotted Leo, Mateo, and Hiro. They were outside the warehouse, off to the side by the crates where they often gathered for lunch. Wylie waved, and all three of them started gesturing him over. Frantically.

Puzzled, Wylie strode over to join them. "Hey, guys," he said, sipping his iced coffee. "What's up?"

"Dude," Hiro said in a rushed whisper. "You gotta bail. Like, now."

"What?" Wylie frowned at his friend. "What're you talking about? Whistle's in, what, twenty minutes?"

"Yeah, it ain't that, man," Mateo replied, also keeping his voice down. In fact, all three of them crouched a bit as if trying to hide. "There's a lady in there looking for you, and judging from her attitude, I don't think you're gonna wanna be found."

"A lady?" Now they had his full attention. "Who? What'd she look like?" His first thought went to Sinead, but why would she be here looking for him—and why would the guys be so worried if she was?

"Tall," Leo supplied. "Built like an Amazon—if they were as dark as Jay. Long hair."

"Hot," Hiro added.

"Scary," Mateo corrected, glaring at his friend.

"Yeah, okay, sure," Hiro amended. "But still hot. In a scary sorta way."

Wylie had listened to this with growing horror. He only knew one woman who looked like that—and he'd only seen her once, from the back, up in Embarrass.

The Hunter.

But what was she doing here in the Twin Cities? And why was she still looking for him?

Unfortunately, he had to admit that he already knew the answer to both questions. It was exactly what he'd feared when Leo had mentioned those murders up at that state park by Duluth, and then Mateo had talked about the others, even closer. Now there'd been even more, closer still—whatever had killed those hunters out in his neck of the woods had made its way down south, just like him. And was in this area. Just like him. And was almost certainly a supernatural.

Just like him.

Which brought back that deep, unsettling notion—what if it *was* him? But he shook that off. Because that couldn't be it. It was just a weird coincidence. Or a whole string of them. But what was clear was that whoever or whatever was doing this was either here in the Twin Cities or headed this way. That had brought the Hunter down here, too, obviously. And since she'd already been asking questions about him up there, she was doing the same down here.

He had no idea how she'd found him, though. Some sort of weird Hunter Sense?

Whatever the reason, the guys were right. He couldn't stick around.

"Where is she?" he asked quickly, ducking down a bit like the others and glancing around him. He didn't see her, but that didn't mean much. There was a lot of ground here and plenty of places she could be hiding.

"In with Ted," Leo answered. "Asking about you. That's all we heard—soon as we did, we hurried out here to keep watch, stop you before you walked into that. Jay's inside, stationed near the office—he'll text if she steps out." He laid a hand on Wylie's shoulder. "You gotta clear out, man. At least until she's gone. We'll text you when she is."

"Thanks." Wylie nodded, then stopped himself. "I don't have a phone," he admitted with a sigh.

The others stared. "What? Why not?" Mateo asked. "It break or something?"

"Uh, yeah," Wylie agreed quickly, jumping on that excuse. "Haven't had time to replace it yet."

"Right." Leo pulled a scrap of paper and a pen from his pocket, scribbled something down, and then passed that over. "That's my number. Just, I dunno, find a phone and text me in an hour or something, yeah? I'll let you know if the coast is clear."

"Cool." Wylie took the paper and stuck it in his pocket. "Thanks, guys."

"Don't mention it," Hiro told him. "Now get going before she sees you!"

Wylie nodded and, quickly exchanging fist bumps with the three of them, turned and hurried back the way he'd come. He glanced back a few times but didn't see anyone following him, and in a few minutes, he found himself back at his truck.

The question was, what was he going to do now?

His first thought, as he climbed back into the cab and tugged the door shut after him, was to just hit the road and go. Swing by the apartment, grab his things, and then drive away.

But to where? Back to Embarrass? Back to his cabin?

He could. She wouldn't look for him up there, not if the murders were happening down here now.

He actually started the truck, revving the engine a bit, and put it in gear to back out of the space—and then stopped.

Because he'd just realized something.

He didn't want to go.

There was nothing waiting for him at the cabin. More importantly, there wasn't anyone, either.

Sure, Roy and Kyra would welcome him back. But it wasn't like they were friends, not really. They were nice people and friendly toward him, but he didn't really know them outside of selling them fish. No, if he went back, it would be returning to the same old routine—living alone, eating alone, fishing alone, driving into town once or twice a month to sell fish and pick up supplies.

He didn't want to live like that anymore. Looking back on it all, he wasn't sure how he'd been okay with it for all those years. Maybe just because he hadn't known any better — sure, he'd seen people with friends and family and jobs and hobbies on TV, but that had been just like watching someone fly a plane or swim the ocean or shoot a laser gun — so distant from his reality it might as well be imaginary.

Now, though — now he had all those things. He had a job he liked, a place he liked. He had friends. People to hang out with, to go to games with, to eat with, to laugh with...

He wasn't about to give all that up.

Knox, Wylie thought suddenly. *He'll know what to do.*

Settling into the seat, he backed the truck out and headed home. Not to Embarrass, though. Not to the cabin. To Mama Rheda's.

His real home.

Once he'd parked and hopped out, Wylie headed for the area where he'd first met Knox. But of course, the Red Cap wasn't there. His street art had been finished over a week ago now. He'd moved on to somewhere new. And Wylie had no idea where that was. Nor did he know where any of the others worked, not specifically. Could he just look up "auto refinisher" or "mechanic" in the area and try to find them that way?

That reminded him of Leo's number and the fact that what he really needed right now — what would potentially solve that and the question of finding the others — was a phone. He'd never seen the need to have one before — it wasn't like he'd ever had anyone to call! — but he could sure use one now!

Spotting a Best Buy, Wylie made a beeline for it. The store was only moderately busy — it was early on a weekday, after all — and a minute after he'd stepped inside, a woman approached him, sporting a name tag on her blue shirt. "Can I help you find anything?" she asked. She was young, with a round, friendly face and short dark curls. Her name tag read "Diane."

"Hi, yeah," Wylie told her. "I need a phone." If he'd had one of those to start, he'd already have Knox's number.

"Sure thing, right this way," Diane told him, leading him down the main aisle to a section labeled "Cell Phones." "Do you already have a data plan with someone?" When Wylie shook his head, she smiled. "That's okay, don't worry about it. We can get you set up with one. It'll only take a few minutes."

As it turned out, she was absolutely right. Which was how, twenty minutes later, Wylie left the shop with a brand-new cell phone clutched in his hand. He'd opted for one of the larger ones—she'd called it a "phablet," whatever that meant—because with his fingers, he figured he'd never be able to manage something smaller. He'd even let Diane talk him into some fancy case that she promised made it waterproof, shockproof, drop-proof—pretty much everything but bulletproof, and even that she said she'd lay even odds on.

The first thing he did, once he'd paused a block or so away, was text the number Leo'd given him. *It's W,* he tapped in clumsily because he had to keep from scratching the screen with his claw tips. He'd already alarmed Diane when he'd tried using one of the test phones—she'd made a joke about "somebody needing to trim their fingernails," but she'd looked a little pale and had kept a little more distance between them after that. *She still there?* he typed in now.

Coast is clear, came the reply a few seconds later. *Come on back.*

That was good news, and Wylie sagged a bit in relief. That also meant he didn't need to worry about locating Knox this instant. They were all meeting up for dinner anyway, so if the immediate danger was past, he could wait to see the Red Cap then. He hurried back home to retrieve his truck and drive back down—but as he reached the building, he saw a familiar, blue-skinned figure coming out. Great. Another person he really didn't feel like running into now.

"Wylie." Brea nodded at him, which meant he couldn't pretend not to see her. Instead, he returned the nod—and then cursed in his head as she turned and approached him. "Thought you'd be at work already," the Ogress asked, glancing at her phone and raising an eyebrow.

"Yeah, running a little late," he answered, feeling like a kid called out by his parents for skipping school. "Had to go get a phone," he added, holding up his new device for her to see. "My boss needs a number for the form."

She studied him a second before nodding. "Good idea. Hard to get by without one these days." Her tone clearly said, "how *did* you manage without one?" but Wylie chose to ignore that.

"Absolutely," he agreed instead. "But now I gotta book. Don't wanna keep him waiting. See ya!" And he pulled the truck door open.

"Sure thing." She didn't move to go, though, and when he was inside, she actually stepped closer, leaning into the window a bit like a traffic cop handing over a ticket. "Hey, real quick—I heard you had a run-in with the *Tori no kotei* the other day." Surprisingly, she didn't sound or look accusing. More... concerned?

"I guess," he admitted. "I mean, it was nothing. I bumped into one. He and his buddies got in my face about it, that was it."

Brea nodded. "Glad that's all it was," she told him. "Just be careful around them, okay? They're bad news."

Wylie stared at her. She didn't really look belligerent or sound like she was trying to threaten him or anything. "Thanks. I will." He ventured a smile. "Appreciate the warning."

That earned him a slight frown, though it looked more bemused than anything. Like even she wasn't sure why she was being so nice to him. "No problem. Just trying to keep the peace." She retreated a step and patted the top of the truck. "I'll let you get to work."

"Thanks." He pulled out and headed back down. Brea was still standing there watching him go as he left. Strange.

When he got back to the warehouse, Ted waved him over. Wylie approached cautiously—he believed Leo, but what if the hunter had said something to turn the foreman against him? But Ted didn't look angry or afraid. More sympathetic.

"Hey," the tall foreman said once Wylie'd reached him. "Guess you heard, huh? About that detective?"

"Detective?" That was a new one. "I heard somebody was looking for me," he admitted. "Didn't know who."

"Yeah, lady detective," Ted told him, keeping his voice low, so it was just between them. "Said something about needing to find you because your aunt died and left you some money?" He shook his head. "Listen, I didn't tell her anything. She knew you'd applied to work here, must have a source at the DOT or something, but I claimed you'd bailed on me this week. Told her I could give you her number if you came back, but she said it was too urgent for that. That you'd lose out if she couldn't find you. Sounded fishy to me. Figured it was all a scam somehow. You're a good worker, Wylie, and from what I can tell, a good guy, so I'm not about to hand you over to some schemer, whatever her game is. All right?"

"Absolutely," Wylie agreed, trying to fight off the relief that threatened to make his knees go weak and his head feel light. "Thanks. No idea why she picked me, but I'm sorry to cause you trouble."

"No worries, man," Ted assured, clapping him on the back. "Better get hopping, though. The guys're already way ahead of you—but I'm sure you'll catch up." And the foreman wandered away, leaving Wylie to rejoin his friends and get to work, which he did with a will.

He told the others what Ted had said and muttered how it was just a scam to get money out of him. Still, even though they were kind enough not to press him on details, Wylie couldn't help but keep looking around for signs the Hunter might still be watching.

And even if she wasn't right now, he got the impression she wasn't the type to give up so easily.

She'd be back.

Plus, there was that other question, which seemed just plausible enough to worry him. He'd have to deal with that, too. Ultimately, it was all part of the same problem.

If he was going to stay in town, he'd need to figure out what to do about that.

Fortunately, for the first time in his adult life, it wasn't something Wylie would have to work through on his own.

CHAPTER TWENTY-FOUR

THEY'D GONE BACK TO BLUE DOOR, THIS TIME SINEAD SQUEEZING INTO the booth with them. Wylie waited until they'd just got their food before clearing his throat.

"Hey," Wylie started, "there's something I need to tell you guys."

The others had all been engaged in a paper football war, flicking little paper triangles at each other and trying to land them in drinks and fry baskets and the like, but they all ceased that and turned to face him. He read the concern on their faces, and that gave him the courage to continue with, "I... I've got some trouble."

"Is it that Minotaur again?" Swift demanded. "Tell Brea, she'll settle him for good this time."

"It's the *Tori no kotei*, isn't it?" Knox suggested. "Man, I warned you about them!"

Sinead didn't offer any theories. Instead, she just reached out and rested her hand on top of his. "What's going on?" she asked.

"It's..." Wylie scowled at the tabletop. Man, this was hard! "I never told you guys why I came here," he answered finally. "Right?" They all shook their heads. "So, I was in this little town up north, Embarrass," he started. "And this woman showed up there, looking for me."

"An old flame?" Knox asked. "Know the feeling, man. I've got a ton of 'em, both sides of the pond."

"No," Wylie replied, feeling his face flush at the very idea of it. "Nothing like that." There wasn't any way to avoid just coming out and saying it: "She was a Hunter."

"A Hunter?" Doug frowned. "Those really exist?"

But Knox was already nodding. "Yeah, they exist," he insisted. "I nearly had a run-in with one myself a few years back. Didn't seem to believe I'd sidestepped my kin's bloodthirsty ways." He tapped his cap with his index finger. "Had to do a runner to avoid winding up another notch in his belt."

"Why was one looking for you?" Sinead asked. "How'd she even know *to* look for you?"

"There were these murders," Wylie answered and quickly added, "I didn't do them! I only heard about them at all when she came to town! And she didn't know about me specifically, not at first. But she was asking about anyone big, strong, solitary, liked the cold—I kinda stood out." He held up his other hand so the others could see his claws. "These didn't help—the murder victims were all torn to shreds."

And again, staring at his own hand, he had that twinge of doubt, only stronger than ever. What if he had killed all those people? What if the Hunter had been right to finger him for those deaths? He was certainly capable of it, at least physically. And those dreams, they'd all seemed so real!

"What's wrong?" Swift asked. "You look like somebody just kicked your cat."

"I—" Wylie turned his gaze toward his friends. "I've been having these dreams," he said slowly. "Nightmares, really. Me, out in the woods. Running free. Hunting." He gulped but forced himself to continue on. "Hunting people. Tearing them apart." He frowned. "I've had them maybe a half-dozen times—and at least a few of those, I heard about murders a day or two later." He glanced at Knox. "Like the other day, when we were getting empanadas, remember? I'd just had one of those dreams the night before." He remembered something else. "I've woken up achy those mornings, too—like I was running all night. Or hunting. And back in Embarrass, I had bark caught in my claws." He groaned. "What if I really am the killer?"

"You're not." That statement made him start. All of them glanced up in surprise because it hadn't come from anyone at the booth. Instead, it had emerged from the tall, broad, blue-skinned figure beside their table.

"Sorry," Brea muttered, leaning on the table, making the sturdy wood creak in response. "I didn't mean to eavesdrop. I was coming over to talk with you"—she nodded at Wylie—"because I heard there was a Hunter asking questions about you this morning."

"Yeah." He didn't see any reason to deny it at this point. "She got my name back in Embarrass, I think. When there were deaths down here the other day, she must've come looking and figured she'd see if I was here, too." He studied the Ogress. "What makes you think I didn't do it?" If anything, he'd have expected her to assume he was guilty.

Brea glanced over at Knox and the Kobolds, and they all slid over, making room on their side of the booth for her to squeeze in. "These are those deaths up at Rice Creek?" Wylie nodded. "It's been all over the news, rabid bear on the loose or something. But the first ones since you've been here, those were last week, right? When you'd just got to Mama Rheda's?"

Wylie thought back. "Yeah, I think so," he agreed finally. "It was — yeah, it was my first night there."

"And I was standing outside your door when you stepped out the next morning," the Ogress reminded him. She laid one hand flat on the tabletop, splaying her fingers upon the scarred surface, and smiled just a little. "Told you I'd be keeping an eye on you. 'Cause I saw you late the night before, like around one in the morning."

"You did?" Wylie didn't remember that, just crashing after being out with Knox and the others that first time, but it would explain why he'd felt tired and sore the next morning!

"Yeah, I was coming back, and you were just heading out," Brea confirmed. "Only you didn't look fully awake, more like you were sleepwalking or something. You headed over toward the river." She ducked her head for a second. "I followed you — sorry, but I didn't know you, so I wanted to make sure you weren't causing any trouble. Anyway, you got over near the water, then climbed up onto one of the buildings right there by the riverbank, four stories hauling yourself up the outside of it like some damn monkey, and plonked down on the edge of the roof."

"And?" Wylie asked, leaning forward.

"And nothing," she replied. "You just sat there, eyes closed, wind on your face, swinging your legs a little. After a while, you climbed back down and returned home. I kept an eye on your door, and you didn't open it again until you found me standing outside it the next morning." She met his gaze. "So you weren't anywhere near whichever park it was that night. Not last night either, 'cause I saw you up on one of those buildings again, sitting there, same as last time. Not doing anything else, and definitely not hurting anyone." She gave him a firm, decisive nod. "You didn't kill anyone, Wylie Kang."

Wylie sank back against the seat, the tightness in his lungs and behind his eyes suddenly vanishing, his breath coming freely for the first time in days. "Thank you." It was as if the weight of the world had just been lifted from his shoulders. He wasn't a killer! And the aches and pains — they'd been from climbing, not hunting. Not killing. Of course, that didn't explain why he'd been sleepwalking like that, but he could deal with that later because Brea's revelation still only solved half his problem. "Now I've just gotta convince that Hunter of that."

"Good luck," Knox muttered. "Sorry, dude. But those guys are implacable. They're like bulldogs. Once they lock onto a scent — or a notion — they never let it go. You'd have better luck teaching a bird to swim or a horse to fly."

"Well, I've gotta do something," Wylie shot back. "Otherwise, she's gonna keep coming after me!" He balled his hands into fists. He could still change his mind and run back to the cabin, but fear started to give way to anger — he wasn't going to let anyone push him around and tell him how to live his life!

"You need to prove it wasn't you," Sinead pointed out softly. She'd retrieved her hand at some point and now had both of them wrapped around her glass, which she was staring at without really seeing. Then she looked up and met Wylie's yellow eyes with her blue ones and spoke very slowly and clearly, despite the rasp: "You need to catch the real killer."

"What?" That was from Brea, who shook her head. "No way. You're not a cop or anything, and you have no idea who this guy is, other than that he's seriously dangerous. You go after him and actually find him, you could wind up being his next victim!"

But Wylie tapped a claw on the table as he thought. "You're right," he told Sinead. "If I can find the real killer and lead the Hunter to him — or leave him gift-wrapped for her — she'll have to believe it isn't me. Then she'll go away and leave me alone for good." He turned to Brea and grinned. "And yeah, whoever he is, he's definitely dangerous. But so am I, when I want to be." Yeti weren't violent by nature, but that didn't mean he couldn't take care of himself.

The Ogress frowned, but Wylie's other friends all nodded. "It's not like you can go to the cops for help," Jeannie agreed thoughtfully. "They wouldn't believe any of this. And this Hunter's not going to believe you without some hard proof. Catching the killer ought to do it, though."

"Yeah," Swift added, grinning. "Time to go all amateur detective on his ass. Team Wylie for the win!"

That got a laugh out of them all, even a grudging half chuckle from Brea. "Thanks, guys," Wylie told them. "I really appreciate the support."

"Of course, dude," Knox agreed. "We got your back." He held out his fist, and Wylie bumped it gently.

"You're going to get yourself killed," Brea warned, sliding back out and to her feet. She paused before walking away and added, "But good luck." Then she was gone.

"Eh, she'll come around," Doug predicted before flicking a football at Wylie. "So, what's our first step, Sherlock?"

"I need more to go on," Wylie replied, considering it all. He sighed. "I guess that means I need to head up to Rice Park. Maybe there are clues where he killed those campers, something that'll lead me to him."

"Rice Creek," Knox corrected, draining his beer. "But yeah, makes sense. Lucky for you, I know the way." He made a shooing motion at Doug and Sinead. "Go on, move out, you lot. Let's get going afore it gets too much later."

"You want to go now?" Wylie asked his friend. He'd been figuring they could trek up there over the weekend or something.

But Sinead nodded, and hipchecked him to get him moving. "Knox is right," she said. "Any evidence that's still there could disappear if there's rain, snow, heavy wind, too many people tramping about—the sooner we go, the better."

"Plus, it'll be easier to sneak in at night," Swift agreed, already on her feet. "What're we waiting for?"

Wylie stood as well, then turned and regarded the rest of them. "I appreciate the offer. I really do," he said. "But are we really all going up there? All six of us?" He could maybe squeeze everyone into his truck, provided a few of them were willing to ride in the back. Then again, it was cold out, and the only one of them equipped to handle that was him. If any of the rest rode outside, they'd freeze solid by the time they got anywhere. So maybe it would be best if they didn't all go?

Jeannie was clearly thinking things through as well. A frown formed on her gold-hued face. "A big group's going to be a lot harder to sneak past any guards," she said after a second. "And I don't know how much help I'd be checking a campsite."

"Yeah, me neither," Swift admitted, though she looked crushed. Then she brightened a little. "But if the trail leads down here, especially to any tattoo parlors, I'm your gal!"

Sinead was clearly torn. "I'm happy to come along if you want," she told Wylie. "But the woods aren't exactly my strong suit."

"Plus, you stand out a bit on a dark night," Doug pointed out. "Sorry. And I'm with you, anyway. Trees and shit? Not my thing either."

"So, just me and the big man, then," Knox summed up, finally escaping the booth himself. "That's cool. Two's definitely better for stealth ops."

"Right." Wylie smiled at the others. "Maybe we can meet up again once we're back, go over anything we found?" He didn't want them to feel like he didn't appreciate their support or couldn't use their help in general.

"Definitely," Sinead agreed, and the others all nodded. "No matter how late. Just text us — or, I mean, Knox can."

Wylie grinned and reached for his pocket. "Actually, I can too," he replied, hauling out his new phone. "I mean, if that's okay."

He nearly lost a finger with how fast Swift snatched the device from his grasp, and a few minutes later, when he and Knox headed back home to collect his truck, Wylie's phone had five new numbers in it. Somehow, despite the fact that it was strictly digital, that addition created a comforting weight against his hip and a warmth deep in his chest.

Evidently, this was what it was like, having friends.

CHAPTER TWENTY-FIVE

"PARK UP HERE," KNOX WHISPERED.

Wylie frowned at his friend but obediently pulled over. There was a drugstore on the corner, and it was that lot the Red Cap had pointed toward.

"First off," Wylie asked as he slid the truck into a space in the back, "why are you whispering when we're the only ones in here? And second, why're we at a drugstore?"

"Because we're only a few blocks from the campgrounds here," Knox answered, popping the passenger door open and hopping down. "Don't wanna pull right up to a crime scene, ya know? This place is twenty-four hours, we can leave the truck here for a bit, and nobody'll notice."

That did make sense, so Wylie didn't argue any further. He stepped out instead but paused in the act of shutting his own door. "A few blocks?" he asked. "Are we liable to run into anybody, do you think?"

"At this hour? Naw," Knox replied. "Residential around here, they've all toddled off to Lalaland."

"Hm. In that case" — bending down, Wylie undid the laces on his boots and yanked one off, then the other. "Ah!" He tossed the footwear back on the floor under the steering wheel, then shut and locked the door. "Much better." He could move a lot faster without boots — especially over natural terrain — and a lot quieter, too. A part of him considered shucking the shirt and jeans as well, but he decided he'd better not risk it, just in case they did encounter anyone on their way. His being barefoot, they might not notice. Him walking around without pants was a whole other matter.

"Right, this way," his friend said and led him back out of the small parking lot and along the road they had arrived on.

"There aren't any back roads?" Wylie asked, glancing around. True, there weren't any other cars approaching, but he still felt a bit unsafe being so out in the open.

"Not really," Knox replied. "You'll see why in a sec."

"A sec" proved to be more like five minutes, but then it became readily apparent, as the houses fell away along the street's south side, to be replaced by water. It was a lake, a small one, but the road ran right along its edge. And a few minutes later, more water appeared on the other side. Were they crossing the water? Wylie wondered at first. But no, the road appeared to be still on solid ground, and the curving banks he saw on both sides suggested they were actually on a narrow spit of land running between two lakes, one north and one south. Interesting.

They encountered a few cars, but no one honked at them, and no one slowed down. There was more than enough space on the shoulder to walk well clear of any traffic, and Wylie knew that his jeans and dark shirt—fortunately, he'd worn a green-and-blue plaid today!— wouldn't stand out much in the dark, nor would his friend's jeans and jacket.

The lake on their left curved away, leaving solid land on that side once more, but the lake on the right continued forward, flowing past them. On the left, however, Wylie saw a turnoff. Off to the side, on the grass, stood a large sign suspended between two sturdy stone pillars. "Rice Creek Chain of Lakes Park Reserve," it read, and below that was a small digital display, which currently stated "Closed until further notice" in cheery orange letters that stood out in the dark. Ahead, the road divided around a small guard post. Wooden barricades had been set up to block passage on either side, the standard white-and-orange stripes often used to denote road construction, but Wylie didn't see that as much of a hindrance.

He started down the turnoff, and Knox put up a hand to block his path. "Whoa, there, amigo," the little Goblin said. "Where d'ya think you're going?"

"We need to get inside," Wylie reminded him, pointing ahead toward the barricades. "That's the entrance, so once we're past it, we're inside. Seems simple enough."

"Well, yeah, of course, but not that way. I guarantee you they've got somebody in that guard station, watching for people trying exactly that," the Red Cap argued. "We go through there, you might as well put on a top hat and tails and paint yourself glitter pink 'cause you'll be under a spotlight in no time."

"Okay, how do we get in, then?" Wylie asked.

"Follow me." Knox turned and headed farther down the street, along the side of the campgrounds. Wylie soon saw his point. There weren't any fences or gates here. Instead, past the road and a stretch of grass, there was a sidewalk. Beyond that was merely more grass and bushes and trees. Nor were they densely packed. Anyone could walk through pretty much anywhere, and without an army of park rangers, there was no way to police the entire perimeter.

When they'd walked another five minutes, and the turnoff was lost in the dark behind them, Knox nodded. "Should be far enough." Then he crossed the road and strolled into the park, with Wylie right behind him.

"Smart," Wylie admitted to his friend, who grinned and gave a little bow. "Okay, now what?"

The little Goblin shook his head, though. "I got us here and in," he explained. "But this is your show, Sherlock. You tell me."

Wylie paused a minute, leaning against the tree as he thought it through. "We need to find where those deaths took place," he said, scratching his nose. "I guess we just start walking, see if we can find them? They're probably taped off, too, so that'll stand out against the grass."

Knox shrugged, removing his cap and tossing it up in the air before catching it and settling it back on his head. "I don't have any better ideas," he admitted, "so sure, lead on."

Wylie started walking. He had no idea where he was going or even what this place looked like, so he just let his feet carry him. It was a pretty place, the campgrounds. Even in early April, a thick layer of snow covered most of the grounds, which felt wonderful on the bare soles of his feet, and traipsing across the mild hills, he felt at home and at peace. As much as living in the city was exciting, this was where he was truly himself.

Something shone off to one side, and making for that, Wylie found himself standing along the shore of a third little lake. It was a good deal smaller than Heikkila back home, barely more than a pond even though he could tell it widened out as it ran to the west, but it was still an achingly familiar sight, the surface smooth and dark under the night sky, like a pane of black glass reflecting moon and stars. Wylie could feel the cold coming off the water. He closed his eyes and took a deep breath, letting that pleasant chill seep into his lungs and throughout his body.

Beside him, he heard Knox shiver. "Man, that makes me cold just watching you do that," the Red Cap complained. "And you ain't even got shoes on!"

Wylie grinned, flexing his toes and digging his claws into the snow, feeling that cold spreading out underfoot like a shadow. He could sense the cool of the water, sharper and deeper than that of the snow—but there was something else up ahead and a bit to the right, like the lake but different. Smaller but more fierce, almost bitter. What was that?

"Follow me," he told Knox and headed in that direction, trusting his instincts to lead him toward whatever it was. They trekked for a good twenty minutes or more, across more ice and snow, around the lake's upper edge. He was so focused on finding the source of that strange cold that, if not for Knox grabbing his arm, he would have torn right through the police tape without ever knowing it was there.

"All right, yeah, good trick, that," Knox told him quietly, releasing his arm once he saw that Wylie had stopped. "How'd you do it?"

"It's cold," Wylie answered, knowing the words to be true even as he said them. "This spot, it's colder than the rest." He breathed in, tasting the air, and frowned. "But it's not right. Something's unnatural about it. It shouldn't be here." The cold was biting, almost acrid, with a faint metallic tinge. More like lightning, almost.

"So, this is where those murders went down," his friend pointed out, tugging the brim of his cap as they stood before a veritable thicket of the yellow tape, crisscrossed every which way. "And there's an unnatural cold here. Got it. Question is, chicken or egg? Which one came first?"

Wylie took another deep breath and held it a second before letting it whoosh back out. "I think—I think the murders came first," he said slowly. "I can't explain it, but it feels like . . . like the deaths brought the cold, not like the cold attracted those deaths." He wasn't sure how he knew that exactly, but it felt right. The cold wasn't old here. It was new, very new, and its birth had been harsh and violent.

Like it had been born out of a brutal murder.

"Let's go have a peek, yeah?" Knox suggested. The trees were significantly closer together here, forming a solid-looking barricade of branches and leaves, and police tape had been stretched across and around them like the trees had been wrapped or tethered together, but the Red Cap didn't hesitate. He leaped up, grabbing hold of one tree and shimmying up its length before pushing away from it and bounding across to another behind it, then springing down from that with a somersault to land within the boundary. "Come on, Wylie!"

Wylie shook his head. There was no way he could match the agile little Red Cap—if he even tried climbing one of those trees, his weight would snap it like a bit of dry kindling. He couldn't fit under the tape, either—there were bushes all around the trees. So, short of slicing the tape to shreds, how was he going to get past it?

Glancing about, he realized that the small clearing beyond the trees backed up against the lake they'd seen, the land jutting out into it to form a U-shape. *Hm.* Following the outer ring of trees down to the water, he peered around and grinned. *There we go.* The police had strung tape across the wide space where the trees met the lake, but they hadn't bothered to be as thorough, figuring no one would be approaching from that side. Only a pair of strands hung there, and they were nearly four feet off the ground. Wylie was able to duck under them without too much difficulty. His feet sank into the snow and wet earth, coming away soaked and muddy, but he didn't mind.

When he straightened up again, he found himself in a surreal space. There was a nice-sized clearing here, with the water in front and the trees all around the sides and in back, forming a private little alcove like a room without a roof other than the stars themselves. A tent had been set up close to those trees, almost nestled under them, its opening facing the lake.

But in the middle of that space, upon the smooth white snow, were short, thin metal poles poking up, with something like string connecting them by their looped tops. Those strings formed rough shapes, and if Wylie squinted, he could just make them out.

People. Two of them. And all within and around those outlines, the snow was still faintly stained red with blood.

"Wow." Knox stood by the water, oddly enough, with his back to those outlines. "What a mess."

"Yeah, it's a mess, all right." Wylie glanced over at his friend, who was standing there with his arms crossed over his chest. "You okay?"

"Me? Yeah, 'course. Just"—the little Goblin shivered. "It's cold here, don'tcha think?"

It was indeed. The same cold Wylie had tasted before, odd and bitter and electric, unnatural but exhilarating. Enticing.

Dangerous.

"The cold definitely came after the death," he said, certain that he was right. "Like they summoned it or something."

He started to say more, but Knox suddenly shushed him. "That ain't the only thing that's got summoned," the Goblin whispered. "Check it out. Behind the tent." He didn't point this time, nor did he glance in that direction himself. In fact, his lips barely moved.

Concerned about this sudden change in behavior, Wylie did glance in that direction. At first, all he saw were more trees and more snow. Then he realized what he'd thought was the dark beneath a half-fallen log was actually far more cohesive than any mere shadow.

Then it twitched slightly, its surface contracting and twisting about as two bright spots suddenly appeared within it.

Eyes.

Someone had burrowed in at the base of the trees, just behind the tent, where they could see into the clearing.

And Wylie had a fairly good idea who. Not the killer, just someone also waiting for them. Hunting them. Only now, she'd found Wylie instead.

The question was, what the hell were he and his friend going to do about it?

CHAPTER TWENTY-SIX

"WE NEED TO GET OUT OF HERE," HE SAID QUIETLY, TURNING HIS HEAD SO their watcher wouldn't be able to read his lips. He hoped.

"Open to suggestions," Knox replied. "Maybe we just run for it?"

Wylie considered. He was fast, but mainly on open snow or ice. If he had to duck and weave through trees and brush, his bulk put him at a disadvantage. Plus, if it was who he thought it was, she had almost certainly carved herself a way in and out—she could get free and circle around while he was still fighting past branches.

"Won't work," he replied finally. "Not for me, anyway." He frowned, studying his surroundings with a different eye now—one geared toward escape. If the lake were frozen, he'd simply charge across it. But even with the cold up here, the water still flowed freely.

Which gave him an idea.

"How are you at swimming?" He asked his friend.

"Me?" Knox lifted one foot, tapping the side of the heavy boot there, which gave a dull thud. "With these things? I might as well be wearing boat anchors!"

"You could kick 'em off," Wylie suggested, but the Red Cap was already shaking his head.

"Trust me, I don't wear these just for fun, or 'cause they're such a styling fashion choice," Knox retorted. "They're required, just like the cap. I ditch either of these, and the Matriarch gets wind of it, I'm toast."

"You get caught here, you could wind up dead," Wylie pointed out, but his friend was unswayed.

"Better that than what'll happen I lose these boots," he insisted. "Next idea?"

Wylie started to argue further, but a new voice cut him off. One that came from behind the tent.

"Hands up!" it ordered. "You're trespassing at a crime scene, and you're under arrest!" It was a woman speaking, and Wylie recognized the voice at once. It was exactly what he'd expected and feared.

The Hunter.

His hands had already started to drift up, but now he forced them back down. "Arrest by who?" he called back. No sense in trying to pretend they weren't here—she had to be able to see them, at least well enough to make out their shapes. The dark clothes that had been so useful walking along the road made them stand out against the snow.

"State police!" came the answer at once, but Wylie wasn't buying it. The one time he'd caught a glimpse of her before, back at Trapline, she hadn't been in any uniform. And if she'd had a badge, she would have flashed it at Linda in the hopes of getting a bit more cooperation. No, this was just a ploy to catch them off-guard, get them to surrender quietly.

Well, he wasn't falling for it.

"Sorry, we were just taking a little late-night stroll, didn't see any signs!" he replied. "We'll get out of your hair!" He was still thinking furiously. Knox couldn't swim, and he couldn't duck. How the hell were they going to get out of this?

Answer—both do what they did best.

"Go," he whispered to Knox, glancing back the way they'd come. "I'll meet you back at the truck."

The little man hesitated. "You sure? I'm not one to leave a mate in the lurch."

"You're not," Wylie promised. "Just go—wait." He dug in his pocket and pulled out his wallet and his keys. Then, from his other pocket, he extracted his phone. "Take these." Doffing his cap, he dumped them all into it and passed the whole bundle to his friend, making sure his back was to the tent so the Hunter wouldn't see. "Now go!"

Knox nodded once and then suddenly lit out. Despite those heavy boots, he certainly moved fast when he wanted to! In a flash, he was at the side of the clearing.

"Hey, stop right there!" the Hunter shouted, but Knox didn't pause. He leaped up and caught hold of a tree. Then, swinging like a monkey, he quickly wove his way into the brush and through it, disappearing from view.

Wylie didn't hesitate, either. As that dark shape rose up behind the tent, still yelling for him to hold still, he turned—and, with two quick steps, reached the edge of the clearing.

Then, taking a deep breath, he dove into the lake alongside it.

Ah! The water was freezing cold, completely still, and dark as a windowless room. It was like plunging into an enormous ice bath, the sudden shock of it like a punch in the gut and an electric shock all at once.

Wylie loved it. He'd swam in the Heikkila almost every day and was nearly as at home in the water as in the snow. Especially good cold freshwater like this. In fact, he'd forgotten how much he'd missed this until just now—he'd have to find a good place to go swimming down in the Twin Cities, or maybe a nice secluded spot where he could take a dip in the Mississippi itself.

Provided he got out of here first, of course.

He dove down until his outstretched hands scraped the bottom. Then he twisted to the left and began to swim, his feet kicking smoothly behind him. He kept his arms moving as well, not only to propel himself forward faster but to push the water up over him and keep himself down near the floor. He didn't want to risk being seen.

The lake narrowed out to the east, just as he remembered, but it was more than wide enough for him to swim through without difficulty. He followed the curve around until he hit the mouth, the banks rising ahead and on both sides.

Then he quickly pulled himself up and out.

Ahead of him lay the road, with a metal railing running alongside it to separate it from the start of the lake. On its far side, past a low concrete barrier, was more water, which Wylie was almost positive had to be that longer lake he'd seen stretching north. Perfect.

He charged forward, jumping over the railing and the barrier past it, across the road, diving over the second barrier and into the lake it bordered. He hadn't seen any headlights or searchlights—the road had been completely dark—and no one had shouted, so he didn't think anyone had seen. Which was good, since he'd have stood out against the asphalt like a snowball atop a tar pit to anyone looking.

Though even if they had, good luck following him! Any normal person would freeze to death in water like this. For him, it was just a pleasant swim. But he was deep enough that his fur wouldn't show through the water, not at night. And he swam a lot faster than that Hunter or any other mundane could walk or probably even run. If she'd had a car handy, of course, she could cut him off—assuming she'd been able to get to it quickly, had some idea which direction he'd gone, and guessed where he was going. Even if she followed him to the end of the first lake, would she really expect him to leapfrog from it into this one?

In the end, though, it didn't matter what she figured out or where she went. He couldn't base his actions on what he was worried she might do next. He just had to stick to the loose plan he'd come up with for himself and let events unfold however they would from there.

He angled southeast as best he could, cutting clear across the lake to its far side. This time, when he climbed out onto the bank, water sluicing off his sopping fur, he could see the backs of houses through the trees beyond.

Moving carefully, Wylie crept between the two nearest houses and out to the small street past them. He really didn't need to run into anyone now—with his hat gone and his fur plastered to him, he probably looked like a giant, bedraggled white gorilla that'd stolen someone's clothes. Not exactly blending in! But all the more reason to get out of here as fast as possible.

He thought he was slightly above where they'd parked, so he started walking south but also going west when the roads allowed. After perhaps another twenty minutes, the little street he was following ran into a much larger one he recognized. He was back on Main Street. And he thought he could just make out a light ahead and to the right. Turning that way, he only went another few minutes before he could make out the welcome glow of the drugstore sign. Yes!

He spotted his truck, still parked there, and as he approached it, Wylie saw a figure seated in the cab. A figure with a dark cap. Knox!

Not wanting to startle his friend, he circled around the truck to approach from the driver's side. He was still ten feet away when Knox cracked open his door and peeked out. "That you, Wylie?"

"Sure is," he answered. His friend shut the passenger door and leaned across to open the driver's side for him. Wylie climbed in, settling into the seat with a relieved grunt. That had been a lot more exertion than he'd expected! "You good?"

"Me? Sure, no worries," the Red Cap replied. "Bolted out of there, got back to the road, trekked back here, and just been worrying myself sick ever since. You?"

"No problem," Wylie said, grinning as he ran a hand over his head. His fur had dried some from the walk back, but it was still damp in places. "Nice night for a swim, is all."

"You—" Knox shook his head. "Better you than me, mate. Better you than me." He locked his door and tugged on his seatbelt. "Reckon we'd better clear out afore that cop comes looking, yeah?"

"Definitely," Wylie agreed, starting the truck. "But that was no cop. That was the Hunter."

"For serious? Shite. I'd known that, I'd've run a lot faster," his friend said as they pulled out of the space. "Well, she can stay up there all she wants." Wylie felt as much as saw his friend's frown. "Though, did we learn anything tonight? Aside from the fact that Hunters're crafty buggers?"

Wylie nodded, most of his attention on the road and the route home. "I think we did," he answered once they were headed back toward the highway. "Some things, anyway."

Now they just had to figure out what those things were, exactly, and how to use them to find this killer.

CHAPTER TWENTY-SEVEN

IT WAS AFTER MIDNIGHT BY THE TIME THEY MADE IT BACK INTO TOWN, but Wylie had promised, and so, after parking at Mama's, he pulled out his phone and texted the others just two simple words: "We're back."

He'd only just sent the message when his phone pinged with a reply. It was Sinead.

You both okay? she asked. *Find anything?*

Yes, and yes, he answered, frowning as he mistyped even that much and the phone decided to change his message to *Yoda ate yummy*. "How does anyone manage to type on these things?" he grumbled.

"Relax, I got it," Knox assured him. The Red Cap had his own phone out in a jiffy, and sure enough, a second later, Wylie received his text, which was also two words: *Taco Taxi*.

"Do I even wanna know?" he asked as they exited the truck, locking it behind them. Not that it was valuable enough for anyone to bother stealing!

"You'll see," was all his friend replied. "Come on."

They walked all of a dozen blocks before Wylie spotted what had to be the place in question. If the bright yellow of its walls and awnings hadn't given that much away, the words "Taco Taxi" in big red and green letters overhead would have done the trick. "What exactly is this place?" he asked as Knox pulled open the door to the tiny little place, whose interior was as glaringly canary-colored as the exterior. "More food?"

"Oh, not just any food," Knox assured him. "Only the best tacos in all Minneapolis—and they're open late, which is perfect for our needs. Hola, Maria!" That last was to the short, gray-haired lady behind the counter, who smiled back at him and then turned to shout orders in what Wylie took to be Spanish over her shoulder at the men laboring in the narrow kitchen beyond.

By the time the door chimed behind him a moment later, revealing Sinead, the tray on the counter already held several large plates, each one with a handful of small soft-wrap tacos arranged upon them around a little plastic cup of salsa.

"Hey," Sinead said, grinning up at Wylie as she joined them. She was out of breath, probably having run there from her apartment, and suddenly Wylie felt like an idiot. Some of that must have shown on his face because she frowned. "What?"

"I'm an idiot," he told her bluntly. "We just parked back at the apartment building. You were probably there already. We should've waited for you."

"Oh." She brushed her hair back behind her ear—she was wearing it loose at the moment, though he'd noticed that earlier she'd had it pulled into a ponytail again—which made her blush clearly visible. "That's okay. But thanks."

"Next time, I promise," he told her and meant it.

"Next time. Sure." Her smile was directed down toward the floor, but it was still bright enough that Wylie felt its warmth on his cheeks.

Then Doug, Swift, and Jeannie rushed through the door in a gold-toned heap, full of their usual energy and enthusiasm. Knox gestured toward a pair of tables right by the front windows. "Go grab those," he instructed. "I'll handle the food." He already had his cap off and was checking around the rim for cash.

"Right." Wylie pulled out a twenty and handed it to his friend, then followed the others back toward the tables. They were tiny, as were the chairs, and he frowned down at them for a second. There was no way one of those flimsy little things would hold him!

Jeannie saw the direction of his gaze and smiled. "Hang on a sec." As he watched, she marched back toward the counter and spoke to the woman there, gesturing toward Wylie at one point. The woman looked him up and down and nodded, then turned and stepped away, back into the kitchen. When she returned, she was carrying a large gray cylinder in both hands. She passed that to Jeannie, who took it, said something more, and then returned to the tables bearing the object.

Upon closer inspection, it resembled a small plastic trashcan. It was cylindrical, slightly wider at the top than the bottom, and made of heavy gray plastic, complete with handles and a lid. "There," Jeannie declared, plunking that down on the floor by the table. "Try that instead."

Wylie sat himself down on it, gingerly at first, but allowing more and more weight to rest on the makeshift stool as it held up under his bulk. "Nice," he said finally, when he was actually seated completely, and it had not yielded. "Thanks."

Jeannie smiled and did a quick curtsey. "The advantage of dealing with small kids all day," she explained, claiming a chair for herself. "Super-teacher powers."

"Ain't she the brainy one?" Swift announced, tackling her sister in a hug and nearly knocking her off the chair. "So smart!" This then turned into a battle of noogies and tickling and tossing napkins, which Sinead and Doug both happily joined in. Wylie just watched and smiled, relaxing for the first time since he and Knox had headed toward the park.

Speaking of the Red Cap, he stepped up to the two tables just then, balancing not one but two trays. "Order up!" he stated, placing one on each table and snagging a taco off the nearest plate before settling into the last chair. "Dig in!"

They all did, as if they hadn't had dinner just a few hours before. Wylie had to admit that the tacos really were excellent, the meat well-cooked and full of flavor, the diced onion and pepper and tomato and cilantro adding just the right balance, and the soft, warm corn tortillas and spicy salsa finishing it all off. The ones he'd had with the guys for lunch—had that really just been earlier today?—were good too, but Knox was right, these were even better.

"Right," Swift stated once they'd demolished more than half the tacos. "Now spill. What'd you find?"

"A whole heap of trouble," Knox started, but Jeannie elbowed him.

"Let Wylie tell it," she said, shushing him with a smile to soften the blow. The Red Cap didn't seem offended. He nodded and tipped his hat at Wylie.

"Right," Wylie started, clearing his throat. He still wasn't used to having this many people all paying attention to him at once or listening to what he had to say. *These are my friends, though,* he reminded himself. They were concerned and wanted to help. "So, we found the murder site," he said, lowering his voice—the only other people in the place right now were a pair of young men who he guessed to be college students and, of course, the staff, but best to be careful. "Two victims.

Lots of blood." He closed his eyes, calling up the scene from memory. "*Lots* of blood scattered about," he corrected. "Like from big slashes rather than just one deep wound."

"That fits with what the papers said," Doug commented, selecting one of the thin radish slices and walking it across the backs of his fingers like a magician's coin trick. "What else?"

"Cold," Wylie replied. "Really cold. Like, right around the site. Colder than the rest of the park—I think the deaths caused it somehow."

Sinead frowned. "Like a summoning spell? Somebody calling the cold, using the blood to activate it?"

Wylie smiled at her. "I was wondering that too. Yeah, maybe. Or the deaths caused it, anyway." He didn't really know how magic worked. Or even if it *did* work. Was there such a thing? There was so much he didn't know!

"We found something else, too," Knox reminded him. "Or someone."

"Yeah." Wylie sighed, picking at a taco. "The Hunter."

"She was there?" Swift whistled. "Doing what?"

"Waiting," Wylie replied. He thought back to a thousand and one movie and TV plots. "For the killer to return to the scene of the crime, I think." He grimaced. "Instead, she got us."

"Which makes you look even more guilty to her," Sinead said softly. "Sorry. Did she see you, do you think?" It was funny how her rasp hardly seemed there anymore—or maybe it was just that Wylie had gotten so used to it he barely noticed.

"She definitely saw us," he admitted. "I don't know how well, exactly." He glanced over at Knox, who shrugged. "I don't think she saw you well enough to make out more than general height and build," he guessed aloud. "Me, though? Even that much, along with coloring, would probably be enough to identify me."

"Sure, but that's all circumstantial, right?" Doug argued. "It doesn't prove you did anything more than trespass at a crime scene."

"If she was a cop, yeah," Knox countered. "But she's not. She's a Hunter. She's not out to prove anything in court—she's out to find and put down whatever supernatural she thinks did this. And right now"—he nodded at Wylie—"that's the big guy, here."

Wylie nodded. It was his fault, of course, but Knox was absolutely right—in the Hunter's eyes, his showing up there confirmed his guilt. Why else would he be there in the middle of the night, skulking about?

Jeannie tapped her fingers on the table, lost in thought. "It's not enough," she said firmly, glancing around at the rest of them. "What do we know now that we didn't before? That there's cold involved? What does that even mean?" She shook her head. "We need to find out more if we're going to figure this out."

"Like what?" her sister challenged.

"I don't know, exactly," Jeannie shot back. "Who the victims were, that'd be a good start. Maybe there's some kind of connection between them. Anything the police found at the scene, stuff that was bagged as evidence, so it wasn't still there when you guys went just now. Any other details we can get."

Swift thwacked her on the arm. "Oh, sure. We'll just call up the cops and ask for copies of their reports. They're bound to hand them over."

"Maybe not," Knox commented, stroking his chin. "But I think I know a way we can get a look at them anyway." He picked up one of the remaining tacos and shoved the entire thing into his mouth at once. "After we eat, of course," he grunted around the food, making the others yelp as he sprayed them with bits of grilled chicken.

"Pig," Sinead muttered, tossing a napkin at him. But she didn't hesitate to snag another taco herself and grinned at Wylie when she caught him watching her.

Jeannie was right, Wylie decided, taking another one of the bite-sized morsels as well. The more information they could get about all this, the better. But it sounded like Knox had an idea how to do that, and he was right, too. If it wasn't something that would disappear in the next few minutes, they might as well enjoy this brief respite. With brutal murders popping up and a Hunter on his tail, this might be the last chance for some levity before things got all too serious. With that in mind, he selected one of the lime wedges that had come with their tacos and lobbed it — in a perfect arc that ended, with a loud splash, right in Knox's cup.

"Hey!" the Goblin squawked while everyone else laughed. That led to a full-on food fight, and they were all still smiling and chuckling twenty minutes later when, having cleaned up after themselves and returned Wylie's makeshift seat, they stepped outside again. It was nearly two in the morning, and the streets were quiet. Wylie was rarely up this late and was starting to feel the fatigue from his earlier exertions, but he didn't argue when Knox rubbed his hands together and said, "Right, who's up for a little late-night visit?"

He was also touched that the other four immediately agreed. So the six of them headed from the restaurant together, with Knox leading the way as usual. He didn't tell them where they were going exactly, but Wylie figured they'd find that out soon enough.

CHAPTER TWENTY-EIGHT

A FEW BLOCKS LATER, WYLIE NODDED. "ELI?" HE ASKED KNOX, WHO grinned over his shoulder at him.

"Eli," the little Goblin agreed. Sure enough, as they reached the corner, Wylie spotted the lights of the cybercafé on the street up ahead. He wasn't entirely sure how the Mara could help them with confidential police files, but Knox seemed confident, and it was probably worth a shot. What did they have to lose?

The café was only nominally more crowded than it had been the last time they'd visited, with a handful of people milling about either on their own computers or the store's laptops. A young man stood behind the counter this time, and Knox headed straight there. "Yo, what's up, Nico?" he asked, raising a hand to fist-bump the dude, who had dark hair shaved short and tattoos up and down his arms. "Eli got a minute?"

"Let me check," Nico replied, though all he did was glance at a screen behind the counter before nodding. "Yeah, head on back."

"Thanks." Knox led the way to that same back door, and the office beyond looked exactly as Wylie remembered, complete with the thin, pale figure lounging behind the desk surrounded by a dozen monitors. "Hey, Eli."

"How goes it, Knox?" The voice sounded as languid as ever, and those eyes were still just as dark and distant. "Wylie, I hope there were no problems with your ID?"

"None," he replied as they all approached the desk. "Worked perfectly. Thanks again."

Those long fingers waved through the air. "Of course. Then I take it this is not a request for a refund?" That dreamy gaze wandered across the others. "A group deal, perhaps?"

"We're after some info," Knox replied. "Was hoping you could help us out." He smiled. "For the right price, of course."

"Hm." Eli's attention had already wandered back to his many screens, and Wylie saw that one of them ran some sort of video, perhaps a movie or show. Another showed the café's outer room. There was one that he thought might be a chat room, from examples of those he'd seen on TV. The rest he wasn't sure about. "And what sort of information do you require?"

"Police reports," Swift told him. "On those deaths up at Rice Park."

That drew the Mara's gaze from his monitors. "Oh? And why would you be wanting those?"

Wylie stepped forward. "Because there's a Hunter out there who thinks I did it," he stated bluntly. "And to get rid of her, I need to prove her wrong. Besides which," he leaned in, planting both hands on the desk, "some supernatural is running around killing people, and I think they need to be stopped."

Eli's dark eyes flicked down to where Wylie's claws dug into the desk's sturdy surface, then up to his yellow gaze. "Yes. Good point. That sort of thing gives us all a bad name," the Mara agreed, a bit more haste to his words than before. "And besides, it is not often I get a challenge like cracking police security." He smiled. "Very well, let us see what we can find, hm?" And he caressed the side of the nearest screen, causing the image to waver and transform as a new window popped up, this one a web browser.

"Whoa," Doug muttered as they watched Eli manipulate the data with his touch. The browser shifted, connecting to the Minneapolis police website.

"Ah," the Mara said as the screen seemed to flicker slightly. "Fortunately for us, it appears they have it set up to allow their detectives to access files from home." He wiggled his fingers in anticipation before returning them to the monitors. "How forward-thinking of them."

"Seriously?" Doug asked. "That seems like a potentially awful idea, putting all their files up where anyone could hack into them."

Eli put a hand to his chest. "Hardly anyone!" he argued, with every appearance of being deeply offended. "They did everything right, the Minneapolis PD. Heavy-duty firewalls, secure sign-on, two-factor authentication, apps locked down to only approved devices. Nearly impossible to crack." He smiled. "Fortunately, they had no way to account for the likes of me."

As they watched, the site's front page melted away, the screen turning darker, with lines of strange text scrolling past. "He's in their system!" Doug exclaimed, eyes still glued to the screen.

"Damn," Swift agreed. "That's one hell of a talent you've got there, son."

A smile spun across the Mara's lips, but he never lifted his gaze as the screen image jumped, new lines and windows appearing and disappearing at lightning speed. "I am indeed in their system," he agreed, flicking windows aside as one might flip through pages in a book or cards in a catalog. "We are seeing their case files now." All Wylie could see was a list of folder names, with dates and sizes beside them. "When were these murders?"

"Friday," Wylie replied. "They were last Friday."

"Hm, yes, all right—ah, only three cases from then," Eli reported. A folder opened onscreen, displaying its contents, and he clicked on one of the files to open it. This, at least, was something Wylie could understand—it showed a computerized form with a whole series of boxes that had been filled out.

He was still reading the first few lines when Sinead sighed. "Not it," she declared in her husky voice. "This one's a car accident."

Eli nodded and tapped the file again, making it disappear with a faint click. He moved on to the next, but after only a few seconds, Sinead shook her head. "Bar fight." Wylie glanced at her, as did the others, and she shrugged. "What? I read fast."

"That only leaves one," the Mara pointed out, opening the third file. The first thing Wylie noticed was that it listed not one victim but two. Then he saw "Cause of Death: animal attack."

"That's it," he said, leaning in to see better. The others all crowded close as well, and for a moment, the room remained silent as they all read through the details.

"I guess this is why there weren't any cops on the scene," Knox said finally. "Animal attack. They don't think it's murder, just a bear or something—more a problem for the Forestry Service than for them."

"Good for the Hunter, bad for us," Jeannie pointed out. "If they'd thought it was murder, they'd have checked for evidence and all that. If it's a bear, though, why bother? Not like you'd worry about finger-prints."

Wylie sighed and stepped back. Was this a dead-end, then?

Sinead continued reading, however, and now she pointed at the screen. "Can you open that one?" she asked, and Eli obliged, causing a second file and a handful of photos to suddenly display.

Knox turned away at once, his face going white. Wylie felt his own gorge rising but forced it back down as he studied the images.

They were photos of the two victims.

It was a man and a woman. Young, he thought, though it was hard to tell since both their faces had been slashed to bits. So had the rest of them, and their chests — those were shattered ruins, little more than torn, bloody messes.

"Listen to this," Sinead said, looking not at the photos but at the report. "Cause of death was exsanguination by massive trauma, multiple blows from what look to be animal claws. Several organs at least partially consumed, bite marks suggest a large cat or wild dog, though possibly a bear."

"Consumed?" Knox sounded as if he were choking, and he still faced away from the monitors. "He *ate* them?"

"Part of them, yes." Sinead didn't sound ill or even disgusted — in fact, as she turned to Wylie, she sounded excited, her eyes bright as she grabbed his arm. "You said something about cold, right?" she asked, her voice rapid. "Around the site?"

"Yeah. The cold was a lot stronger there than anywhere else," he said, remembering how it felt. "Not natural, either. Bitter, biting. Like it came from the deaths."

"Or maybe like the killer made it cold after he killed them?" she asked.

"Could be," he agreed.

"Then," Sinead said, turning to face them all, "I think I know what did this." She took a deep breath as everyone studied her but didn't back down or look away or hide her face. Instead, she lifted her chin as she told them firmly, "I think we're dealing with a Wendigo."

"A wendy-what?" Doug asked, only to have Swift elbow him in the ribs. "Come on, not like you know what that is either," he complained.

Wylie watched Sinead closely. She looked more energized than he'd ever seen her, but he realized it wasn't anything like getting off on the sight of blood or the thought of grisly murder. It was the thrill of solving a puzzle. "Okay," he said, smiling at her, "what's a Wendigo?"

"It's a Native American supernatural," she told him. "It feeds on human flesh. Not just that, it's made up of equal parts hunger and cold — and that's all it is, a creature of infinite rapaciousness and constant chill." She frowned. "They say it grows in proportion to its meal, so it's always hungry, never full, no matter how much it consumes. And all it eats is people. It was human once itself until it was starved and ate human flesh for the first time. Now it can't get enough."

Knox whistled. He'd turned back enough to look at Sinead without facing the screens. "What're you, some kinda Wendigo groupie?" he asked. "Or just a bookworm in general?"

That made the Banshee laugh, and she still didn't back down as she replied, "Yeah, guilty as charged on the latter." She shrugged. "I read a lot. And I read a lot of weird things. So what?"

"Good for us," Wylie told her. "Otherwise, we'd have no idea what this thing was." He frowned, glancing back at the screens, which still showed those reports. "Okay, so we're looking at a Wendigo. And it's not just killing people. It's eating them, too." He scrubbed at his face with one hand. "Great."

"Well, knowing is half the battle, right?" Jeannie pointed out. "Now we know." She smiled at Sinead before looking at Wylie. "Question is, what do we do with that knowledge now we've got it?"

"What do they look like?" was Swift's question. "Can we, I dunno, put out an APB on him or something? 'Look for the guy with the big claws and fangs that likes to eat people?'" She glanced over at Wylie and flushed, turning her skin more bronze than gold for a moment. "Sorry, dude."

Sinead paced back and forth in front of Eli's desk — Wylie noticed the Mara was as absorbed in this conversation as the rest of them. "They're supposed to be gaunt," she said, her long pale hair streaming behind her as she moved. "Like pale, living skeletons, almost. But furred, too. Like great white apes that've been starved."

"That shouldn't be too hard to spot, then," Knox commented, but Sinead was already shaking her head.

"They wouldn't be — if they were always that way," she corrected. "But I don't think they are. They were human until they let their hunger take them over. That's how the stories go. What if that's the *only* time they're like that, when they give in to the hunger?"

Wylie got her meaning at once. "You're saying this guy, he may only look like that — only be like that — when he's on the hunt," he said slowly. "And the rest of the time, he's just some ordinary guy?" He sighed. "Great. So, we've got no way of finding him except when he's in full Wendigo mode—and that means he's out to kill and feed."

Jeannie suddenly straightened. "You were worried earlier," she recalled, talking to Wylie. "You thought you could be doing this without knowing it because you kept having these weird dreams, waking up tired, all that." He nodded. "And the last time that happened was Friday, right? When was the time before that?"

He thought back. "Tuesday," he answered finally. "And Saturday before that." Because Sunday was when he'd woken up all stiff and sore. And all he'd done the day before was go to the ball game with the others, which had been amazing but hardly strenuous.

But the Kobold had already switched her attention to their current host. "There were other murders in the area," she told Eli. "Other animal attacks. Can you see if any of those were last Tuesday night?"

The Mara nodded, gently dabbing at the screen with his fingertips. Folders closed and opened and shuffled until he'd settled on one and began flipping open the files it contained. This one held more, so it took him six tries before he found the right one. "Yes," he stated, the screen displaying a similar-looking set of reports and photos. "Tuesday night, in Solana State Forest. Two more. Almost identical." Unasked, he tapped a bit more, and an additional screen appeared. "And the previous Saturday. Savanna Portage State Park."

"That's the connection," Jeannie announced. She looked over at Wylie. "Every time the killer turns Wendigo, you feel it. You feel his cold."

Wylie considered that. Yes, it made sense. He'd always been sensitive to the cold, after all—not in the "overly affected by it" sort of way but in the "aware of it" type. He could sense not only how cold it was but where the cold came from, and even pick up subtle differences in the sensation depending upon its point of origin. He could also predict snow and ice with more accuracy than any weatherman. Not just when they would hit but from where and how much they'd accumulate. "So, I've got a cold-sense," he said now, "and this guy, he sets it off because he's generating a whole lot of cold all by himself. So much so that it makes me sleep-walk toward it—only I can't get across the river, so I just park myself somewhere facing it for a while."

Swift laughed. "You're like a cold compass!" she declared, slapping him on the back. "So, all we gotta do is wait for him to Wendigo out, and then you can lead us straight to him!"

"Yeah, maybe," Wylie agreed. "If he stays that way long enough for me to find him." It'd be like someone switching on a beacon, he realized — and if he stayed awake, he might be able to consciously follow the light to its source, but only if it stayed on the whole time. Once it shut off, he'd be in the dark again.

Sinead stepped over to Eli. "Could you look and see if there are more files like these?" she asked him. "Not here, but up north? You said there was one up near where you were before, right?" she asked Wylie.

"Yeah, out by Embarrass," he replied. "A little over two weeks ago, now." He remembered the conversation with Brea. "And there must've been one that Wednesday night, too."

"I shall look," Eli promised. He gave them all a smile. "This project intrigues me, so I will not even ask for payment."

"Thanks, man," Knox told him. "You're a gem." The Red Cap yawned. "I'm guessing that'll take a while, though, and I don't know about the rest of you, but I'm beat — Wylie and me were running all over hither and yon tonight. So maybe pick this up again on the morrow?"

Wylie nodded, feeling the fatigue himself. And he had to work tomorrow! "Yeah, sounds good. Thanks, Eli." The Mara waved as the rest of them traipsed out of the office and then out of the café altogether. "Catch you guys tomorrow," Wylie told the others. "And thanks."

"Later, dude," Swift said, giving him a quick hug and a thump on the arm. Jeannie did the same minus the thump, and Doug and Knox both fist-bumped him before the quartet wandered off, leaving Wylie and Sinead standing there together.

"Shall we?" he asked, dipping into a bow and then holding out his elbow.

"We shall," she agreed with a throaty laugh. She threaded her arm through his, and together they started back toward home.

Despite everything, despite the grisly murders and almost getting caught by the Hunter, Wylie knew a broad smile currently graced his face as the two of them walked, chatting along the way.

In the end, it had been a very good night.

CHAPTER TWENTY-NINE

WYLIE WAS STILL TIRED WHEN HE DRAGGED HIMSELF INTO WORK THE NEXT morning—and concerned, since he'd had more of those dreams, which meant the Wendigo had struck again. At least he knew it wasn't him doing it, though! Still, the fatigue was probably why he didn't fully register his friends gesturing at him to turn around as he approached the loading bay. Instead, he walked into the warehouse, only partially awake—and stopped in his tracks at the sight before him.

It was RT. The musclebound bully was talking to a tall, Junoesque woman with dark skin and a long, thick braid. And, as Wylie stared, RT glanced up, grinning widely—and pointed right at him.

Even in his befuddled state, there was little question as to who the woman was. He had seen her only the night before, after all, though under much dimmer circumstances.

It was the Hunter. She'd come back for him.

He studied her as she left the smirking RT behind and approached him. Tall, broad-shouldered, strong features. Dressed in a heavy waffle-knit shirt and a sturdy, hip-length leather jacket over dark jeans and solid boots—sensible, comfortable, durable. No weapons in evidence, but he had no doubt she was armed, probably heavily so.

She was inspecting him in turn, and he saw her eyes flick to his hands, then back to his face. So. She was worried about what he might do to her if she got too close. Fair enough. He could work with that.

"That's far enough," Wylie declared when she was still ten feet away. "You really don't want to get any closer."

She stopped, and her left hand slid under her coat, disappearing behind her. She must be carrying her gun in the small of her back. "This doesn't have to get messy," she replied. Her voice was tight but level, controlled. She was nervous, on high alert, but hardly panicked.

"I agree," he replied. "Why don't we take this somewhere a little more private?" And, taking a risk and turning his back to her, he walked out of the warehouse and toward the docks proper.

"Stop!" she called from behind. "Or I'll—"

"No, you won't," he replied, not slowing at all. "If you didn't care what people saw or thought, you'd have shot me already." She didn't say anything, but a second later, he heard the sound of footsteps behind him.

The paved stretch between buildings and water was wide here, and there were large pallets spaced apart just shy of the edge, each piled high with boxes, bales, canisters, and containers. Wylie headed for the next nearest of those, angling away from the warehouse so no one back there would be able to see where he went. Once he was well back along the stack of wrapped shapes, he slowed to a stop, twisting about to face the way he'd come.

When she stepped into view a moment later, she did so with her back straight and her head high. If she was afraid at all, she covered it well, though she did draw her gun as she moved behind the concealment of the pile. Wylie wasn't a gun person, had never owned or even fired one—what did he need something like that for?—but he could tell that hers was quite large. It probably put impressive holes in people.

Clearly, she was counting on it being able to do the same to him.

"Okay," he said slowly, holding both hands up so she could see he wasn't trying anything funny. "So. I'm Wylie, Wylie Kang. But you knew that already. And you are?"

"Hailey," she answered after only a few seconds of staring at him like he was nuts. "Hailey Robards." She had her gun up now, clasped firmly before her with both hands, that cavernous hole at the barrel's end aimed straight between his eyes. "Give yourself up now, and I promise to bring you in alive."

He couldn't help it—he laughed. Which made her eyes widen and her trigger finger twitch, he noticed. *Okay, maybe tone down the amusement a tad, Wylie,* he chided himself. Even so, he was sure it laced his words as he replied, "Bring me in alive? To who? It's not like there's a Wanted poster up or anything. What're you going to do? Drag me to Fish & Game and say, 'here's your bear'? I don't think so." He spread his hands before lowering them — slowly — to his sides. "Besides which, I didn't do it."

"Uh-huh. So why were you out there last night, then?" she demanded. Still, she hadn't actually shot him yet, so — progress?

"I was—" he sighed, knowing how this would probably sound. "Look, I was in Embarrass, right? You know that already. That's where you found me. Only, I live there. Lived there. Just minding my own business, not causing any trouble, keeping to myself. But you showed up and started asking around. I figured you weren't gonna believe any of that, no matter what. Right?" He leaned against the pallet, propping an elbow on it. "You know what I am?"

She frowned but otherwise didn't move. No, wait — had she relaxed her stance just a little? "Big, white fur, claws, likes cold — I'm thinking Yeti," she replied.

"Got it in one." He was impressed despite himself. Hell, even Knox and the others hadn't figured that out. "You ever met one of us before?" When she shook her head, he continued. "Yeah, there's a reason for that. We keep to ourselves, mostly. Don't look for trouble. Don't cause any, neither. We're not violent — we only fight to defend ourselves, and only when there's no other way out."

Yes, she'd definitely come up out of her half-crouch a bit now. "Y'all don't normally live in town and wear jeans and boots, neither," she pointed out in what he took to be a deliberate drawl. "That makes you an anomaly, in my book. And if you're already different from the rest of your kin in one way, why not another?"

"So just because I like toilet paper and sleeping in a bed, I gotta be a serial killer, too?" he demanded. "That makes no sense."

"Maybe not," she admitted. "But the facts are, all the deaths up until Embarrass, all nineteen of them, were up north of you, spread all around up there. Then, after I flushed you out, a whole string of them, each heading further south, ending with Rice Park and now last night's in Elm Creek, actually within the Twin Cities. And you right here." Her gun had lowered, aiming at the ground near his feet, but it rose again. "How else'm I supposed to read that?"

"I don't know," he admitted, keeping himself where he was by sheer force of will when every instinct in him said to cut and run, to climb the pallet and disappear over the side or just flat-out bolt past her and around the corner. "But I'm telling you, it wasn't me. I've never hurt anybody. And I didn't know a thing about those deaths until you showed up." Nor had he known where last night's was until she'd mentioned it just now. Not that she'd believe him.

"Yet there you were last night, poking around the murder scene," she reminded him. "You and some kid. I thought at first he was your next victim but considering how he bolted, I'm guessing no. Accomplice, then?"

"Just a friend," Wylie answered, not entirely sure why he was even telling her that much. Maybe he was just hoping his honesty would impress her somehow. "And we were there for the same reason you were — trying to figure out what really happened and who did it. Well," he corrected himself, "the same reason you should've been. Since it seems you've already made up your mind who's responsible."

"I haven't seen anything to make me think otherwise," she replied. "Including our little tete-a-tete here. Though I'll admit," and again the barrel lowered some, "this is the first time my prey's ever stopped to chat me up." He thought he saw just a hint of a smirk tug at her lips for a second, but if so, it vanished before he could be certain.

Wylie could see she still wasn't swayed, but he wasn't ready to give up just yet. "Look, I get it," he told her instead. "You see me, you know what I am, I'm capable of doing that, the area fits, I've got no alibi, you figure case closed. Hell, I even worried for a while that I *was* killing in my sleep or something. But I'm telling you, I'm innocent. And I knew the only way to convince you was to catch whoever'd really done it — that's why I was up there." He decided it was time to play his ace in the hole. "And I know what it was, too."

"Oh?" This time her second hand came off the gun completely, and she lowered it to her side, standing straight once more, though he wasn't fooled — he knew she could bring that weapon back up and fire before he could push off from these crates. Still, at least she was curious. "And what's that?"

"A Wendigo." He watched her closely as he told her. There — the way her eyes narrowed, losing their hawklike focus on him for an instant as she considered before nodding once. She knew exactly what they were!

"Plausible," she conceded slowly, clearly against her will. "Fits the profile."

"Better than a Yeti does," he challenged.

She nodded reluctantly.

"True." Her eyes speared him once more. "But I don't see a Wendigo anywhere around here. All I see is you."

"He's here," Wylie promised. "I don't know where yet. But I can sense him, his violence, his cold. I'll find him. I'm working on it. I just need some time."

This time she was the one who laughed, though it was a bitter little bark without any real humor to it. "So, what, I'm just supposed to let you go? Under the assumption that you're actually working to clear your name? This isn't some TV thriller. It's real life, and I can't risk anybody else dying because I gave you the benefit of the doubt." She raised her gun again.

"Just give me a few days," he pleaded. "Look, I'm not going anywhere! You know where I work now. You can find me if you need to." For half a second, he considered giving her his phone number, but even he wasn't that naïve. "I'm innocent, and if you really care about justice, instead of just putting another notch in your belt, you'll let me prove it."

They studied one another across the barrel of her gun, neither of them moving—until she nodded and, in one smooth motion, not only lowered it again but tucked it back away behind her, her hands emerging empty a second later. Damn, she was good at that! "You've got forty-eight hours," she told him. "Prove your innocence or settle your affairs, whichever. But when your time's up, I'm coming for you. And I'll be watching you, meantime."

She pivoted and marched away, disappearing around the corner with a handful of quick, strong strides. Wylie stayed where he was another second or two before finally slumping.

Well, that could've gone better, maybe. Forty-eight hours wasn't a whole lot of time.

Still, it could've gone a lot worse, too. She hadn't shot him, at least. Yet.

A whistle sounded nearby, jerking him out of his reverie. Shit, he was late for work! He leaped away from the pallet, racing back across the way toward the warehouse. Ted must have seen that she'd come back, or else one of the other guys had told him because he nodded at Wylie and continued giving the day's marching orders without pause.

Leo and the others welcomed him back, of course. "Sorry, man," Hiro said. "We tried to flag you down, but you breezed right on past."

"No worries," Wylie assured them. "I needed to face her down, anyway. It's all good." For two days, at least, he reminded himself but didn't say.

RT looked downright pissed, of course. Wylie made sure to give him a big, shit-eating grin, which only made the bully grumble and scowl and stomp off.

That helped Wylie's mood immensely, and he was able to get through the rest of the workday with only glancing around for any sign of her two or three times a minute and only jumping a little at every strange noise or sudden appearance.

CHAPTER THIRTY

THE FACT THAT HE DIDN'T SEE THE HUNTER—*HAILEY,* HE REMINDED himself. *She has a name now*—at all throughout the rest of the day did little to put Wylie at ease, and he jumped at shadows and sounds as he made his way back to his truck after work ended. He'd begged off going out for drinks with the guys that night, and they had all nodded sympathetically—given that they thought Hailey was a private detective or a scam artist, it was actually really considerate of them to give him some space, and he appreciated that, but really, he just didn't want to drag them any further into this mess than they already were. Which also made him wonder if he should cancel dinner with Knox and the others tonight. What if she was following him and spotted all of them there? Would she decide they were accomplices, too? They all had lives here. He couldn't be responsible for them having to give those up!

At the same time, they were his friends, and they were helping him figure all this stuff out. Where would he be without them? Would he have even a chance of solving this and avoiding having to run again himself?

He was still weighing those arguments as he unlocked the truck and slid behind the wheel. Backing out of the space and heading for the highway, he kept expecting at any second to glance around and see Hailey. The whole way on the road, he eyed every passing car with suspicion—and the ones that stayed just behind him, even more so. She'd said she'd be watching him, after all. He had to assume she really was. The fact that he didn't see her anywhere just meant she was better at shadowing him than he was at spotting her, which made sense—this was her, what, job? Mission? Calling? Something. Whatever it was, she had a lot more practice at it.

The closer he got to the turnoff that would take him back to Mama Rheda's, the more anxious he became. If Hailey was watching him, could he really risk bringing her straight to an apartment building owned by another supernatural and inhabited by so many others? That would potentially put all of them at risk, including Sinead.

At the thought of the pretty Banshee, Wylie perked up. Sinead! She would know what to do!

Taking the next exit, he pulled over at the first available spot and dug out his phone. Good thing she'd given him her number! He called it, and she picked up after only two rings.

"Hey," she said, her voice as raspy over the phone as it was in person. He'd yet to tell her that he'd actually started to like the way it sounded. "Everything okay?"

"Not entirely, no," he admitted. "I... had a bit of a run-in today." He told her about his encounter with Hailey.

"Oh, wow," Sinead said when he was done. "That's intense. But at least she's backing off for now. Not a whole lot of time, though."

"No, it isn't." He took a deep breath, then blurted out, "I'm worried she's following me or something. I didn't see her anywhere on the road, but she'd be dumb not to be, right?"

"Yeah—or she's smarter than to trust she can keep you in sight," Sinead replied. She paused a second. "Listen, can you meet me someplace? I'll text you the address."

"Uh—sure," Wylie responded, though the request had him confused. Especially since they were all getting together for dinner later anyway.

"Great. See you in a few. And don't worry, okay? It'll all be fine." She hung up, and a second later, his phone buzzed with a text. It was an address in Whittier, just the other side of 35W from Phillips. The address was highlighted, and when Wylie clicked on it his browser opened to display a business: Manny's Auto Works. *Okay*, he thought as he restarted the truck and pulled back out, balancing the phone against the steering wheel so he could see the location on the map while he drove. He knew Sinead worked at a garage—her dad's, in fact. Was that what this was? Why did she want him to meet her there?

Manny's proved to be a long, one-story white building on a corner lot—one side had four bay doors, all open at the moment, while the angled front had large plate-glass windows on either side of a glass door. Wylie wasn't sure exactly where he should go, so he pulled up in front to avoid blocking the bays, several of which had cars up on lifts inside them. Climbing out, he headed for the front door instead.

The inside was small and sparse, just a single big desk and a few chairs. The floor was black tile, the walls white, and there were framed pictures of various people and vehicles in different combinations. The guy behind the desk was older, his dark curls and neat beard starting to frost at the tips, but despite that and his slight build, he looked fit and focused. The gaze he gave Wylie was friendly but searching. "Help you?" he asked as Wylie let the door shut behind him and his eyes adjust to the indoor lighting.

"Yeah, hi," Wylie replied, approaching the desk. "I'm looking for Sinead. I'm supposed to meet her here."

"Yeah?" The man thumbed a button on the phone in front of him. "Sinead, I need you up front," he said, and Wylie heard the call echo through the open door beside the desk, beyond which he could see the garage area. He stood there in awkward silence, neither of them speaking. A moment later, the Banshee in question came rushing in.

Wylie stared. He couldn't help it. He was used to seeing Sinead with her hair down, loose and flowing like a white silk banner or a cape, and dressed in loose, comfortable clothing. Right now, however, she had her hair tucked up under an old baseball cap that said "Manny's" across the front, and it was as smudged with dirt and grease and oil as her dark gray coverall. A few spots were on her cheeks, and her hands were black. Her smile, however, shone bright, if a bit hesitant, as she glanced between him and the man at the desk. "Hey," she said. "There you are. Wylie, this is my dad, Manny. Dad, this is Wylie. I told you about him. Keys." That last part was to Wylie as she held out her hand.

Guessing she meant the keys to his truck, he dropped them into her open palm.

"Got it. Back in a bit." Then she moved past him and out the front door, rounding the truck to the driver's side. A second later, Wylie heard it cough to life.

"So," Manny said, and Wylie returned his attention to the room's other occupant. Sinead's dad. He should have guessed that—not that they had the same coloring or anything, but there was maybe a little something around the eyes. Plus, there was the name stitched onto the breast pocket of his coveralls. "You're the one who took my daughter to that ballgame the other week."

"Yessir." Wylie held out his hand. "Nice to meet you."

"Hmph." Manny's hand was firm and callused, and his grip solid — he definitely didn't just sit behind the desk all day! "She had a good time," he admitted after a minute. "And I hear she's been hanging out with you and your friends a lot since then."

"Yessir." Wylie gulped under the man's sharp stare. He definitely wasn't used to this! "She's great," he added.

That earned him a little bit of a smile. "She is, isn't she?" Manny said with clear pride. "The best." When Wylie nodded, the man's gaze darkened a bit again. "If anything ever happened to her, anyone hurt her, I'd..."

"Me too," Wylie promised, frowning not at her dad but at the thought of anything happening to Sinead. "Trust me, I'd never let that happen."

Manny studied him a second before nodding once. "Yeah, I guess I can see that. Good." He sighed and seemed to deflate slightly, or at least relax a little. "Her mom... she died when Sinead was real young. It's always just been her and me. I know I'm probably overprotective and all. I just... I can't lose her." His smile now seemed slightly sad. "And she's not too outgoing, usually. Never had a whole lot of friends. So," he steeled himself and returned all his attention to Wylie, "thank you for getting her to come out of her shell some."

"My pleasure," Wylie replied, smiling. "She really is great. And she's definitely part of the gang now. Not that we're a real gang or anything," he hastened to add. "Just, you know, a group of friends." He glanced down at his hands, which he'd placed on the edge of the desk. "I never had a lot of friends either, so this is all new to me, too," he confessed. "But it's great having them now, and I'm really glad your daughter's one of them."

Manny nodded again, and now his smile seemed more friendly. "Glad to hear it." He tilted his head to the side, a gesture Wylie recognized as having seen Sinead do as well. "So, you're a sports fan?"

That led to a whole discussion about local teams, with Manny apparently happy to educate Wylie fully on the strengths and weaknesses of each one once he discovered that Wylie was more enthusiastic than knowledgeable. He was still holding forth on the virtues of how the Minnesota Lynx, the Twin Cities WNB team, was criminally underrated and was all set to wow people this coming season when Sinead reappeared from the garage.

"Okay, you're all set," she told Wylie, tossing him his keys, which he fumbled and barely caught. "Good to go."

"Oh? Cool, thanks." He wasn't sure what that meant, exactly, but fortunately, she'd already turned to her dad.

"He was having some issues getting her turned over," she explained. "I told him to bring her in. Alternator wire was loose. No biggie."

Her dad nodded. "Yeah, I heard it when you started her up." He glanced at the clock across the room, which read 5:40. "You outta here?"

"Yep." She leaned in and gave him a quick kiss on the cheek. "Heading home." She glanced over at Wylie, and this time he got the hint.

"I can give you a ride if you want," he offered. "We're neighbors," he explained to Manny, who nodded like he already knew that. Which he probably did.

Sinead smiled. "That'd be great. Give me just a sec." And she disappeared through the door again.

"It's really nice to finally meet you," Wylie told her dad once she'd gone. "She talks about you — well, not a lot, but what she says, it's obvious how close you guys are."

That had Manny practically beaming. "Yeah? Good to hear. Thanks." He offered his hand again. "Nice to meet you too. Don't be a stranger, okay?"

"I definitely won't," Wylie promised. He hoped that he'd be able to keep his word on that.

When Sinead returned a few minutes later, she'd lost the cap and the coveralls, her hair loose again, as usual, her garb now the poncho Wylie had seen her in before over black, star-spangled leggings, her bag slung across her. "Let's go," she said, giving her dad a hug. "See ya, Pops. Love ya."

"Love ya too, sweetie," Manny replied. "Have a good night."

She'd apparently pulled the truck back in front, or someone else had, because it was waiting again right where Wylie had left it. They climbed in, and Sinead turned to him as soon as the door was closed. "Sorry about that. Hope he didn't give you too hard a time."

"Who, your dad? Naw, all good. He seems really nice." Which he had, once he'd decided Wylie was okay, but he left that part unsaid. After all, he imagined that if he had a kid, he'd be even more protective than that.

"Oh? Cool." The truck started smoothly, and Sinead smiled. "You really did have a loose wire. But that's not why I wanted you to bring it in." She held up her phone, an image of some sort of small metal box displayed on the screen. "This is."

"What's that?" Wylie asked as he pulled out into traffic and headed toward home.

"A tracker," his passenger explained. "She must've found your truck at some point and wired it on. That's why you never saw her following you—she didn't need to when she could keep track of you from a distance instead."

"Oh. Wow." He'd seen stuff like that in tons of movies, of course. Just never in real life. "So, what'd you do with it? Destroy it?"

"No, then she'd just know you'd found out, and she'd come looking for you again," Sinead told him. She grinned. "I wired it to somebody else's car instead. Don't worry, guy's a jerk, always pulling up unannounced and insisting we drop everything to work on his precious baby this second, even though most of the time it's just stupid stuff like him stripping the gears. Serve him right if she pulls him over or something."

Wylie laughed. "Yeah, I'm sure that'd go over well for all concerned."

"From the sound of it, she wouldn't hurt a mundane," Sinead assured him. "She'd figure out what'd happened then, sure, but she'd blame you, not him. Still, it should buy you at least a little time free of her. I'm guessing she won't figure it out until tomorrow when the tracker doesn't head down to the docks." And she won't figure out where we live, Wylie knew they were both thinking. That was huge.

"Nice. Thanks." He smiled back at her. "You know, I really appreciate all your help. Pretty sure I'd be screwed without you and Knox and the rest."

Even with her hair falling about her, he saw her cheeks pink. "Happy to. Thanks for—thanks for including me." She glanced away as she said that last part, but he heard the pain in her words.

"Are you kidding?" he told her as gently as he could. "Asking you to that game is probably the best thing I ever did." His truck chose exactly that second to sputter a bit, and he patted the dash. "Well, except maybe buying this old heap, of course."

That wrung a laugh from the Banshee. "She's not so bad," she said, laying a hand on the dash as well, "Just needs a little TLC. Still runs great, though, and solid as a rock. You could do a lot worse."

"True." Neither of them said much for a few minutes after that, but it was a companionable silence, and Wylie didn't mind. He still wasn't so used to being around other people, but with Sinead, he felt like he didn't have to fill the air with words every second. They could just both be here in the truck, driving home, and it was all good.

It was just the world outside the truck that he found filled with craziness and chaos.

But Wylie felt—he hoped—that each step they took brought them that much closer to getting some of that straightened out.

CHAPTER THIRTY-ONE

Dinner that night was Sinead's choice, a place called Gandhi Mahal. It was a bit more of a walk than most of the places Wylie had been so far, across the highway and then up to Franklin and almost to the river, but he didn't mind — it was a nice night out, and they ran into the others on the way over there.

"Cool," Swift said as they approached the two-story building, which was whitewashed up top but painted a variety of bright colors below. "Haven't had decent Indian food since we hit the Twin Cities, believe it or not."

Knox nodded as well. "I'd heard they burned down," he offered as Sinead led the way to the front door with its oval window.

"It did," she confirmed, ushering them all inside. "They moved here in the interim while they rebuild."

It felt a bit interim to Wylie, with its plain walls — one of them white-washed brick and the other a solid yellow-green — and tile floors and exposed ducting overhead. Still, the smells that hit him as they entered, rich and spicy and creamy and filled with scents he'd never encountered before but that had his mouth watering, all seemed to point to good things.

The woman at the front smiled when she saw Sinead — and that smile widened as she took in the others. "With friends this time, Sinead?" she commented and pointed them toward a long table nearby. "Very nice."

The lighting was bright enough to make out Sinead's blush. "I come here a lot," she admitted as they followed the hostess.

"Then we know it's gotta be good," Wylie assured her. He frowned at the chairs—no benches here!—but they looked sturdy enough. His groaned a little but held up as he lowered himself onto it.

After a waiter—who also greeted Sinead by name—brought them all glasses of water and two baskets of flat, round bread the others called "naan," Wylie filled the rest of them in on his encounter with Hailey the Hunter.

Knox whistled when he'd finished. "Look at you, on a first-name basis with your stalker!" he marveled. "Maybe you should invite her along, too," he added with a grin, which turned to a yelp as a small balled-up piece of dough hit him square in the forehead, thrown with impressive accuracy by a scowling Sinead. A second piece followed from Swift, thrown less precisely but with more enthusiasm, and the Red Cap quickly raised his hands in surrender.

"What?" he managed between laughs. "I'm just saying, our boy here's good at meeting people!"

That earned him more glares and an elbow from Doug next to him, but Jeannie actually nodded. "Wylie's very sociable," she agreed. "But in this case, it's also real smart. It's like they say for kidnap victims, make sure your kidnapper knows your name. That humanizes you to them—you're no longer just some faceless body, you're a person, and that makes it harder for them to hurt you."

Everyone nodded at that, though Wylie snorted. "Not so sure that'll work with her," he argued. "She seemed pretty set on getting rid of me. But I figured it couldn't hurt."

"At least she's backed off for two days, right?" Swift offered. "Better than nothing."

"She did put a tracker on his truck," Sinead countered. Then she smiled. "But I took care of it."

That earned her a fist bump from Swift and a high-five from Doug. They were all still grinning when the waiter returned to take their orders.

After they'd finished dinner—which was amazing, something called Rogan Josh—they trekked back to East Phillips and then over to Eli's.

It was fun walking all together, talking and laughing along the way, and Wylie could see his friends' personalities on display in the way they moved and interacted during the journey. Swift was the most animated, of course, constantly shifting position within the group, flitting from topic to topic just as easily and often grabbing Jeannie or Sinead or Doug to twirl around with them. Doug was more sedate, tending to stay in the same spot unless someone else moved him but not objecting if they did. Jeannie was clearly supportive, migrating to fill in any open spot so no one was left walking alone, even for a minute. Sinead stayed next to Wylie except when Swift dragged her away, though she always laughed and gave in whenever that happened. Knox stayed out in front, leading the way, but often turned and walked backward so he could participate more fully in the conversation. And Wylie? He brought up the rear, since he could easily see everyone even from there, and let the chatter flow around him like a swift river, enjoying the feel of it and tossing out comments from time to time but just as content to take it all in.

"Dude," Swift told him at one point, sliding in between him and Sinead, "you gotta loosen up some! Live a little!" And she hauled on his arms, trying to get him to dance with her.

It was like a cricket trying to budge a log, of course, but Wylie allowed himself to be moved in a lazy circle, laughing. He even attempted to mimic her moves, lifting his feet and hopping from one to the other in an effort that made the sidewalk shake.

"Okay, don't bring the house down!" Swift exclaimed, but she smiled as she said it. That was the thing about them, Wylie had learned early on—they teased each other a lot, especially Swift, but it was always friendly, like a sign of affection. The people they didn't like, they'd never bother giving trouble like that.

"I can't dance either," Sinead confided once Swift had turned her attention to her sister and cousin, dragging the two of them into an impromptu jig. "Don't worry about it."

Wylie smiled down at her. "It's fine," he promised her. "I don't mind. But thanks." He patted his stomach. "That food was amazing, by the way. Thanks for introducing me to it."

It was harder to tell out here under the night sky, with only spread-out streetlamps and the occasional car for light, but he thought she might have blushed again. "No problem. Glad you liked it."

A question he'd had earlier popped back into his head, and he blurted it out without thinking. "So why don't you have a car, yourself? I mean, you're into cars, you work on them, but you don't have one?"

Fortunately, she didn't seem to take any offense at the minor interrogation. "I can drive, of course," she agreed, "and I can borrow one from my dad if I need it. But here?" She shrugged. "Easier not to have one. I can get anywhere in the city without it."

That made sense, of course. Wylie wasn't sure he'd want to deal with the trek down to the docks each day and back on the train, but Sinead's work was a bit closer to home, and he guessed her dad probably lived somewhere near the shop, too. "I guess I need to get more familiar with the trains and busses," he said. "The only time I've been on it was to the game and back."

"We'll show you the ropes," Swift promised, suddenly appearing and looping arms with them both. "No worries, you'll be a pro straphanger in no time." Then she was off again.

"Boundless energy, that one," Wylie muttered, and Sinead laughed as they all continued on.

Eli's was no more crowded than before, with a handful of people camped out at various spots and the same guy, Nico, behind the counter. He nodded when they entered and told them, "He said to go on back whenever you got here."

"Thanks, man," Knox replied, already heading for the hallway and its private door.

"Greetings," the Mara called as they stepped into his long office. He didn't look as if he'd moved since the last time, though Wylie noticed his shirt was different. "I've been waiting for you." He wiggled those long fingers of his. "I have a good deal of information to impart."

"You found more deaths that match?" Sinead asked, and when Eli nodded, Wylie recalled something from his conversation with Hailey.

"Nineteen in all, right?" he asked, and the hacker's eyebrows rose.

"I believe that was the number, yes," Eli agreed after a second of studying him. He tapped the righthand monitor, and a series of files appeared, one after the other. "They date back well over a year, and all are north of here, though spread about from east to west in what strikes me as a fairly regular pattern." Another touch, this time to the adjacent screen, and a map appeared, with dots strung in a rough arc that ended at Embarrass and then dropped down to Rice Park and another spot nearby, a new one, Elm Creek Park Reserve. The one Hailey had mentioned.

"Nineteen deaths in under two years?" Knox whistled. "How'd nobody care about this before now, then?"

"Because they're all classified as animal attacks," Jeannie said. She'd moved closer to read the top file, which Eli had open. "No sign of human involvement, so it wasn't murder, just an unfortunate accident each time."

Sinead examined the map. "And they're spread out enough," she pointed out, "that it wouldn't be obvious. You've got a month or two between each one, and they're not just in Minnesota, either—some are in Wisconsin, some in North Dakota." She shrugged. "So, nobody made the connection."

"Until Hailey the Hunter got suspicious," Doug added. "Maybe figuring this was weird, even for a bear or boar?"

"Can you pull up the one from Embarrass?" Wylie asked. The Mara nodded, flicking a finger across the screen to bring a particular folder to the front and open its files. Eli was still scanning its contents, though, when Sinead nodded.

"There." She indicated a line in the report. "One victim was found halfway up a tree, the other nearly a mile away. I'm not much on wildlife, but that doesn't sound like a bear attack to me."

"It isn't," Swift told her. "Going after you up a tree, maybe, though they're more likely to leave you and chase after anyone on foot. But a mile away? Unless you seriously pissed them off, they'll lose interest once you're out of their immediate view. I watch a lot of nature shows," she added defensively as Knox and Doug both stared.

"So that's what caught her attention," Wylie said. "She heard about that and figured it couldn't be an animal, but it wasn't human, either. That left supernatural. Which led her to me."

"What else've we got?" Knox asked, pacing alongside the desk. He'd barely even looked at the screens, but Wylie had already figured out that the Red Cap wasn't much on technology beyond phone texts. "Anything that could lead us to our Wendigo?"

"Well, we know he's getting worse," Jeannie offered. That got everyone's attention, and she gestured at the map. "Eli, can you add the dates of each attack?" He did so with a quick nudge, and after a second of studying them, Wylie saw exactly what she meant.

"It's happening more often." Sure enough, the first two had been nearly two months apart. And the gap between the others had steadily decreased as they went. The last ones, Rice Park and Elm Creek, were separated by mere days.

"Yeah. He's escalating—or, in this case, his hunger is," Sinead said. "So, we know he's gonna have to hunt again soon. It's literally eating away at him until he does."

"And he'll probably stay close, too," Doug added. "That arc, it's centered on here. He's been venturing up and out to hunt, but lately, he's been too desperate to go that far."

"So, he probably lives here," Wylie agreed. "Somewhere. We just need to find him."

Eli hemmed under his breath, drawing their eyes. "I might have something else," he said slowly, reaching out to a third screen and bringing up another file. "This one is not part of the list. I wasn't even sure if I should mention it. It doesn't fit the general pattern. Still, there were a few points of similarity, enough that it tripped my search filters."

They all moved around to the desk's other side to read it. "Man dead of natural causes," Wylie stated. "Fell down a ravine." He frowned. "Doesn't seem like them at all."

"His body was picked apart by animals," Sinead pointed out, having read ahead. "Though it looks like that was postmortem, or maybe while he was dying."

"Happened during a snowstorm," Jeannie noted. "And it was a few months before the first death. So that could track."

"Yeah, lower down than the others, though," Doug corrected. "Still—are there pics, Eli?"

"There are." The Mara called those up into view, and Wylie noted that Knox immediately turned away. He began to suspect his little friend couldn't stomach the sight of blood.

Not that there was much in evidence here. The man's body had obviously frozen. Still, Doug moved in, studying the images. "Can you enlarge it a bit there?" he asked, gesturing at one spot.

A tap to the screen and that portion zoomed in. Wylie wasn't entirely sure what he was looking at, but Doug whistled softly. "Ouch," the Kobold muttered.

"What's wrong?" Jeannie asked him.

"This is," her cousin answered. "All of it." He shifted to look at the report again. "Look, this guy was on a hunting trip with his wife, right? They got caught in a snowstorm, trapped in their tent for a week, ran out of food—starving, yeah? She said he decided they needed food and went out to try getting some game and didn't come back. Storm ends.

She digs out, can't find him, and slogs to the nearest town. They send out a search party, find him a few days later down in that ravine, figure he fell, broke his neck, then some animals found him, figured it was a free lunch." His face twisted up a bit as he added, "Tragic, awful, but just a freak accident."

Wylie watched as the usually laid-back artist practically stabbed at the onscreen image. "Except for this, right here." He waved a hand toward the top of the grisly sight. "All this, it's where his chest was. Torn open, organ devoured — yeah, an animal could've done that. But not this." He returned to the first spot. "That's a clean cut, there. With a knife. The only straight line in the whole mess."

"And what is that, exactly?" Sinead asked softly, and the look Doug gave her was... sympathetic? Apologetic?

"It's his junk," he explained in a whisper. "Somebody castrated him. Probably before he died, too."

"Dougie did a year in med school," Jeannie explained quietly to the rest of them. "Before deciding he hated it." She nodded. "So, it's not animals, it's not even the fall, it's probably that cut that killed him. And the only other person up there — "

"Was his wife." Eli touched another monitor, and a woman's face appeared, clearly a driver's license photo or the like — sturdy, broad features, blond hair, gray eyes. "Elizabeth Duran. Thirty-eight. Lives here, over in Lynnhurst. She is an IT technician for" — he read a line and smiled. "Amberson Electronics. They specialize in pharmaceutical machines. They're in almost every major pharmacy in the region."

"So, she'd have a reason to travel up north a lot," Knox stated. "Going up to check on machines in town drugstores and the like."

"If they were trapped in that tent and starving, and she ate... parts of him," Sinead said, choking a little on the end of that statement, "that could have been enough to make her a Wendigo. Especially if they'd fought — anger and hunger and cold, all mixed in together."

"So, she kills him, makes it look like an accident, claims he wandered off to his death, and then comes back home," Wylie agreed. "Only now she's a Wendigo. After a few months, the hunger's too much, so while she's up on a business trip, she turns and goes hunting. That's her first time." He nodded at the map. "And she's been doing it ever since." He shook his head. "All this time, I was assuming it was a guy. Stupid."

"Normal," Jeannie corrected. "Most serial killers are men—at least, most of the ones who've been caught."

"Yeah, 'cause women are smarter," Swift added. "And so was she. Until the hunger got to be too much, and she got sloppy."

Wylie studied her picture. She looked so normal! Then his eyes drifted from her face to the details displayed below that.

Her address and phone number.

"Right," he declared, clapping his hands together and making everyone else jump a little. Even Eli. "Well, we know who she is—and we know where she is. What say we go get her?"

CHAPTER THIRTY-TWO

IT WAS, UNSURPRISINGLY, JEANNIE WHO OBJECTED. "OKAY, HOLD UP," THE Kobold said, coming around to place herself bodily between Wylie and the door. "You can't just 'go get her.' What're you going to do? Just walk on up to her and say, 'ha, gotcha!'?"

"Why not?" Swift asked, circling around her sister toward the exit. "Like the big guy said, we know who she is and where she is. And there's a lot more of us than there are of her." She stopped, cocked her head to the side, frowned, then shrugged. "You know what I mean."

"Jeannie's right," Sinead cut in, and for just a second, Wylie thought he saw something like a pout or a sulk on Swift's face. "It's not that simple. Remember, she looks completely mundane unless she changes. And it's her neck of the woods, not ours. If we go charging in there, all she has to do is call the cops, say we tried to mug her or something." She waved a hand to encompass their group, in all their jeans and leather and studs and hair dyes. "Who do you think the cops'll believe, her or us? Especially when we tell them, what, that she actually turns into a legend that feeds on flesh and cold?"

"Oh." Now Swift did visibly slump. "Well, yeah, when you put it that way, sure." Retracing her steps, she perched on the edge of Eli's desk, which the Mara raised an eyebrow at. "So, what's the plan, then?"

"First thing we need to do," Jeannie answered, "is make sure she's even there." Pulling out her phone, she started typing something in, glancing up once or twice at the information displayed on Eli's screen, but he stopped her, his arm proving quite long as he reached out and wrapped those spidery fingers around her hand, phone and all.

"Perhaps best not to use your own, traceable number, hm?" The hacker suggested, and Jeannie flushed a little. "Try this one instead." Releasing her, he retrieved and offered a cell phone from a desk drawer.

"Thanks." Taking the proffered device, Jeannie started again, then held the phone to her ear.

"You really think she'll answer an unknown number?" Doug asked.

But Wylie had a different question. "Even if she does, how does that tell us she's home?" he asked. "Couldn't she be anywhere?"

"She could," Jeannie replied with a wink. "If I was calling her phone." She held up a hand for silence, and her voice changed slightly, becoming more serious, her words more pronounced. "Yes, hi, Elizabeth Duran, please. Apartment fourteen c. Thanks." She waited a few seconds more, then hung up. "She's there."

"Who'd you call?" Doug demanded, but his cousin just smiled at him.

"I used to have a few students in that area," she explained, tapping the phone against her cheek. "A lot of those apartment buildings have someone at the front desk twenty-four-seven, just like at a hotel. So, I called the building and had them connect me. She answered." She shrugged. "No idea what to do next, though."

"I do." Knox stepped forward and held out his hand. "Phone, please." Jeannie relinquished it to him with a flourish, and he grinned back before keying in the number off Eli's monitor. "I know about your husband," he stated a moment later. "Northwest corner of Lynnhurst Park, one hour. Five thousand, cash. Come alone." Then he hung up and tossed the phone back to Eli, who snatched it out of the air as easily as one might pluck a flower from a bush. "All set. Let's go."

"What's Lynnhurst Park?" Wylie asked as he followed his friend out of the office, pausing to call back, "Thanks, Eli!"

"Let me know how everything turns out," the Mara replied. "Assuming you can, of course."

They all did their best to ignore that last part as they exited the café, back into the cold night air. "It's the only park in Lynnhurst," Knox replied, still on the move. "There's a hockey rink, baseball diamonds, ice skating, a whole bunch of stuff."

"And like a zillion entrances," Doug pointed out, trotting along beside them. "We can't exactly box her in there."

"Maybe not, but it'll give us room to move, and it's night, so there won't be as many people about," Knox countered. "I also told her one corner, so we don't have as much ground to cover."

"Ever been there?" Sinead asked. She was right behind him and Wylie, walking with Swift and Jeannie.

"No," the Red Cap admitted. "But it's a park. How hard can this be?"

"Okay, so not too terrible a choice, right?" Knox asked as they approached the park. They'd wound up catching two busses, the 21 across Lake Street and then the 4 down Bryant Avenue. That had been a new experience for Wylie, and he couldn't say he liked it entirely—the bus was even more jerky than the train, and a good deal narrower, though at least on the 4, they'd managed to claim the back section, and he'd been able to sprawl out across a row of seats. They'd gotten out at West 50th Street, and from there, it had been only a dozen blocks to the park itself.

Wylie could see what the others had meant about the neighborhood. There were a few big apartment buildings clustered together, but most of the area was houses, each one only one or two stories, with a nice big yard and massive old trees out front. It all looked very cozy, very suburban, like so many shows he'd watched. And the few people he saw out and about at this hour were all better dressed than him and his friends, and most of them older. They really did not fit in here.

The park was bigger than he'd expected, easily a block or two on each side. There wasn't one baseball diamond. There were four, spread out at the corners of a wide, open lawn, with the only trees around the edges and at the corners. The park's east side was taken up by what looked like administrative buildings, with a walkway separating the two uneven halves and a loop on the south offering a handful of parking spots.

"We're gonna have to keep an eye on each direction," Wylie pointed out, scanning the place. There was no cover at all, which was both good and bad—good because it meant they'd see her coming, bad because she'd probably spot them right away, too. Well, they'd just have to make it work. "I'll wait here," he decided, stopping at a wooden bench beside the sidewalk, just shy of the corner. It faced the diamond, a bit short of first base. "You guys spread out, watch for any sign of her and be ready to cut her off if she tries to run." He worried what might happen if his friends did try to hold her off—he had no idea how tough any of them might be or how much of a handful a Wendigo was, but didn't really want to take that chance, which is why he added, "If she does run, let me handle her."

"We'll watch the south approach," Swift announced, looping her arm with Sinead's. "Come on, girly-girl." And she dragged the Banshee off down the sidewalk with her.

"Doug and I'll cover the southeast, by those buildings," Jeannie offered, heading off and taking her cousin with her as she followed her sister—Wylie wondered at first why she didn't simply cut across the lawn, but that would have made the pair of them a good deal more visible to anyone who happened to be watching. As it was, Jeannie was the most conservatively dressed of them, so the most likely to blend in—provided no one noticed all of Doug's tattoos peeking up under his collar and out from his cuffs. "Be careful, okay?" Wylie nodded and held up a hand in a wave.

"Guess that leaves me with the northeast," Knox said. "Text if you need anything, okay?"

"Will do," Wylie promised. His friend nodded and clomped away, stepping off the sidewalk and following it on the grass instead so his iron boots would make less noise.

Then Wylie was alone.

It was strange, he thought. Before he'd come down here, being alone was all he knew how to do, the only way he knew how to be. It didn't bother him at all, not having anyone else around. He was used to it. He liked it.

Or at least, that's what he'd always told himself.

Now, sitting here on the bench by himself, he realized that he didn't, actually. And that maybe he never had.

Oh, he'd been content enough, he supposed. He'd managed. And it wasn't that he wanted to have people around every second of the day—he still needed some private time, just him and his thoughts and maybe his fishing pole. But now, having friends to talk to, laugh with, plan with—to turn to when he needed help—he hated the idea of not having that. He felt weird, uncomfortable, anxious, being cut off from his new support network, even for a few minutes.

He could handle it, of course. But he didn't enjoy it. Not anymore.

Too anxious to sit still, Wylie stood and began pacing back and forth in front of the bench. Where was she? Had it been an hour yet? He didn't wear a watch—he'd never needed one before moving down here. His phone showed the time, of course, but that meant hauling it back out again. He'd just wait.

There were a few people about, though not many. It seemed the shows were right about one thing—life in the suburbs tended to shut down early! He did spot a small cluster out on one of the other diamonds, the one clear across the lawn from his location—they didn't seem to be actually playing, more just horsing about and running the bases, but whatever.

And off to his left, he saw a single figure approaching along the sidewalk from the east, moving quickly and glancing about frequently.

Bingo.

Wylie stopped pacing and stepped out onto the grass a little, where he'd be more visible. He didn't want her to think no one was there to meet her. He heard a shout from across the field, but his attention was locked on the woman moving toward him. He could now make out her blond hair, blowing in the evening breeze above the long, puffy winter coat and under the knit cap. That had to be Elizabeth Duran. The Wendigo.

"Hey!" The shout sounded again, a little closer now, and Wylie glanced up—to see the people who'd been on the other baseball field heading toward him. There were four of them, and as they crossed the grass, he could make out what looked like splashes of blood at their foreheads and waists.

No, not blood—sashes. Dark red ones.

Crap.

"Yeah, you, furball!" one of them yelled at him. It was the emaciated-looking leathery gray dude from the other night. Swell. Wylie also recognized one of the others, the one with the bat-wing ears. Just what he didn't need right now.

He looked to the left and saw that Duran had stopped, staring at the scene before her. *No, keep coming,* he wanted to scream but didn't dare—that would only spook her further.

She was close enough now—level with that side of the diamond—that he could clearly see when her eyes finally locked onto him. And when they widened in shock.

Then she turned and bolted.

Great.

"Stop!" Wylie bellowed, charging across the field. He could still cut her off, and if the others heard or saw, they could intercept her, too.

But the *Tori no kotei* got in his way.

"What's your hurry, big man?" one of them said, stepping directly into his path. "You're not bugging out on us, are you?" Wylie didn't recognize her, but she had bumpy green skin, and her eyes were as yellow as his but wider set and more slanted, giving her a definite reptilian look.

"Yeah, my man here says you disrespected him the other day," another added. He was shorter, more on par with Batwing, but extremely wide, and his face had a blocky look like he'd been carved from stone and only roughly. His fists looked like massive boulders when he raised them in Wylie's direction. "Can't be having that."

"Listen, it was a misunderstanding," Wylie said quickly, his eyes still locked on the fleeing Wendigo. "I'm really sorry about that. I've gotta go, though. There's someone—"

"Nah, you ain't going nowhere," Leatherman replied, chuckling with a sound like coughing. "Not ever."

They'd continued approaching amid the taunts and threats, and Wylie suddenly realized they had him surrounded, right out on the dirt of the diamond. "Okay," he said at last, sighing as he gave up on following Duran for the moment and turned his full attention toward the matter at hand, rising to his full height. "Let's just—"

Something big and heavy bashed into the back of his skull. The impact drove him off his feet, and as he crashed to the ground, he heard someone say, "Dump him in the lake. Nobody disrespects the *Tori no kotei*."

Wylie tried to object, but his mouth wouldn't move properly. Neither did his limbs. His eyelids felt heavy, his whole head fuzzy, and he closed them, just for a second, just for a quick rest.

He hoped the others were able to follow Duran. And that they weren't close enough to get mixed up in this little fracas.

Then the darkness settled around him like a heavy blanket, and he was out.

CHAPTER THIRTY-THREE

WYLIE WOKE WITH A SHOCK WHEN HE HIT THE WATER.

It was like a slap in the face—intense cold washing over and around him, enveloping him, the chill seeping instantly in through fur and flesh, deep into blood and bone.

He found it exhilarating.

His eyes flew open, but all he saw was darkness. Not black, however. No, this was a deep, dark green. Wylie knew that color well, the hue of fresh water, a lake or pond or river. He'd started to take a breath, instinctively trying to gulp air to clear his head further, but he restrained that impulse just in time, clamping his mouth shut instead and hoarding what little oxygen he still had.

The words he'd heard came back to him in a flood: "Dump him in the lake."

The *Tori no kotei*. They'd blindsided him, knocking him out from behind—his head still pounded from that. Then tossed him in here, wherever here was—was there a lake near the park? He felt he might have seen one off to the right as they'd approached earlier but couldn't be sure. No doubt they'd done this before, many times. Dispose of the evidence, dump the body, problem solved.

They'd obviously never met a Yeti before.

What little light was around him came from above. Good, that meant he was already face-up. He could simply push off from the lake floor, shoot to the surface, catch his breath, and look around.

Except that, if they weren't completely stupid, the gang members would be nearby, on the shore, watching. Just in case he didn't stay down.

The question was, which way was the shore? Wylie concentrated, studying his surroundings. There was little to go on—no change in light, no noticeable current, and no motion above or below.

Ah, but there was one thing, faint but present:

The cold.

It was marginally colder to his right. The water would be cooler at the center of the lake, away from the shore, which acted as an insulator. That meant land must be closer on his left. Accordingly, he turned that way and kicked behind him, scooping with his arms at the same time to propel himself forward even faster. His lungs had already started to ache, which meant he needed to hurry.

They hadn't thrown him very far, it seemed, because it only took a few strokes before his hands ran up against a slope, solid but yielding in that way that only damp dirt and sand could be. Good, he'd found the shoreline. Picking at random, he turned right and swam a bit farther, his left hand trailing along the hard-packed earth to keep him close while he took care to stay where the water was still deep enough to cover him completely.

When his lungs began to burn and his head to throb, Wylie finally thrust himself up toward the glimmer of light above. He broke the surface as quietly as he could, tilting his face up so he could open his mouth and breathe in deeply. *Ah! That was better!*

He hadn't heard any shouts at his sudden appearance, so he leaned back and floated for a moment, letting the night air tickle his cheeks and forehead. Then he reached out, grasped the lip of the dirt just above the water, and hauled himself up and out onto dry land. There proved to be a thin strip of grass there, with a paved path past that, and he made very little sound as he planted his feet and stood, shaking water from him like an enormous dog.

Now, where had those "street emperors" gotten to?

Closing his eyes, Wylie listened closely. There! Muttering, laughter—a group of people somewhere nearby, talking. At this hour, that had to be them, especially since anyone else near the water had probably fled upon seeing the gang members. Particularly if they'd been dragging a large body between them.

They were to his left, from the sound of it. Past the pavement ran another strip of grass, a little wider this time, with trees spaced along it, and then a slightly wider paved way, perhaps a bike path. Even more grass lay beyond that, and Wylie quickly crossed to there, his strides long enough that his feet never touched asphalt. There were trees here as well, and he did his best to creep from one to the next since his fur would stand out all too well in the dark. Good thing they'd thrown him in fully clothed, or he'd look like a dove in a pack of ravens!

The sounds grew steadily louder as he approached, and soon enough, he could see figures. They were perched, sprawled, or pacing around a bench along that first path, right where the bike lane widened and turned, cutting across the second median and toward the road. He suspected that road led straight to the park, meaning they had hauled him by the simplest and straightest path. Which made sense—he was heavy enough that it had probably taken all of them to carry him this far.

He'd have to thank them for being so gentle about it. He hadn't felt a thing.

"How long you think we should give him?" One of them was saying as he reached, not a tree, but a big, heavy metal trash can stationed between two of them. Ducking down behind it, he thought it might almost conceal his bulk, especially with no lights around.

"Give it another few minutes, to be sure," another replied. Wylie recognized the voice—it was his old friend, Leatherman.

Well, a few minutes sounded nice, but really, why wait?

With a roar, he sprang up from his hiding place and charged forward, straight toward the bench. All five started at the sudden bellow, and the two standing up turned, staring as Wylie came barreling toward them.

But they weren't his first target.

He'd run still hunched over, his hands practically dragging on the ground. Now he lowered his shoulder further and slammed it full force into the bench.

This was no flimsy little piece of lawn furniture. It was solidly constructed, with concrete supports cemented into the ground and bolted for added stability. Thick wooden slats formed the back and seat.

Wylie crashed into it and ripped it clean out of its moorings, splinters and chunks exploding outward as he sent the entire mass of concrete and wood flying forward.

The three gang members who had been seated upon it went sailing as well.

One of them—Batwing—flailed his arms and managed to slow his progress, pitching to the side and crashing down onto the grass inches from the water.

The two who'd been next to him—a thin fellow with skin like tree bark and the lizard woman—weren't so lucky. Both of them soared clean out over that last bit of land and hit the water with a mighty splash amid pieces of the wrecked bench.

Wylie would deal with them later—if they made it back to shore.

Leatherman and Rocky had both been standing. The bench had clipped Rocky, but he'd kept his feet, whereas Leatherman had been bowled over. That made Wylie's next choice of action an easy one.

He turned toward Rocky.

"I think I owe you one, pal," he told the stout fellow. "Figure you're the one who cracked me upside the head before, right?"

"That's right," the *Tori no kotei* member replied, raising his fists. "And I'm about to do it again."

"No, you're really not." Wylie hauled off and backhanded the man right across his blocky face. It was like hitting a brick wall, but that was fine. Wylie was more than capable of tearing through one of those. The force of the blow knocked Rocky off his feet and sent him flying back several yards before landing hard with a sound like a small avalanche. He groaned, struggling sluggishly to rise, before collapsing in a heap.

And then there was one.

Wylie turned to find Leatherman clambering to his feet. Perfect. "I didn't have any beef with you," Wylie told the cadaverous man. "We bumped into each other, you got nasty, but whatever. No biggie. This, though—" He shook his head. "Bad enough you try to bump me off, but you just messed up something important. Something big." He advanced on the gray fellow. "That really ticks me off."

"You think I'm scared of you?" Leatherman declared, though he backpedaled as he did, nearly tripping over his own feet in an attempt to stay out of Wylie's reach. "I ain't! We're the Torei no kotei! Nobody messes with us!"

"Yeah?" With a sudden burst of motion, Wylie lunged forward, one hand grabbing the scrawny gang member by the front of his shirt and hoisting him up into the air, drawing him close at the same time, so they were face to face, even though Leatherman's feet flailed just above the ground. "Well, I'm Wylie Kang, Yeti, and nobody messes with me!"

And with that, he flung the gray man from him, far out toward the center of the lake, like a boy might throw a football.

Turning, he did a quick scan of the area and the situation. Rocky was still down and out. Lizard Girl and Treeboy still splashed in the water. Neither seemed to be making much progress at swimming ashore just yet. Leatherman landed well past them and had just sputtered to the surface. No trouble from any of them any time soon.

Batwing, though — he'd caught himself before getting dunked and had picked himself up off the ground.

Wylie advanced on him, hands loose at his sides, claws out, teeth bared.

The coal-skinned gang member held up his hands.

"Whoa," he said quickly, stopping where he was, hands still up and out, fingers splayed. "We're good."

"Are we?" Wylie asked softly, narrowing his eyes and seeing the smooth-scalped man flinch. "You sure? 'Cause I don't feel like we're good." And he rubbed the back of his head meaningfully. Though, truth be told, it was only a little sore now. That swim in the lake had done him a world of good!

"Sorry about that, man," Batwing replied. "Seriously. But I didn't do that. You and me, we got no issues."

"Yeah?" Wylie studied him a second. "Good," he said finally. "Keep it that way. Because next time? I won't be so forgiving."

He walked away without a backward glance. Maybe the Torei no kotei would leave him alone from now on. Maybe they'd come after him with twice as many next time. He didn't know, and right now, he really didn't care. What mattered was, he'd lost Elizabeth Duran. And he had no idea where his friends were or if they were all okay.

Those were on his mind as he headed down the road. He could see the park up ahead, which meant he could find his way back to the bus. But first things first. He dug his phone out of his pocket. Good thing Diane had talked him into that case! He just hoped it was as waterproof as she'd claimed. Flipping it open, he thumbed his phone to life and began typing out a message.

Time to regroup and come up with a Plan B.

CHAPTER THIRTY-FOUR

HE'D ONLY MANAGED A WORD OR TWO—HIS FINGERS WERE NOT MADE for this!—when shadows suddenly rose up from the side of the road, under the trees. "Wylie!"

He tensed, raising his hands to defend himself, as two figures burst from the foliage to grapple him—and stopped just short of hauling them off him as his brain belatedly recognized the raspy voice and then identified his two assailants, one tall and slim and pale, the other shorter and more golden.

"You're okay!" Sinead said, still hugging him. "We were freaking out! Okay—I was freaking out!"

"Not just you," Jeannie agreed, also still with her arms around his middle. She disengaged and backed up a pace with a warm smile. "But you're okay."

"Yeah, had us going there, big guy," Swift agreed, stepping in to punch him in the arm. Her eyes were bright, though, and not just from her usual glitter.

"I am okay," he agreed slowly as Sinead also peeled herself away, her cheeks pink and clearly damp from tears. "Thanks. Sorry." Knox and Doug joined them as well from the group's apparent hiding place, and Wylie exchanged fist bumps with them.

"Looks like you took a dunking," the Red Cap stated, studying Wylie's still-wet clothes as he twirled his cap on his index finger. "Sure you're good?"

"Yeah, I'm fine," Wylie promised. And he felt it. His head had stopped hurting at some point. He glanced around them. "Maybe we should get somewhere we can talk," he suggested.

Knox nodded; his suspicious frown quickly replaced by a grin as he restored the red cap to his head. "Fortunately, I know just the place, and it ain't far. Come on."

"I'm gonna go out on a limb and guess it serves food," Doug suggested as they all fell in behind the Red Cap again, making their way back toward the park.

"You know me so well," Knox admitted. "But we gotta move, they ain't open all that late."

Sinead placed herself beside Wylie. "What happened?" she asked, peering over at him. "You disappeared, and then you didn't answer your phone."

Wylie glanced down at the phone, still in his hand, and realized for the first time that there were little icons on the top he hadn't noticed there before. "Oh. Sorry. Didn't hear it, I guess. Still figuring this thing out." He managed a smile, and Sinead returned it with one of her own, visibly relaxing as she saw that he really was all right. Her concern and that of the others warmed him. It was nice to know people cared!

Knox took them down past the park to Fiftieth again and along that, back toward where they'd exited the bus. A few blocks shy of there, however, he stopped. "Here we go."

The building in front of them had a tall but shallow green awning and a big sign along the side. "The Malt Shop Restaurant," Wylie read aloud. "Cool." He'd heard of malteds but had never had one.

The interior was a good deal darker and warmer-hued than he'd expected, with a tan marbled floor and tall wooden beams. It wasn't crowded, and they were able to claim a pair of tables tucked in back. A waitress stopped by, and everyone ordered a malt plus two orders of fries to split. "Okay, so spill," Swift demanded as soon as the waitress had gone. "What the hell happened? We were down at the south corner" — she indicated Sinead, who nodded — "and heard shouting, then we got a text from Knox saying Duran was doing a runner."

"We hurried across the field to where he was," Sinead picked up, idly shredding a napkin as she spoke. "But he wasn't there. And neither were you."

"We got the same text," Jeannie agreed. "And we headed up, too. Ran into Swift and Sinead, then Knox a few minutes later, coming back."

"Yeah." Knox rapped his knuckles on the tabletop. "I was keeping an eye out, and all of a sudden, I see her go flying past me. Duran, had to be—nobody else out, and she fit the bill, plus she's clearly running scared. I go after her, but she's well ahead of me. We get past the park, and suddenly there's a cab driving by, of all things! She flags it down, practically throws herself in, and that's it. She's gone." He shook his head. "I headed back and ran into everybody else. Everyone except you."

They were all looking at him, and Wylie sighed. "Yeah. About that." He rubbed the back of his head, despite it feeling fine now. At least his clothes had dried on the walk over here! "That shouting you heard? I ran into some mutual acquaintances. The kind with bad attitudes—and red sashes."

"Oh, shit," Knox muttered. "The *Tori no kotei*? Here?"

Meanwhile, Jeannie gasped. "That's who was on the baseball diamond!" she said to Doug. "We saw some people out there, but, well, they sounded drunk, and we decided just to avoid them. Didn't want to cause a scene and scare Duran off."

"That was them," Wylie agreed. "And when she showed up, and I stepped forward so she could see me—they saw me too. It was two of the same guys I ran into before," he told Knox. "And I guess they figured, five to one, they liked those odds." He allowed himself a bit of a smirk. "Not so sure they still feel that way, though."

"You took 'em out?" Doug asked, following that statement with a whistle when Wylie nodded. "Damn, dude!"

"Not before they took me out first, though," Wylie admitted. "Knocked me out, dragged me up to the lake, and tossed me in. Guess that was supposed to do the trick, but all it did was wake me up and piss me off. I was heading back to look for you guys when you jumped me."

Sinead poked him in the arm. "We were worried!" she pointed out. "Nobody knew where you were!"

"Yeah. They must've carted me off while you were all chasing Duran." Wylie frowned. "And now she's gone, and we've got nothing. I'm sunk."

"Maybe, maybe not," Jeannie said. "She's in the wind, sure. But it's not like she packed up and left town, right? She hopped in a cab. She's probably too spooked to head back to her place, which means she's got whatever she had on her at the time. She'll be laying low, but I'm betting she's still here in town."

"She won't get far, either," Sinead agreed. "She can't. She was probably already starting to get hunger pangs again—it's been a few days since the last time, and she needs it faster and faster. Getting spooked can't help with that, either. I'm betting she'll need to feed again, and soon."

That sparked a thought, and Wylie turned to Knox. "You have Eli's number, right?" he asked, and the Goblin nodded, hauling out his phone. "Call him." Knox did, then passed over the phone.

"Eli? Hey, it's Wylie."

"H'lo, man," the Mara replied, sounding as dreamy as ever. "How'd that go? You bag the Wendigo?"

"Not yet, no." Just then, the waitress came back, carrying a tray of tall glasses and two plates of golden fries. "Listen, can you pull up those files again and check something for me?" He turned away slightly and lowered his voice. "Can you check the... the time of death?" he asked as quietly as he could. "See if they match?"

"Yeah, sure, I got 'em all right here. Hang on." He heard a soft tapping, almost like a slow drumbeat. "Huh. Yeah, they're all after dark, dude. How'd you know?"

"Lucky guess," Wylie replied. "Thanks." He hung up and handed the device back to Knox, then waited until the waitress had gone before filling the others in. "I was thinking," he started, "she's like any other predator, right? She's got her habits, her patterns, when she hunts best, stuff like that. Eli says all the deaths happened after dark. Which makes sense. She's a nocturnal hunter." He toyed with a fry. "And that's why I kept having those dreams. She turns at night."

"It's colder," Sinead offered. "Moon instead of sun. That all tracks."

"Right. So, she's gone to ground, for now, probably," Jeannie put in. "And dawn's not that far off. Which means she'll hunt tomorrow night. Soon as the sun goes down."

"Yep. She'll go Wendigo. Try to find her next meal," Knox said, popping a fry into his mouth. "So, what, we find her first and bag her instead?"

"We'll have to," Wylie replied. "I don't have much time left, plus we can't let her kill anyone else."

"How're we gonna get her, though?" Swift asked. "Just lay in wait and pile on her when she shows?"

Wylie shook his head. "Won't work, I don't think." He remembered how Duran's eyes had widened at her first real look at him. "She's got the Sight, I'm pretty sure—after all, she's one of us now, too. If we come within a hundred feet of her, she'll see us and spook."

"Not all of us." The quiet rasp drew the whole table's attention as Sinead raised her chin. "I look like a mundane."

"No way," Wylie, Swift, and Jeannie all said at once. But the blonde Banshee quieted them all with a resolute look.

"It can't be any of the rest of you," she argued. "Like you said, she'll see you a mile off. But not me. I can be the bait." She smiled. "Don't worry, I'm not about to be Wendigo-chow."

They all grumbled about it but, in the end, had to admit Sinead was right. None of the rest of them stood a chance at drawing Duran out the way she did.

"So, you stand around, looking all dinner-like," Swift said, earning her a fry in the face from Sinead, which she batted aside with only a little chuckle, "and then what? We tackle her?"

"*I* tackle her," Wylie corrected. "Same plan as before, for that. I can hold my own. The rest of you get Sinead clear and leave it to me."

They all nodded, though it was clear to him that the others weren't thrilled about not being able to help with that. Which he appreciated but having them in the fray with him would only make him have to worry about their safety. Better this way.

"Okay, so we've got a plan, sort of," Doug said, taking a long pull from his malt. Wylie tried his own and groaned happily as the icy chocolate liquid filled his mouth. Ah, that was good! "We just need to figure out where she's gonna go, so we can get there first," the tattooed Kobold added.

"She'll want someplace quiet, right?" Swift asked. "And cold?"

"Yeah, and as much like wilderness as she can get," Wylie agreed. "Snow and trees and not a lot of people around." He frowned, sipping at his malt, as he mulled over those details. It was a lot like fishing, in a way—or hunting, as he'd told the others. You figure out your prey's pattern, where they like to go, when they tend to be out, how they behave, and you plan around that.

Quiet, cold, trees and snow—he straightened, setting his nearly empty cup down on the table with a loud *thunk*. "I know where she's gonna go," he announced. He winced, though, as he turned to Knox. "And I think I'm about to need your help, 'cause we're gonna have to talk real fast to pull this one off."

CHAPTER THIRTY-FIVE

KNOX SHOOK HIS HEAD, THEN TILTED IT BACK TO PEER UP AT WYLIE beside him. "This," he declared, "is a truly terrible idea, mate. I mean, legendarily bad."

"I know," Wylie agreed. "But what're our options otherwise?" He gestured ahead of them. "Tell me I'm wrong about this."

The little Red Cap sighed. "No, you ain't wrong," he admitted grudgingly. Then he reached up and tugged down the brim of his cap. "Fine, if we're gonna do this, let's do it. Better'n standing around here all day."

It *was* day, too. After explaining his idea to the others over the remains of their malts and fries and suffering through a round or two of "That's a bad idea. Okay, come up with a better one. Crap," they'd agreed that, if they were seriously considering this, they'd be better off at least waiting until daylight. Then it didn't seem *quite* as monumentally stupid.

So they'd all traipsed back up to Phillips and then split up to head to their respective homes—making Wylie realize that he had absolutely no idea where the others lived besides Sinead—to get some rest. Now here it was, a little after ten in the morning, Wylie had called in sick to work, as had Sinead and Doug and Swift just in case they were needed—Jeannie couldn't get away with that as easily—and everyone was as ready as they were ever going to be.

Which probably wasn't saying much.

"Come on," Knox muttered and stomped ahead down the paved walk. That stopped a few feet later, or rather disappeared beneath the same snow blanketing the rest of the park.

Elliott Park. The one place in the city Wylie knew would have trees, snow, and no one else around.

Well, no one except for the antagonistic gang they were now deliberately trying to find.

"Hallo, the park!" Knox called out, cupping his hands alongside his mouth to project further. "Anyone in there?"

For a moment, there was no response, not even an echo, as the snow and the leaves swallowed up the sound of his call. Then a small figure dropped down from one of the nearer trees. "Whaddya want?" he demanded. The creature interrogating them was smaller than Knox and slighter, with greenish skin and sharply pointed features. His voice sounded shrill. The Goblin could easily have been one of those Wylie had encountered the last time he was here.

He hoped this interaction went better than the one before.

"Sorry to intrude on your space," he said now. "But we need to talk to the Green Goblins. All of you."

"All of us?" the Goblin laughed. "Pal, you couldn't handle all of us." Grinning, he put two fingers to his lips and blew a sharp whistle that cut through the air. An instant later, three more emerged from the tree branches, landing on the snow without a sound and without even denting its surface. "Happy now?"

"Look," Knox cut in, "we need the boss, okay? This is serious stuff."

"So far, it's just two idiots trespassing on our turf," one of the newcomers replied, pulling out and flicking open a knife. "And we can make short work of that."

"You really can't," Wylie warned, stepping forward and tensing in case they attacked. "But we're not here looking for trouble. We need your help."

"Our help?" That had all four of them laughing, the sound as high and sharp and grating as their voices. "Dude, we're the Green Goblins," the one in front told him. "We don't help — we help ourselves!" The others cracked up anew at that little witticism, and Wylie looked back at Knox, who shrugged.

"Help us to help you, then," the Red Cap suggested. "'Cause there's trouble coming down the pike, mate. And it ain't the sorta trouble you want, believe me. We're here to sort it for you, though. No thanks needed."

"What sort of trouble?" The question emanated from up among the leaves, and then four more Goblins leaped down. Three of those were bigger than the rest, though still shorter than most human adults. The fourth one was small, but his jacket was forest-green leather instead of the standard black, and he had large gold hoops dangling from both ears.

It seemed they'd found the gang's leader.

"A Hunter," Knox explained, dipping his head in a sign of respect as the bigger three placed themselves out in front of their superior, arms folded. "Here in the area now, tracking a killer, a Wendigo."

"What's that got to do with us?" the lead Goblin demanded. "I don't even know what that is, but it sure as hell ain't here, and we ain't letting it in, neither."

"It's coming anyway," Wylie told him. "It's hungry—that's all it knows, really, is pain and hate and hunger—and it needs to feed. On flesh." He glanced past the gang leader toward the trees. "And it's looking for someplace quiet, and cold, and untouched. That's your park here."

"So let it come." The Green Goblin chief bared his teeth, which looked very sharp. "We'll show it not to mess with us."

"You don't understand," Knox said. "This thing, it's a killer. Strong, fast, clawed—it'll go right through you. And then there's the Hunter, too. You really don't want to get caught between the two of 'em."

"So, we scare this thing off," one of the other Goblins put in, "the Hunter goes after it, problem solved." The others all nodded.

"It's not that simple," Wylie insisted. "It's beyond thought at this point. Just consumed by hunger. It'll come, and it'll attack. And yeah, maybe you can fight it off. But how many of you'll die in the process?"

The chief considered this. "So, what is it you want?" he asked, hands on his hips.

"We just need to borrow your park for the night," Knox started, but the gang's laughter drowned him out before he'd finished the statement.

"You want us to go, but you can stay?" one of them asked. "And mess up all our pretty snow? No way!"

"I'm the only one who can take on the Wendigo," Wylie replied. "And believe me, I'm even better with snow than you are. Clear out, let us settle in for the night, and when it shows, I'll deal with it. Then you can have your park back, nice and clean and safe."

He could see the chief mulling this over. But finally, the Goblin shook his bald head. "Naw, we take care of our own problems," he stated. He nodded to one of his trio of bodyguards, who pulled out a cell phone and tapped something into it. Now what?

That question was answered a moment later when a large, battered green-and-white van came screeching up to the curb. Wylie hadn't seen one quite like it before—it had windows all along its side, and in the front, the white sort of swooped down and in, forming a V. Between that, the round headlights, and the curved front bumper, it looked like a face, smiling at him.

There was nothing friendly, however, about the van's inhabitants. Once it had pulled up, the doors flung open, and a veritable wave of leather-jacketed little green men and women came pouring out. They spilled across the sidewalk and into the park proper, swarming up behind their chief like oversized ants until as far as Wylie could see, the snow was covered with gang members.

"Think that Wendigo can get through all this?" the chief asked, smirking as his warriors formed up behind him.

"Maybe not," Wylie agreed. "But you'll lose a bunch in the process. Is that really what you want?"

The chief didn't budge, though, and his smirk didn't fade.

"This ain't working," Knox muttered. "We need a Plan B."

"Great, what's that?" Wylie whispered back. "Threaten 'em? Bribe 'em? Maybe we can rent the place for the night?"

"Worth a shot," his friend agreed, then raised his voice. "Look, of course, you can handle yourselves," he called to the Green Goblins. "We're not questioning that—nobody is. But we need to be the ones to deal with the Wendigo. And it's gotta be here, tonight. What'll it take to get you to let us have it for that long?"

"You want us to vacate our park and leave you alone in it for the night?" the chief replied. "Why would we do that?" He grinned. "Unless you got a million bucks tucked up under that cap of yours."

He laughed, and all the other Green Goblins laughed with him, a wave of biting sound. They'd evidently left one to mind the van, too, because whoever was in there started honking the horn to complement the others' merriment, though that strange blatt of noise hardly improved the cacophony. Wylie winced at the sound and glanced back toward the vehicle. It had clearly seen better days—probably before he was even born.

But that gave him an idea.

Grabbing his phone, he sent a quick message, and a minute later, Sinead and Doug and Swift appeared across the street, having waited around the corner of a building half a block down, where they could be here fast if things went sideways.

"What's up?" Doug asked as the trio drew nearer, but Sinead's eyes had gone to the big green vehicle by the curb.

"Whoa," she whispered. "Is that the real deal?" She approached the battered old van slowly, carefully, like someone trying to sneak past a sleeping lion—or like someone reverently examining a great work of art. "It is!" she practically crowed when she was near enough to lay a hand on the hood, just above the headlight. "A nineteen sixty-seven Volkswagen Transporter! Awesome!"

The Green Goblins had been watching all of this quietly but curiously, and now their chief spoke. "You know this van?" he asked.

"Oh, yeah," Sinead replied, patting the front affectionately. "It's a classic. First released in March of nineteen fifty." She reached up and lightly tapped the windscreen. "You can tell it's the original style, the Type Two it was called, from the split windshield." Now Wylie realized that she was absolutely right. The van's front window was two pieces of glass instead of one, with a thin strip of metal between them. "In good shape," Sinead added, "this beauty's worth a pretty penny." Then she frowned, taking in the scratches and dents and the faded paint and cracked windows. "Shame it isn't *in* good shape."

"But it *could* be, right?" Wylie asked her. She met his eyes, noted his raised eyebrow, and nodded, smiling.

"Definitely," she agreed. "Give me a week, and I could have this thing looking like it was new and purring like a kitten."

Wylie peeked back at the chief. Yes, he was definitely interested.

"Doug," he called next. "That's a lot of blank canvas for you, isn't it?"

Their Kobold friend was not slow to catch on. "Yeah, it is," he agreed, eyeing the wide stretch of green all along the van's side. "I could do a real nice mural on that. 'Green Goblins' in big letters across the top, maybe all of them glaring out below that."

Knox had figured out the game plan by now, too. "So," he said to the lead Goblin. "Whaddya say? Let us borrow the place for the night, and in return, we'll clean and soup up the van for you, trick it out, the works."

The Goblin chief rubbed his pointed chin. "You're not gonna damage any of our trees or nothing?"

"Wouldn't dream of it," Wylie promised him. "I'm guessing there's a space a little farther in that's more open, like a courtyard or something?" The Goblins nodded. "Great. That's where I'll be." And, with any luck, it wouldn't ever get beyond that point.

Another minute passed. Then the gang leader nodded. "Fine," he announced. "The place is yours from dusk to dawn. No more." He pointed a finger at them. "And our van becomes a work of art."

"Deal." Wylie nodded back, then turned and grinned at his friends. They'd done it! They had the place.

"Okay," Swift said as they walked away. "So, Step One, done. Nice. Now, what about Step Two, the plan?" She cocked her head, peering up at Wylie. "You *do* have a plan, right?"

"I—yeah. Yeah, I do." Which, in fact, he did, the notion coming to him right then and there. "Let's grab a table somewhere, and I'll go over it." He frowned, glancing at Knox. "Brea, too."

"Yeah?" His Red Cap buddy was only surprised for a second. "Good idea. I'll buzz her. Lucé's?"

Wylie nodded, but right now, food was the least of his concerns. Still, "an army marches on its stomach" and all that—might as well get in a good meal before everything went nuts.

"Okay," he said once they were all at the pizzeria and their food had already been delivered. "So, here's the plan. Sinead and I'll wait in the park after dark. She'll be out in the open. I'll be hidden in the snow nearby. With my fur, I'll blend right in, and it's not like the cold'll be a problem. When the Wendigo shows, I jump out and grab her. Sinead takes off. I subdue the Wendigo. We hand her over to the Hunter. That's it."

"What're you gonna subdue her with?" Swift asked, pointing a fry at him like a mic. "Rope? Bungees? Fuzzy handcuffs?"

"I—don't know," he admitted. "I don't have anything like that." That produced giggles from the girls and a smirk from Doug, presumably over the last item she'd named.

"Right, new part of the plan," Knox offered, ignoring all that. "We hit the hardware store, get some bungees or something. You know the rest of us ain't just gonna be sitting at home watching TV while you two are putting yourselves at risk, right? We'll be nearby, just in case. So, I'll have the restraints with me. When you've got her down, holler. I'll come running. We tie her up good and tight. Bob's your uncle."

"How're we gonna know you're ready for that?" Doug wanted to know. "Just in case we can't hear you when you yell for us."

"I'll have my phone on me," Wylie suggested. "I can call when it's all done."

"And I'll call too, soon as I'm clear," Sinead added. "So, we'll all know to be ready with the ropes." She didn't flinch even a little bit at the idea of being bait, though Wylie certainly hated the notion of putting her in danger, even for a second.

"What if she gets past you somehow, though?" Jeannie fretted. She'd joined them when she'd finished work, and they had filled her in on the scene at the park. "Hate to be a buzzkill, but let's be honest, if she gets past you, there's no chance the rest of us'll be able to stop her."

"I know," Wylie agreed. "But we know one person who might." And he turned his gaze to their newest dining companion, who sat stonily in a chair at the end of the table.

"Let me get this straight," Brea stated, her voice flat and as harsh as her gaze. "First, you bring a Hunter to my city —"

Knox snorted at the "my," but Sinead jumped in over the sound. "The Hunter's here because of the deaths," she pointed out. "And those aren't Wylie's fault, remember? That's all the Wendigo. Who lived here long before Wylie showed up."

"Yeah, Ms. Hunter Chick was gonna wind up here eventually, no matter what," Swift agreed. "If anything, we're cutting down the eventual body count and hopefully running her out of town all the sooner."

The Ogress stared at them all a second but finally nodded. "All right, fine. So you need me to play back-up. I can do that."

"From outside the park," Wylie reminded her. "You can't come in, not even for a second, no matter what."

She waved a hand at that. "Yeah, yeah, I got it. She sees me, she'll rabbit for sure," she muttered. "Fine. I'll stake out the perimeter, make sure she doesn't get by. You can count on it." And Wylie believed her.

There wasn't anything more to add after that. They finished their meal, then picked up the earbuds and the bungees.

Now all they had to do was set the trap — and wait.

And hope everything worked.

CHAPTER THIRTY-SIX

WYLIE FROWNED. "YOU STILL GOOD WITH THIS?"

"I'm good," Sinead replied, her usual rasp muffled slightly by her hood, which was up over her head for once. "Let's just get to it."

He sighed. They stood by the north edge of the park, right where they'd met with the Green Goblins earlier in the day. Now, however, the sun was setting, streaks of color decorating the sky. No one else was around, as promised, and he'd even been able to park his truck right along the side, not far from the corner entrance itself. Knox and the others were stationed across the street, far enough away that Duran hopefully wouldn't see them when she showed but close enough to rush in at the first sign of trouble. For the moment, though, it was just Wylie and Sinead.

And he was about to get naked.

"Turn around," he ordered as he shucked his cap, pitched it into the truck's cab, and started unbuttoning his shirt. His boots he'd already removed and placed on the floor there.

Sinead obediently swiveled about so her back was to him. "What's the big deal, anyway?" she asked, giggling just a little. "I mean, you're covered in fur, right? It's not like you're entirely covered except your crotch, is it? 'Cause that'd be weird. Though maybe you're manscaping. Yeti-scaping?" The giggling increased. Wylie suspected at least part of that was nerves, but it didn't make him any less embarrassed.

"I'm all-over fur," he confirmed, getting the shirt open at last and tossing it onto the seat as well. "It's just—I'm not used to not wearing clothes around here." *Or around you*, he added silently, unbuttoning his jeans and peeling them down off his legs. But there was no way this would work if he was clothed, so naked it was. Once he'd finished and added the jeans to the loose pile in his pickup, he shut the door. No point in locking it, and the others were nearby anyway. "Okay."

He steeled himself as Sinead turned back around to face him. "Don't worry, I'll keep my eyes above the waist," she promised with an impish grin that made her eyes sparkle even under her cowl. Then she studied him a second. "Huh." Reaching out slowly, like one might to a skittish cat, she brushed a hand over his shoulder. "You seem taller. Weird. Your fur's nice and soft, though. I bet you go through conditioner like mad, huh?"

"That *is* weird, and yes, yes, I do," Wylie agreed, fighting the flush he could feel heating his face. "Okay, let's go. Ladies first," he added because the idea of Sinead walking behind him and seeing his bare butt—even though it was fur-covered like the rest of him—made him want to just keel over and die right there on the spot.

She didn't argue but laughed and led the way into the park. Within fifty feet, she was crunching through ice and snow, her boots sinking deep with each step. "Knox wasn't kidding about them scaring off the cleaners," she remarked as she slogged along, Wylie holding her elbow to give a little added support. "Thanks."

"Guess not," he agreed. They were past that first ring of trees now, and if he turned, he could only just make out the streets beyond the park's edges. Facing forward, he saw nothing but snow and foliage. Perfect. "A bit further, I think."

They kept going and, a few minutes later, came upon what the gang must have been talking about—a blank area, perhaps forty feet across and slightly mounded from snow, with benches placed in a circle under the trees. "Looks like the place," Sinead remarked, selecting a bench.

"Yeah. Here, let me." Wylie reached past her and brushed the snow from it.

"Thanks." Opening her shoulder bag, she pulled out a small, battery-powered space heater and set it down, turning it to face the rest of the bench seat and then switching it on. Next, she extracted a book. Then she pulled out Wylie's phone and handed it to him. "Here you go."

"Thanks." The phone had a new addition, courtesy of another quick stop to Best Buy—a set of earbuds that plugged into the headphone jack at the phone's top. He wedged those into his ears, brushing the fur aside first. They felt odd, and for a second he worried that he wouldn't be able to hear anything around him with those little silicon cones shoved into his ears, but he could still make out the faint hum of the heater and the rustling as Sinead settled onto the bench beside it. *Okay, good.* "Calling now," he informed her and clicked on her number.

She had her own phone out and in her hand, earbud wires trailing out from under her hood, and after a second ring, she picked up. "Hey." It was funny hearing her voice both through the earbuds and in person — the rasp seemed more pronounced through the tiny headphones, and given the way she ducked her head, he suspected she didn't like talking on the phone much.

"Hey. Okay, here I go." Turning away from her — and trying not to think about presenting her his backside — he waded out into the middle of the little clearing, careful to walk lightly so as not to leave prints. Then, when he was a good ten feet away, he turned and, facing her, crouched down.

And then he slowly, carefully, began tunneling down into the snow.

It was piled so high, fortunately, that he still hadn't hit whatever dirt or concrete or asphalt lay beneath by the time he was deep enough to lay down and bury himself completely. "How does it look?" he asked once he was ensconced, scraping away a little right in front so he could still see her on the bench up ahead.

"Good," she replied after a second. "Really good. I can't tell you're there at all."

"Great." He forced his body to relax a little so he wouldn't stiffen up. "Now we wait."

It was not, he freely admitted, the most sophisticated of plans. But beauty in simplicity, right?

"So," Wylie asked after a few minutes. Normally, he could sit still and silent for hours on end, but now he was hidden in a snowdrift watching his friend pretend to relax and read on an isolated park bench, waiting for a killer. He had to fight to keep from fidgeting, and the quiet was killing him. "Still glad I invited you to that ball game?"

He'd meant it as a joke, and Sinead laughed, raising her book to cover her mouth as she replied. "Hell, yes. This beats sitting home alone any day."

"You'd be warmer at home," he pointed out. He didn't mind the cold, of course — being buried in snow was really comforting, in fact, all snug and cozy — but he could see Sinead's breath misting in front of her when she spoke, and she looked to be shivering, even with the space heater glowing at her side.

"Only on the outside," she answered seriously. "And that'll warm up again. I'm thinking a hot chocolate the size of my head oughta do the trick."

"Add whipped cream the size of mine, and you're on," Wylie promised. Despite where they were and why, he couldn't help smiling. Who'd ever have thought he'd be here, bantering with a friend like this? Not him, that's for sure!

Now he just had to make sure she stayed safe and he stayed free so they could continue to joke around.

Something crackled nearby — not right by him, but within the park, definitely. "Did you hear that?" he asked.

She shook her head. "Is it her?"

"Not sure." Just then, his phone vibrated. Wylie couldn't exactly check to see what it said, but he could guess. "I think so. You ready?"

The book trembled in the Banshee's hand, and he could see her body tense. "Ready."

"Remember," he told her again, "When I pop out of the snow, you run. Don't stop, don't look back, don't worry about me. You just get clear." Once he knew she was safe, he could concentrate on taking down Duran.

More noises emerged, the faint crackle of someone stepping on pristine snow, breaking that thin top layer of ice and sinking into the softer snow beneath. The sound came from the side, and Wylie twisted a little to see better in that direction — just in time to watch a figure emerge from between the trees and step out through the circle of benches. He recognized the long puffy coat and the knit cap, and the blonde hair beneath.

It was her.

She was still a bit too far from him yet, so he waited, gathering himself for the leap. She took a step, then another, her attention fixed entirely on Sinead there upon the bench, still pretending to read, supposedly unaware her privacy had just been invaded and her life put in danger.

Duran took another step — and began to change.

Wylie stared, frozen by the sight unfolding before him. As he watched, the woman seemed to stretch, growing upward like a fast-forward of a flower sprouting. Her skin paled, turning a grayish-blue, and the pale gold bleached from her hair, leaving it ghost-white. Her cheeks sank in, and her lips peeled back even as her teeth extended, growing longer and sharper. Her eyes, which had been an indeterminate color before, glowed red like fire. Her hands, now extending well past the cuffs of her coat, were larger, longer, and tipped in long, talon-like claws. Her feet were the same, literally bursting through her boots, tearing the leather and fabric to shreds in the process. Her next step left those tatters behind even as she shed the coat, revealing a pale body clad only in the remains of what he guessed had been some sort of pale gray dress.

The Wendigo, nothing human left about her now, tilted back her head, her mouth gaping open, and let out a fearsome howl, somewhere between a screech and a roar. The sound echoed through the clearing, shaking snow from the trees. She loped forward, eyes locked upon her prey, who glanced up, genuinely startled by the sound if not the sudden appearance of this strange, fierce creature.

As she moved past Wylie, he coiled, yanking the earbuds from his ears. "Now!" he shouted, bursting up from the snow and flinging his phone toward the waiting Banshee. The Wendigo turned, startled by the yell and the sudden motion in her peripheral vision, but too late. Wylie barreled into her, sending her flying several yards before she hit the snow. "Sinead, go!" He bellowed as he raced after the creature. He put himself between his friend and the Wendigo even as she picked herself back up, spitting and shaking off snow with a growl.

"Gone!" Sinead agreed behind him. She bent down for an instant, then straightened and took off, back the way they'd come. The Wendigo watched her go, that growl increasing as the Banshee disappeared between the trees, and Wylie grinned.

"Sorry, she's not for you," he said, showing his teeth. "But I'm right here. Let's do this."

That drew those red eyes back to him, and she snarled, baring her fangs right at him. Good. She was too hungry to think straight, to realize he wasn't easy prey. That had been his one concern, that she might still possess enough cunning to know when to run.

Now, as she stalked toward him, flexing her hands in anticipation, he knew that wouldn't be an issue.

He extended his claws as well, crouching a little, arms wide as he stepped to meet her —

—and something wide and heavy settled around them both, connected strands that were metal-cold to the touch but produced a painful zap when they brushed his fur and skin. Wylie couldn't help yelping in pain, his body contorting from the shocks lancing into him from multiple spots. Beside him, the Wendigo shrieked as well, her body also writhing in unexpected pain. Tears came to Wylie's eyes as he struggled against his confinement. Each contact with it produced yet another jolt.

What the hell was this?

CHAPTER THIRTY-SEVEN

"WELL, WELL, WELL..." THE VOICE THAT EMERGED FROM THE TREES WAS only too familiar and sent a chill through Wylie that had nothing to do with the temperature. "Look what we have here," Hailey the Hunter declared, her boots crunching in the snow as she made her way toward them. "I thought, from studying the maps, that this seemed like the perfect place for a little night-time murder spree. Guess I was right." She chuckled, but it was a sound with little humor to it. "Wylie Kang, as I live and breathe. And this must be Mrs. Kang. Did I catch you two at a bad time?"

"Hailey, you idiot," Wylie managed to gasp out, his own words punctuated by gasps of agony from the frequent shocks still stabbing into him. "Back off and let me handle her!"

"Yeah, sorry, can't do that," she replied, stopping perhaps a dozen feet away. "You'll have to settle your little marital spat some other time." Now that she was closer, though, she frowned, studying her two captives. "Huh," she said after a minute. "I guess beauty really is in the eye of the beholder, huh?"

"She isn't my wife, you fool," Wylie roared. "She's the Wendigo I told you about! I was about to catch her!"

"Oh, yeah? Well, now I've caught you both," the Hunter shot back. "Two for the price of one, you ask me." She grinned, drawing a large, bulky-looking gun with a rounded barrel from under her coat. "Not sure how many tranqs it'll take to put either of you down," she explained as she raised the weapon. "But don't worry, I've got plenty. Now, who's first?"

The Wendigo had been half-whimpering from pain during this conversation, but those sounds had slowly grown both louder and more sharp-edged as anger and hunger overwhelmed the pain. She had also continued tugging at what Wylie now realized was some sort of weighted, electrified net. She kept twisting about, trying to get her limbs free of its confines so she could bring her claws to bear.

When he heard the shriek of tearing metal, Wylie knew she had.

"Look out!" he shouted as the creature ripped her way through the strands on her side, shredding them and clawing her way out. Doing so seemed to short out the entire contraption, which sparked and hissed and then went dead. Wylie was able to shrug it off easily now that there was no longer any tension from the one side. He flung the tangled net away onto the snow and turned—

—just in time to see the Wendigo launch herself at Hailey, arms out, claws glittering in the dim moonlight.

"NO!" Wylie leaped after her, flailing—and managed to latch onto the creature's ankle. He crashed down onto the snow, his weight stopping her mid-air and dragging her down with him. "Get out of here!" he shouted at the Hunter as he yanked hard and tossed the Wendigo to the side, just shy of the bench Sinead had so recently vacated. "I've got this!"

Hailey didn't move. She seemed frozen. But at least she didn't shoot him as he rose to his feet and turned his back to her, facing off against a howling-mad Wendigo. The fall evidently hadn't hurt Duran any, and now she flung herself at him instead. Her glowing eyes narrowed in hatred. Her sharp teeth gnashed as if she could already taste his flesh.

He moved to bat her aside, but she was faster this time. She darted past his sweep, and her claws arced out, tearing a sharp, burning line across his middle. Wylie had never felt such agony. He staggered, one arm wrapping around his stomach, the fur there instantly soaked with blood. He lashed out reflexively, backhanding the Wendigo away like a meddlesome fly. He curled in on himself for a moment, his sight blurring from the intense pain.

"Ah, damn it!" he muttered, gasping for air. The cold seared his lungs but in a good way, like ice crystals coating a burn, soothing it. The pain in his belly receded slightly. Okay, that helped some. He drew in more deep breaths, letting the chill seep through him. With each one, his wound hurt less. After a moment, he straightened and took his arm away. The fur still dripped red, but he could not see an actual cut. It was completely gone.

Wylie remembered the lake last night and how his head had felt better after he'd emerged from it. It hadn't just been the water and the adrenaline helping him, he realized now. It had been the cold. That had been what healed him.

He didn't just thrive in the cold. It super-charged him. It made him stronger, tougher. Maybe even bigger, he thought, remembering Sinead's earlier comment.

And the Wendigo gave off intense cold, stronger than any he'd encountered except in the bitterest winters.

Glancing over, he watched her climb to her feet once more, shaking her head to clear it from the blow he'd landed. "Hey, ugly!" he called, and her head swiveled up, those red eyes fixing on him again. "Let's finish this!"

She howled and threw herself at him. Spitting and shrieking and biting. Claws extended to rend and tear. Wylie met her head-on. He didn't try to dodge or block. He flung his arms wide, barreled forward, and wrapped them tightly around her. Heaving, he lifted her clear off the ground. Her feet scrabbled at his shins as she struggled for purchase. Her claws flattened against his chest, and she dug in deep. She lowered her head to tear chunks of fur and flesh from his neck and shoulder, but Wylie held on tight, squeezing harder and harder, dislodging her claws from his flesh and driving the air from her lungs.

And her cold sank into him, deeper than her claws or fangs, giving him strength. The wounds she made healed the second she carved them, the pain so fleeting he barely felt it.

With a bellow that shook the trees, Wylie shifted his grip and raised the Wendigo high over his head. She struggled, but she had nothing to grab onto, and his hands had her arms clamped tight at her sides, her claws pinned.

Then he flung her with all his might. She flew through the air, shrieking as she went, and slammed into one of the trees, hard enough to dump all the snow from its branches. Something cracked from the impact.

Hurrying over, Wylie saw that she lay stunned on the ground. Her eyes blinked but were unfocused, and her arms thrashed and twitched, her chest heaving for air — but her legs did not move.

The collision had broken her back.

She was no longer a threat, but he couldn't be sure that would last. What if she could heal like he did, only slower? If she recovered from this, she'd just attack again and again.

No, Wylie realized with a heavy heart. He had to end this. Not just the threat of her but her suffering.

With that in mind, he dropped to his knees beside the wounded creature, reaching down and grasping her head gently but firmly between his hands. Then, with a quick wrench, he yanked it to the side. Tears sprang to his eyes as he heard the sharp snap. Her whole upper body convulsed once, twice, before going limp, the glow in her eyes fading as they turned glassy.

It was over. The sound of a high, haunting song rising from somewhere nearby confirmed it. The Wendigo was dead. And despite the horrors she had committed, and the fact that she had just tried to kill not only him but Sinead, Wylie couldn't help mourning over what he had just been forced to do.

A cough from somewhere nearby made him glance up, finally. It was Hailey. She had approached so quietly he hadn't noticed and now stood only a few feet away. The tranq pistol dangled from her hand as she met his gaze.

"You saved my life." It wasn't a question, but he could see the one in her eyes.

"Yeah." He rose to his feet and brushed the snow from his knees. "I told you I wasn't the one you were after." He gestured down at the dead Wendigo. "She was. Her name was Elizabeth Duran. Her first kill was her husband. That's when she turned. The hunger's been getting stronger ever since."

Together they studied the creature. She had not changed back to her mundane form after her death. Wylie wondered if that was just because he'd killed her in this form or because she'd been so far gone the change had become permanent. He'd never know.

"Big, pale, long white hair, claws, fangs," Hailey noted. "You can see why I thought it was you." It wasn't exactly an apology, but he suspected it was as close as he would get.

Wylie nodded. "Yeah. But like I told you, Yeti aren't violent. We just wanna be left alone."

"A Yeti in the big city, though?" Now the Hunter studied him, and for a change, he saw no hatred in her eyes, only curiosity. "Never heard that one before."

Despite everything, he grinned at her. "Guess I'm just special, then."

"Guess so."

The sound of rapid footsteps arose from nearby. Both of them tensed, Hailey's pistol snapping up as five figures burst from the trees and raced toward them—three of them gold-skinned, one tall and blonde, and one short with a bright red cap.

"Don't," Wylie warned, reaching out and gently pushing the barrel back down. "They're friends."

"Wylie!" Sinead was in the lead, her legs longer than the others'. She hurled herself at him, ignoring Hailey to hug him tight. "You okay? I started singing and... well, I'm glad it wasn't you I was singing for." She glanced down at the dead Wendigo by their feet and shuddered. "Wow. Gotta admit, when she changed—I nearly lost it."

"You did great," he promised her, returning the embrace. "And it's all over now." He looked at Hailey over Sinead's head, and after a second, the Hunter nodded.

"Guess it is," Hailey agreed slowly. "Thanks." But she let her gaze sweep across the others. "Looks like there's a lot more going on in the Twin Cities than I realized, though."

Knox tensed, balling his fists, and the Kobolds all glanced down and away, but Sinead turned, disengaging from Wylie to glare at the Hunter, head held high.

"It's all good," Wylie assured the woman quickly. "Nothing you need to worry about."

"Yeah?" She considered that and him another minute before nodding. "I'll hold you to that," she warned. "But for now, I'll take care of this." She took a step closer to the body.

"All yours," Wylie promised, backing away from it and dragging Sinead with him—the Banshee looked ready to start a fight, and that was the last thing they needed right now, though he certainly appreciated her willingness to defend him, and the others.

"Be seeing you, Wylie Kang," Hailey called out as he walked toward the entrance with his friends. "Stay out of trouble, you hear? Oh, and—thanks."

"You're welcome," he yelled back but didn't turn around. No one said anything else until they'd made their way back out of the park and over to his truck, where he quickly donned his clothes once more.

"Right," he said then, glancing around at the others. "That's that." Accepting his phone back from Sinead, he grinned. "Now, I don't know about the rest of you, but I could really go for some pie. And I believe I promised someone here a hot chocolate the size of her head."

"Don't forget the whipped cream," she reminded him as he tugged the passenger door open and ushered her in. The others looked mildly confused by this, but nobody argued, and Knox rubbed his hands together as he slid into the truck, leaving Doug, Jeannie, and Swift to pile into the back.

"I know the perfect place," the Red Cap announced. Yanking off his cap, he felt around inside it and came up with a much-folded fifty-dollar bill. "And I'm buying!"

CHAPTER THIRTY-EIGHT

THEY WERE AT KHAN'S THE NEXT NIGHT, CELEBRATING, WHEN BREA appeared, stomping her way between the tables to theirs. "You need to come with me," she told Wylie bluntly, arms folded over her chest. "Now."

Wylie frowned up at her since he was already seated and halfway through his second bowl. "Nice to see you too, Brea," he remarked, grinning at the Ogress. "Pull up a chair." She hadn't turned up after the events in the park, but Knox had texted her to tell her what'd happened, and she'd replied that she'd make sure the Hunter took care of things and then left quietly. Evidently, that had worked out somewhat, though her expression suggested it hadn't gone perfectly.

She scowled and opened her mouth to bark something, but Knox cut in before she could. "What's the big deal, Brea?" the little Red Cap asked. "You have any trouble last night?"

That made her slump ever so slightly and shake her head. "No," she admitted. "No trouble. You all did good." Then she straightened. "But Wylie still needs to come with me. He's been requested."

"Requested? By who?" Sinead asked, and the Ogress turned toward her, seeming a little surprised to find the Banshee beside Wylie. "Is he in trouble?"

Again, Brea shook her head. "No. At least, I don't think so." She sighed. "Look, I don't know all the details, okay? I just know that I'm supposed to bring him." She tapped her foot on the floor. "Now."

"Bring me?" Wylie pushed back from the table so he could study her more fully. "Where? And why?"

"Actually, I think I know," Knox offered, also watching the Ogress closely. "And if I'm right, you actually should go." He grinned. "Don't worry. We'll hold onto your bowl for you."

Wylie wasn't too happy about this strange apparent summons, but he trusted Knox to know more about the inner workings of the Twin Cities than he ever would. If the Red Cap thought he should go with Brea, he'd go. So he rose to his feet, slurping down one last bite and chugging half his glass of beer before grabbing his cap off the back of the chair. "Fine," he said. "Let's get this over with, then— whatever 'this' is."

As Brea led him away, he saw Knox lean in, whispering something to the others. But Wylie couldn't make out what it was.

Hopefully, it wasn't anything like, "that poor sap. It was nice knowing him."

"Where to?" he asked Brea once they'd exited the restaurant. It wasn't terribly late yet, and the air felt cool and crisp, the sky clear. There were some people out and about, but most of them were bundled up and hurrying toward their respective destinations.

"This way," his guide replied, leading him south a block to Lake before turning west. "Don't worry, it's not too far."

As they walked, Wylie tried to figure his companion out. She didn't seem as angry at the moment as she had in their first few encounters, though still brusque to the point of rudeness, but that could just be an Ogress thing. She was clearly determined, very mission-oriented, but maybe not entirely hostile toward him anymore, especially after last night? He considered trying to talk to her, seeing if maybe he could break down the wall completely, but then decided it might be better not to risk it. Their silence felt almost companionable, and for now, maybe that was enough.

Their destination turned out to be none other than Midtown Global Market. "I thought it was shut for the night," Wylie asked as they approached the massive building with its bright yellow awnings.

"It is," Brea confirmed, but she headed straight for the front doors anyway, pushing them open without pause. They hadn't been locked, apparently, and Wylie could only assume that had been carefully planned. It wasn't like they were just going to leave this place open all night for anyone to wander in off the streets!

She continued on, past shops and stalls, all closed up tight. There was no one else here, but as they walked, Wylie thought he spotted a faint glow up ahead. Could that be their goal?

Sure enough, a few minutes later, they stepped out into a wide-open space. Massive yellow columns bordered it, supporting an enormous peaked skylight through which he could see the stars. There were tables and chairs here, and he guessed that normally they filled much of this space—the shops all around it appeared to be restaurants, and this some sort of communal eating area, like the public space Knox had taken him to when they'd first met. Only now, all but two of those tables had been shoved to the sides.

And at those two tables, which were side by side in almost the center of the cleared space, sat a handful of men and women.

Not exactly men and women, though. Or least, not all of them. He recognized Mama Rheda right off, of course. His landlady smiled at him, her colorful headscarf shifting slightly. Beside her sat a tall, slender woman so bleached-out she made Sinead look dusky; a big man with rugged, almost craggy features; a tall, skinny man in what looked like an old rain slicker and matching cap; a small, slight woman, neatly attired and with her silver-streaked hair up in a bun; a much bigger woman with oddly feathery hair and large, dark eyes; and a tiny, wizened old man with olive skin. The seven of them were all seated along the same side of the two tables. Brea marched straight toward them, stopping a handful of paces away.

"Here he is, as instructed," the Ogress stated. Then she pivoted with all the precision of a soldier on parade and stepped to the side, taking up a stance against the nearest pillar, one foot propped up against it, so she could see both Wylie and the table.

Wylie had followed her forward and now found himself the center of everyone's attention. He shifted from foot to foot, hands thumping against his sides. What was this all about?

"Hello, Wylie," Mama Rheda said, her tone friendly and her smile kind. "How you fitting in these days? We hear you got a job down on the docks. And of course, I already know you got a place. You liking it there?"

"I—yeah, it's great, really great. Thank you," Wylie answered after clearing his throat. "I like the job, too. It's good—keeps me busy, good exercise, nice people." Her expression encouraged him to keep talking, so he went on, "And I've made some other friends, too. Knox, Jeannie,

Swift, Doug. Sinead." He swallowed, feeling like this was some sort of interrogation. "I do like it here. I want to stay."

Up until that exact second, there had always been the thought, lurking in the back of his head, that after everything calmed down, he might want to head back up to Embarrass. But now, with the trouble past and the Hunter gone, Wylie realized that was no longer the case. His mind was already made up. That little cabin might have been where he lived all those years, but that's all it had ever been.

This was home. And he wasn't about to give it up without a fight.

Some of that belligerence must have shown on his face because Mama Rheda laughed and made calming gestures with her hand. "We're all glad to hear that," she replied. "Yes, we are. It's good to settle in, put down roots. Ain't that right, y'all?" A few of the others nodded, but some did not respond. "Now, let's talk about other things."

"The Hunter," the big woman said, her voice sharp and almost shrill. "And the Wendigo."

"Yes," the smaller woman agreed, and she was the opposite, her words silky smooth. "Tell us about that, please, Mr. Kang." She smiled, but it held no warmth, just superiority and secrets.

"Those murders that've been happening," Wylie explained, glancing at his strange audience. "They were this Wendigo, Elizabeth Duran. She lived here. Mostly she hunted farther north, but she grew more desperate and more careless, striking closer to home. She killed some campers up near Embarrass, where I was living at the time. A Hunter showed up, trying to catch the killer. She heard about me from some locals, figured out what I was, and decided I must've done it. That's why I came here, to get away from her. But the murders started happening here too, and then she came looking and found me again." He resisted the urge to bow his head or sigh. "So I caught the Wendigo. The Hunter was there—she saw it all, admitted she'd been after the wrong person, agreed to leave me alone. Leave all of us alone," he added, remembering what she'd said when he'd told her it was all good in the Twin Cities: *"I'll hold you to that."*

The big woman and the tiny one both nodded as if they could hear his thoughts. "You handled yourself well, young man," the little man at the table told him then. "Not easy, catching a killer like that. You were clever and brave. And you had good friends backing you up. That's important, too."

"But now this Hunter knows about us," the craggy man added. "That's not good. She'll be watching for any signs of trouble."

"Yes, she will," the pale woman agreed. "And she'll be watching you, Wylie Kang, to see how you handle it all." She smiled, and she was lovely, almost blindingly so, but cold and distant like an evening star. "You're going to have to stay on top of things from now on."

"What?" That came from Brea, but Mama Rheda quieted her with a raised hand and a tremor to her scarf.

"It's true," the Kishi confirmed. "Like or not, Wylie's now the one that woman's looking at to keep the peace." She smiled at him. "So, if you wanting to stay here, that's exactly what you gonna do. You think you can handle it?"

Wylie frowned, trying to follow the conversation that had apparently just bulldozed over him. "So, you want me to, what, make sure nobody causes any trouble so that Hunter doesn't have a reason to come back?" he asked slowly, and this time all seven of those people nodded. "But isn't that Brea's job?" Which certainly explained why she'd complained just now. If they were offering him her job, he could hardly blame her!

"Brea keeps us apprised of things and helps settle trouble, yes," the little man agreed. "But we have never defined her duties, and she does them out of her own sense of obligation, not any decree from us."

"Plus, you are the one who noticed what was happening with the murders," the craggy man added. "You took steps to find and stop the Wendigo. We need that kind of initiative."

That seemed a bit harsh, but Wylie couldn't entirely argue it. He considered the offer instead, thinking about the *Tori no kotei* — who this council must know about but clearly wasn't doing anything to rein in — and the Green Goblins and Darius the Minotaur. It was clear *somebody* needed to keep an eye on things, put some rules in place. "I'm not giving up my job," he warned them. "But, yeah," he said, lifting his chin and meeting the seven's collective gaze. "If you want me to keep the peace, I can do that."

It actually felt good, the idea that he might suddenly have some responsibility for this, his new home. And why shouldn't he keep everybody safe and happy? He'd stopped the Wendigo, after all. How hard could this be?

Glancing over and seeing the ferocious glare Brea leveled at him, though, Wylie wondered if maybe he hadn't just bitten off more than he could chew. Maybe he could find a way to work with her instead of butting heads?

Well, time would tell. For now, he smiled at his seven questioners and one furious guide. "Was there anything else?" he asked. "Because, if not, my dinner's getting cold." And sometimes, even a Yeti liked his food to be fresh and, yes, moderately warm.

ABOUT THE AUTHOR

FIRST SIGHTED IN THE WILDS OF NEW JERSEY, THE CRYPTID KNOWN AS "Aaron Rosenberg" or "the Gryphon Rose" has been seen as far afield as New Orleans and Lawrence, Kansas, but for the past twenty-five years has been primarily found in and around New York City. Though a sociable creature, Rosenberg has been known to unleash cutting wit and biting sarcasm, often upon those pulled into his expansive social circle. When not utilizing such weapons on the unwary, or camouflaging himself as the web content manager for a financial trade organization (previous disguises have included "college professor," "animation studio creative director," "film studio script supervisor," and "children's book publisher desktop coordinator"), the Gryphon Rose can most often be found pounding the keys of a battered laptop or equally dilapidated desktop, engaged in his most beloved activity — writing.

Over the past thirty years, Rosenberg's particular brand of storytelling has been traced to more than two hundred publications, including roughly four dozen novels in a variety of imaginative genres, from horror to comedy to action-adventure to mystery to various shades of science fiction and fantasy. His unique approach has been conclusively linked to the bestselling sci-fi comedy series The Adventures of DuckBob Spinowitz, the Anime-esque epic fantasy series the Relicant Chronicles, the space-opera series Tales of the *Dread Remora*, the period cryptid mystery *Gone to Ground*, the pirate fantasy mystery adventure *Deadly Fortune*, the historic dark fantasy *Time of the Phoenix*, and, in a rare collaboration with unsuspecting human David Niall Wilson, the occult thriller series OCLT. Rosenberg is also believed to be responsible for the award-winning *Bandslam: The Junior Novel*, the bestselling *Finding Gobi: Young Reader's Edition*, the #1 bestseller *42: The Jackie Robinson Story*, and the original children's book series STEM Squad and Pete and Penny's Pizza Puzzles.

Nor has this strange and prolific creature limited himself to original work. Rosenberg has also inveigled himself into various tie-in worlds, producing novels for such properties as *Star Trek, World of Warcraft, Warhammer, Stargate: Atlantis, Shadowrun, Eureka,* and *Mutants & Masterminds,* and short stories for *The X-Files, James Bond, Deadlands, Zorro,* and many more. The Gryphon Rose has even made his mark on roleplaying games, writing the original games *Asylum, Spookshow,* and *Chosen,* and doing work for games by Wizards of the Coast, Fantasy Flight, Pinnacle Entertainment, and many others—he won an Origins Award for the book *Gamemastering Secrets* and an ENnie for the Warhammer supplement *Lure of the Lich Lord!*

When Rosenberg is not writing at breakneck speeds, working alongside regular folk, or deploying snark against those who call him friend, he can be found reading, watching TV and movies, eating, and spending time with his mate "Jenifer" and their two offspring.

To follow more of this strange creature's adventures, monitor him through his site at gryphonrose.com, observe him on Facebook at facebook.com/gryphonrose, and watch his antics on Twitter @gryphonrose. Just be prepared for frequent dad jokes and daily writing updates.

FRIENDS OF OUR COVERT CRYPTIDS

Adam Nemo
Amanda Nixon
Andrea Hunter
Andrew Kaplan
Andy Hunter
Anonymous Reader
Aramanth Dawe
Austin Hoffey
Aven Lumi
Aysha Rehm
Bea Hersh-Tudor
Becky B
Benjamin Adler
Bess Turner
Bethany Tomerlin Prince
Betsy Cameron
Bill Kohn
Bill Schulz & family
Brad Jurn
Brendan Coffey
Brendan Lonehawk
Brian G
Brian Quirt
Brooks Moses
Carol Gyzander
Carol J. Guess
Carol Jones
Caroline Westra
Carolyn and Stephen Stein
Carolyn Rowland
Cathy Green
Chad Bowden

Charles Barouch
Charles Deal
Chris Bauer, novelist,
    Blessid Trauma series
Christopher J. Burke
Christopher Weuve
Cori Paige
Craig "Stevo" Stephenson
Cristov Russell
Dale A Russell
Dan Persons
Daniel Korn
Danielle Ackley-McPhail
Danny Chamberlin
Darke Conteur
Darrell Z. Grizzle
David Goldstein
David Lee Summers
David Medinnus
Debra L. Lieven
Denise and Raphael Sutton
Dennis P Campbell
Diana Botsford
Donna M. Hogg
Dr. Kat Crispin
Edwin Purcell
Ef Deal
Elaine Tindill-Rohr
Ellery Rhodes
Elyse M Grasso
Emily Rebecca Weed Baisch
Eric Slaney

Erin A.
Fantasy Supporter
Gary Phillips
Gav I.
Glori Medina
GraceAnne
    Andreassi DeCandido
Greg Levick
Heidi Pilewski
Hollie Buchanan
IAMTW
Isaac 'Will It Work' Dansicker
J. Linder
Jacen Leonard
Jack Deal
Jack Deal
James Hallam
James Johnston
Jason R Burns
Jeffrey Harlan
Jennifer L. Pierce
Jeremy Bottroff
Jim Gotaas
jjmcgaffey
John Keegan
John L. French
John Markley
John Peters
John Schoffstall
Jonathan Haar
Josh Ward
Jp
Judith Waidlich
Jules
Julian White
Julie Strange
Kal Powell
Karen Krah
Kate Myers
Katherine Hempel
Katie

Kay Hafner
Keith R.A. DeCandido
Kelly Pierce
Kelsey M
Kerry aka Trouble
Kimberly Catlett
Kit Kindred
krinsky
KT Magrowski
Lark Cunningham
Lawrence M. Schoen
LCW Allingham
Lee Jamilkowski
Linda Pierce
Lisa Kruse
Lisa Venezia
Lori & Maurice Forrester
Lorraine J. Anderson
Lowell Gilbert
maileguy
Maree Pavletich
Marilyn B
Mark Bergin
Mark Newman
Mark Squire
Mary Perez
Matthew Barr
Maureen Lewis
Mauria Reich
Megan Murphy Davis
Melanie Ball
Michael A. Burstein
Michael Brooker
Mikaela Irish
Mike "PsychoticDreamer"
    Bentley
Mike Bunch
Mike Crate
Mike Zipser
Mina Ellyse
Miriam Seidel

Nathan Turner
Nathaniel Adams
Nicholas Ahlhelm
Pat Knuth
Patrick Purcell
Paul Ryan
Paul van Oven
Pepita Hogg-Sonnenberg
Peter D Engebos
pjk
Pookster
prophet
Raphael Bressel
RAW
Rich Gonzalez
Richard Novak
Richard O'Shea
River
Rob Menaul
Robert Claney
Rochelle
Rose Caratozzolo
Ross Hathaway
Ruthenia
Sally Wiener Grotta
Saul Jaffe
Scantrontb

Scott Elson
Scott Thede
Sheryl R. Hayes
Sidney Whitaker
Steph Parker
Stephanie Lucas
Stephen Ballentine
Stephen Cheng
Stephen Lesnik
Stephen Rubin
Steve Locke
Steven Purcell
Stuart Chaplin
Svend Andersen
The Creative Fund
The Reckless Pantalones
Tim DuBois
Tina M Noe Good
Todd Dashoff
Tom B.
ToniAnn & Kyle
Tracy 'Rayhne' Fretwell
Ty Drago
Vee Luvian
Will "scifantasy" Frank
William J. Donahue

CPSIA information can be obtained
at www.ICGtesting.com
Printed in the USA
BVHW070858250123
657071BV00004B/66